All That I Own

*Finding Faith, Family, And
Love In The Old West*

Jean M. Teasdale

Executive Writers LLC

ISBN: 9798839526730

Cover design by: Art Painter
Library of Congress Control Number: 2018675309
Printed in the United States of America

I dedicate All That I Own to my daughters, Chris, Kathy, Karen, and Sarah, and to my dear friend, Katy White. They have supported me with their excitement and enthusiasm over all the stories that I have written. Thank you, girls, for acting like you are my biggest fans.

There are so many people that I would like to thank for helping to make this story possible. Lisa Davidson, I figured if I could get you to approve of the love scene, I would have it made. Thanks for approving.

Thanks, Carol Roberts, for reading the first few pages and telling me to keep it up. I had a story.

Thank you To Mike, Julie, and Michael Christopher Thompson. for hanging in there with me for all of these years. With Rocky and three babies later and the death of our daughter, Kathy, it looks like we are finally getting it finished. Thanks Julie for listening and being my friend, and inspiring me to get back to work. Thank you, Cheri Marundi, for not hesitating to critique my work.

And so many other friends that have come and gone in my life but always have given me positive input after reading my stories.

And of course, my dear husband Major T, who has supported me in any way he could and has always believed that I could do anything that I set my mind to. His wonderful dry sense of humor has kept me laughing for over fifty years. He has shown in so many unselfish ways his love for his family. His faith in God and his love and concern for hurting people have been a constant testimony to me.

I would like to give God all the Glory, Honor, and Praise for any talent that I might have. I would be nothing or have nothing without Him and His precious Son, Jesus. I thank you for all that you have bestowed on me through the power of the Holy Spirit.

Jean M. Teasdale
Jean M. Teasdale,
Teasdale/All That I Own 2011, 2022.

Contents

Foreword

I was immediately enthralled by "All That I Own" as I was reading and editing through it. It has a way of taking you into the story. I often wondered what was going to happen next. Jean does an excellent job of storytelling and holding the reader's interest captive as the narrative unfolds. Readers will find this novel gripping. This is a story that will appeal to both men and women in that it's not overly sappy or sentimental. It also portrays day-to-day living as you would expect in the Old West.

The characters are imperfect people in virtually every way. They aren't perfect physically speaking, for example, you see people with weight issues and people with scars. They aren't idyllic emotionally, either. No one in the book is perfectly composed or always in control at all times. Nor are they spiritually perfect. Even the heroes are flawed, much like the ones in scripture. Yet, they rise to the occasion, such as Ned, to pull things together in a greater divine plan.

Though this is a faith-based story, it doesn't in any way come across as preachy or overly moralistic. You see, a more subdued sharing of deeper truths that naturally flows through the storyline.

The story has realism about it as well. Jean tries to stay historically accurate and down to earth. I found myself researching some of the information in the story to see if it was historical in nature, and it was. The story is not fanciful or improbable in the slightest. She keeps it grounded!

Editor,

<u>Jay W. Spillers</u>
Jay W. Spillers
June 6, 2022.

Chapter 1

SOMEWHERE IN COLORADO 1888

The narrow dirt road stretched out before them, appearing to go only as far as the next curve. Chris wasn't certain what was beyond the curve or the bend after that, but she was confident she had to continue until she got to her destination. For the girl's sake, she had to try.

She trudged on, paying little attention to the brave crocuses that were pushing up through the gray snow, showing by their bright colors that spring was on its way. The only thing she noticed, with unease, was the wind, chasing the branches of the numerous trees lining the road.

"Sis, can we stop for a while? I'm tired."

Chris turned and watched as the little girl caught up to her. Karen had been lagging behind, and she did look tired. But Chris was exhausted too. She had been carrying Sarah on her shoulders for the last hour.

"No, Karen, we have to hurry." Chris gestured

apprehensively toward the sky and the black, rolling clouds. "From the looks of it, we're in for a storm."

Chris felt as if there was a storm brewing in her stomach. She was scared! What if he didn't agree, what would they do? And then again, what if he did agree? What would she do? Mrs. Perkins had always said appearance didn't matter, but it was how you acted toward your fellow man that mattered. That made her worry even more because from what she had heard about Dylon Clay, it appeared that he didn't care about his fellow man at all. His appearance was close to frightening. His unruly, yellow-blonde hair hung down to his massive shoulders. The ragged-burn scars that disfigured his cheek pulled at his left eye and ran down into his bushy beard, making him seem even more invincible. Chris shivered, not knowing if it was from the wind whipping around her or from what she was about to do.

Why did this have to happen? She wondered. Mrs. Perkins was a good woman and there were a lot of bad people in this world that could have died in the influenza epidemic. Why her? When she died she left two small girls and no family to take care of them.

As Clara Perkins laid in a fevered daze, she feared for Chris's safety. Now that she was eighteen, Clara knew that eventually, Jack Slade would come for her. Clara knew she was dying, so she had told Chris to go to Mr. Clay's and ask him to marry her and take care of the girls.

Chris thought back and remembered that horrid night. Clara had weakly clutched her arm and pulled her close and rasped. "He's lonely and a good man. I know he'll do good by you and the girls." Chris hadn't paid much attention at the time, thinking it was the fevered railings of a sick woman.

For as long as Chris could remember, Dylon Clay had paid Clara Perkins to do his washing and ironing. Although they were not what one would call friends, Clara had always liked him. He would drop his wash off and bring her fresh eggs, then pick it up a couple of days later along with the fresh bread she had baked for him. He and Clara would spend a few minutes talking, mostly about gardening. He would always speak nicely to the little girls, throw Chris a brisk nod, and then mount his horse and ride out.

Chris couldn't figure out why Mrs. Perkins would think he would want to marry the likes of her. Now, three weeks later, with no food left and the threat of her being sent back to the unknown with Jack Slade, she knew she had to at least try, or lose the only family she had ever known.

Chris's mother, Megan Spencer, was classified as the town whore. She worked for a cruel, greedy man by the name of Jack Slade who had a lot of money and held a great deal of power in the community. He had made a fortune from many different adventures and didn't seem to care if they were legal or not.

When Slade found out that Megan was pregnant, with Chris, he brutally knocked her to the ground and he viciously kicked her as he shouted, "any whore worth their money needs to learn how to prevent these kinds of mistakes!" When he threatened to toss her out on the streets, Megan agreed to enter into a contract with Jack. She had to have a place to stay for her and the baby. So she and her child became Jack Slade's bondservants.

After Chris was born, he saw that the child was boarded out in exchange for her mother's service in his establishment. Chris was ten when Megan died and for the next five years, Slade paid for her board and saw that she was taken care of. He realized that there would be a huge financial profit in owning an innocent young girl's contract.

When Chris turned fifteen, her life changed for the better. Slade sent her to live with Clara Perkins. It was the only time he had ever really spoken to Chris, and she knew she had good reason to be fearful of him.

"You work hard for her." He ground out, shoving his finger in her face. "And do what she says, or you'll be sorry."

Chris was never sorry she was sent to Clara's. Clara was kind and gentle and hardworking.

Clara Perkins was a widow who supported her family by washing and mending clothes for people of the community. She had two small girls, Karen and Sarah. It wasn't much loss when her husband was killed in what people said was a hunting accident. It was also said that Jack Slade killed him after he saw Clara's battered face.

Jack Slade had loved Clara since they were children. He loved her not only for her beauty but also for her kindness, gentleness, and unselfishness, all the things that he wasn't.

Jack was just twelve when he was thrown into the orphanage. Having had a free run of the streets up until then, he was rebellious to all authority. He was constantly being punished by having his meals withheld or by being locked in a dark closet. Clara, who was five years his junior, could never remember any other home but the orphanage. She had a tender heart and felt sorry for Jack so she would sneak him food and drink.

Jack ran away from the orphanage not long after he was placed there, but he had always remembered Clara. Ten years later, after he had struck it rich, through much double-dealing, he came back to town in hopes he would find Clara. He did, but she was already married and carrying her first child.

So Jack invested in a saloon and settled down, wanting to be near Clara.

When Clara's husband died, Jack approached her and asked her to marry him. And, although Clara cared for Jack very much, she knew that a man like him could never change. Her daughters were the most important things in her life and she would not allow them to grow up with the stigma of their mother being the wife of a man like Jack Slade.

Jack knew that other than a few jobs washing and ironing for people, Clara had no visible means of support, and he also knew that she would not take money from him. So he hired her to do the washing, ironing, and sewing for the women he had working for him. He also offered the use of his young bondservant, Megan Spencer's girl. Clara jumped at the chance. Anything to get the child out of the clutches of a man like Slade.

"Sissy, I'm hungry." Chris turned around and walked toward the pretty little dark-eyed, black-haired girl. Kneeling down, she gently set Sarah on the ground, only to have her grab at Chris's skirt and stick her thumb in her mouth.

"Me tho I'm hungthre." Chris smiled as she stroked her baby-fine black hair. "All right," she answered wearily. "We'll rest for a minute, but I only have one biscuit left for each of you, so eat them slowly. We'll get a drink of water at Mr. Clay's."

She patted Critter's head as their big black dog rubbed up against her. "Sorry, boy, none for you. You'll have to go catch yourself a rabbit." Chris could feel the rumble in her own stomach. It had been a while since she had eaten.

***

Dylon pulled the reins on the plow horse, bringing him to a stop; untying the bandanna from his neck, he mopped his brow as he peered at the darkening clouds. Feeling the strength of the wind hit him full in the face, he hurriedly unhooked the plow, slapped the horse's rump, and shouted. "Come on, Moses, best be gettin' back before we get rained out." As he was leading the horse into the barn, he noticed some people coming down the road toward the cabin. It appeared to be a woman and some children. "What now?" He wondered.

Dylon Clay was a private man, and he liked his solitude. His mother died when he was born and left him and his brother with a father who drank too much. When Dylon and his brother Dan were old enough, they struck out on their own. They were going to work hard and save every penny they earned, then buy some good farmland and settle down. Being deprived as a child, material possessions had become very important to Dylon. His plan was to have a big home, a beautiful wife, and a bunch of kids. The plan just about succeeded too; after six years of hard work, he and his brother had saved their money, found their land, and picked out their future wives.

Then disaster struck! They were working on a farm, helping bring in crops, and sleeping in the barn with the other hired hands. No one really knew how the fire started. It was late and they were all sleeping. Dylon heard the shouts and ran to safety. When he couldn't find his brother, Dan, he dashed back toward the barn. As he got to the door, a burning log fell and knocked him face down into the flames. Some of the men grabbed him by the feet and drug him to safety just as the barn caved in. He was unconscious for days. When he awoke, the side of his face was a mass of scars, and the woman he was to marry had left him. Worst of all, his brother, Dan, was dead.

When he was strong enough, he came out west and eventually bought this prime farmland. Then he built his cabin by using the logs on his property. That had been eight years ago.

Then Dylon Clay allowed his heart to become more scarred than his face.

***

Chris noticed he was taller than she remembered. His broad shoulders and muscular arms made him appear powerful. But it was those piercing blue eyes that she couldn't forget. She thought they had held a look of mistrust and now, being this close to him, she was certain of it. Fear shook her whole body and for an instant, she considered grabbing the girls and running.

"You're Miz Jenkins' hired girl. Ya lookin' for my laundry?" He questioned, as he towered over her.

"N…no sir! Mrs. Jenkins died two weeks ago."

Yanking his hat off of his head, he wiped the inside rim with his bandanna and appeared embarrassed. "Oh, yeah, I heard, sure am sorry, she was a good woman." Then, shooting her a mistrustful glare, he continued. "What business you got with me?"

Chris inhaled a deep breath and began speaking rapidly. "Well…sir, Mrs. Jenkins said that you were lonely and needed a wife. I thought that you and me could maybe get hitched up and take care of these little girls. I know I'm not much to look at, but I'm a good cook and work hard, and well, I don't want the girls to go to the orphanage."

Stunned, Dylon gawked at her, then he thundered. "Are ya crazy, girl? I don't even know what you're talking about!"

Karen and Sarah jumped with fright when he yelled and with puckered faces threw their arms around each other and began wailing loudly. Exasperated Dylon pointed his huge finger toward them, glanced quizzically at Chris, and shouted louder. "What's wrong with them?"

Upset by his harsh attitude, Chris took a protective stance and, with a voice that sounded surer than she was, yelled back. "They're hungry and tired and you're scaring them!"

Swiping his hand through his hair, he expelled a loud sigh while trying to control his voice. "Well, you better head on back home before the storm starts." Moving toward the shrieking children, he waggled his huge hands at them. "Go on now." He said in what he hoped was a calm voice. "Go on home!"

Chris could feel her temper rise; protection for these babies over-ruled any fear she had for this gigantic creature. "Don't you dare talk to them like that!" She raged, her hands planted on her hips. "Why you're nothing but an overgrown bully and I wouldn't marry you now for all the money on earth!" Whirling around, she picked up Sarah. "Come on, Karen." She instructed with a dignified air. "Let's go. This place is starting to stink."

Dylon's face furrowed into a questioning glare as he watched her walk away. Who did this piece of brown fluff think she was? She was as plain as a mud puddle, brown hair, brown eyes, and brown dress. She was also a bit chunky for his taste. "Good riddance!" He muttered as he stomped through the cabin door.

Dylon had a hard time falling asleep that night. The wind was howling and he could hear the rain beating against the roof. Usually, rainstorms made him sleepy, but tonight he felt on edge. It wasn't every day a young girl came to his door with a ready-made family to propose marriage. Every time he closed his eyes he could see them, the children sobbing, their huge dog barking and her standing up to him like a she-bear protecting her young.

His heartfelt sadness for the death of Clara Perkins, she had always been friendly to him. On lonely nights, her slim figure, silky black hair, and friendly smile crossed his mind, but he had never got up the courage to try courting her. He remembered speaking to the girl once or twice, and the children always gave him a friendly hello. Sure wasn't enough to form a marriage on. Mashing his pillow with his fist and turning on his side to find a comfortable position, he lay in his lonely bed, trying to clear his mind and find sleep.

Suddenly, he heard a noise. At first, he thought it was thunder, and then realized it was coming from the barn. Jumping to his feet, he went for his gun, remembering the bobcat he had seen a couple of days ago. Not bothering to put on his pants or shoes, he rushed to the barn. "Whoa...boy!" He soothed, "that's it-steady now!" The horses seemed skittish, but not frightened enough for the presence of a wild animal. The barn door was open, and the wind was whipping it back and forth. He realized that was what had frightened the horses, but he was certain he had latched it before coming in for the evening.

Hearing a low moan in the stall at the back of the barn, he raised his gun and crept slowly toward the noise.

Chris was peeking through the stall knothole when she saw his massive bulk with nothing but his long johns on advancing toward them with rifle raised. She realized she had better make their appearance known or he would frighten the girls. Standing, she quickly rushed out and whispered loudly. "Don't shoot, please; the girls were tired and wet." She threw him a pleading gaze. "We didn't mean no harm, we was just going to rest here until the storm was over."

"Jeez!" Dylon exclaimed as he laid the gun against the far post. "You scared the daylights out of me."

"I...I'm sorry, but Karen's got a fever. I think she's bad sick."

Dylon watched the woman standing before him. She was shivering, and he felt a twinge of guilt, not knowing for sure if she was really that cold or just downright scared of him. Realizing how frightening he must look to her, with his grotesque face, almost naked body, and gun in hand, ready to do harm to a woman and two small children. "Come on." He said, quickly taking the situation in hand and glancing toward the children. "We better get them in the house." He walked over to where Karen was lying on a bed of clean straw. "I'll carry the bigger one." He told Chris. As he reached down to pick the little girl up, he could hear her teeth chattering, and he noticed how hot she was to the touch. He could never remember holding a child before and was surprised at how light she was. Glancing toward Chris he noticed she was having a hard time picking the baby up.

"Wait here." He whispered. "I'll carry this one in and come back for her." She wearily nodded her head as she watched him dash toward the cabin.

Dylon placed Karen on his bed and covered her, then slipped into his pants and boots. He grabbed his jacket from off the peg by the door and ran back out to the barn. The girl was sitting on a bed of hay, trying to soothe the crying baby.

"Here, give me the child and you put this on." He said, handing her the jacket. "The rain's letting up a little." As Dylon was walking out of the barn, he tossed her a glance over his shoulder. "Be sure to latch the barn door on your way out." Then, with the baby securely tucked in his arms, he ran to the cabin.

Not wanting to put the baby with the sick child, he sat her in the big rocker and wrapped a blanket around her. "There, little one, this should warm you up." He said as he gently brushed her hair back from her face, grinning as he watched her thumb pop into her mouth.

As Chris entered the cabin, she felt the warmth from the blazing fire engulf her. But she had little time to enjoy it. "Thithy, Thithy," Sarah called out as she stuck her thumb in her mouth and held her other arm out toward Chris.

Kneeling before her, Chris whispered, "Listen, darling, you need to be a good girl and sit here while I take care of Karen, she's sick." Taking Sarah's arm, she wrapped it again in the blanket and smiled. "Will you do that for me?"

Gazing at her with sorrowful eyes, Sarah whined. "I'm hungthry, Thithy."

Dylon noticed the concerned expression on the girl's face as she tended to the child. He also saw the dark circles under her eyes. The realization of what she had been through the last couple of weeks finally dawned on him. He swiped his hand across his face and let out an exasperated sigh. Sending a woman and two small children out in a storm was unthinkable. What kind of a person was he becoming?

He glanced over at Sarah and forced a smile. "You're hungry, huh! Well, we'll fix that." He said, as he turned to the big cast-iron stove, opened the lid, and stirred the coals. Then, dipping in the water bucket, he filled the teapot. Chris watched as he opened the door next to the large rock fireplace and disappear. Her mouth watered when moments later he came out with a slab of bacon. Placing it on the sideboard, he began cutting thick slices, laying them in the big cast iron frying pan he had taken from the cupboard. While the bacon was frying, he sliced bread and set it on the table, along with some whipped butter and a jar of strawberry jam.

While Dylon was busy cooking, Chris went into the bedroom to see about Karen. She was sleeping fitfully and her fever seemed worse. Sitting on the edge of the bed, Chris shuddered with fear. "Oh, God, I don't know if you're there or not." She prayed. "If you are, please don't take her too." Hearing a noise, she glanced up and saw Dylon standing at the door with a bowl of cool water and a clean rag.

"I thought maybe you'd want to sponge her off. It might help to bring the fever down." He spoke softly as he entered the room.

She was sitting on the opposite side of the bed and as he handed her the bowl, their eyes met. It was the first time he had ever really looked at her. She wasn't plain at all. She reminded him of an autumn morning. Her hair hung down her back in a thick braid, with wisps of curls teasing her forehead. Except for the hints of red, it made him think of the rich brown soil turned over by his plow. Her complexion was as smooth as silk, with a smattering of freckles across her nose and a hint of pink brushing her well-rounded cheeks. Her luminous golden-brown eyes spoke volumes and he knew she couldn't keep much hidden. He felt an overwhelming urge to comfort her and tell her everything would be all right.

Her small hand brushed his as she took the bowl. "Do ya think it's the influenza?" She spoke softly and looked into his eyes as if to find an answer there.

Dylon glanced down at the little girl and saw that she had pushed her arm out from under the blanket. He grasped it gently in his large, calloused hand and studied it, noticing again how delicate she was. His face held a bewildered look as he glanced at Chris and asked. "What are these red spots? That's not from the influenza, is it?"

Chris also appeared puzzled. "No... I don't think so." She answered as she started sponging the child's fevered face.

"I'll ride for the doctor in the morning," Dylon said as he covered the child. "But right now, you need something to eat."

Chris was famished and didn't hesitate when Dylon offered her more food. Sarah was so tired she almost fell asleep at the table, so Dylon made up a mat for her on the floor next to the fireplace. After Chris tucked her in, she went to the bedroom to check on Karen while Dylon cleared the dishes. It was late, so he decided to check on the horses and make sure the barn door was latched. When he came back into the cabin, he went into the bedroom to see how the sick child was. He found Chris sitting in a chair with her head on the bed, in what looked like an uncomfortable position, sound asleep. "Jeez!" He muttered under his breath, and then he gently picked her up as if she were nothing more than a feather pillow, and carried her to the couch, covering her with a quilt.

The only place left for him to sleep was the big wooden rocking chair. Reaching for a blanket from the closet, he settled his big frame into the chair, trying to find a place for his head. When a scratch on the door interrupted him, he uttered another Jeez, got up, went to the door, opened it, and saw a large black dog. Dylon recognized him from this afternoon as part of the group that was now invading his home. The dog ran past him and went immediately to the couch and nuzzled Chris, only to have her sleepily bury her head deeper into the blanket. He then went, as if by instinct, to the bedroom and, with his front paws on the bed, sniffed Karen thoroughly. Satisfied, he went and settled himself beside the baby, who was asleep on the floor.

Dylon sank back in the chair, glared at the dog, and sarcastically whispered. "Make yourself at home. Everyone else has."

He had finally fallen into an uncomfortable sleep, with his

head back, mouth open, and his legs sprawled out in front of him. He awoke with a jerk when he felt something tapping on his stomach. Straightening his head and wincing at the kink in his neck, he reluctantly opened his eyes and there was the baby standing in-between his legs, one hand patting him and the other with her thumb stuck in her mouth. She gazed at him with her huge brown eyes and lisped. "Pothy, pothy."

Dylon reached down and gently tugged the thumb from her mouth, thinking that it was permanently glued in there. "What did you say?" He asked.

Sarah answered back quickly, "Potty! Potty!" While she moved her small body in what looked like a ritual dance. Her thumb shot back into her mouth, although the dance continued.

Agitated by this new event, Dylon glanced over at the dog, which was setting attentively watching the scene. He would have sworn he saw amusement on the stupid dog's face. He instantly knew he'd get no help there, or he realized from the sleeping girl on the couch.

His full attention went back to the child, who was by this time holding herself with one hand, sucking with the other, and still performing her ritual dance.

Knowing he had better do something fast, he ran to the cupboard, grabbed an old, rusted pot, and put it on the floor next to her. Sarah gazed up at him quizzically. Dylon pointed to the pot and with frenzy in his voice, muttered. "Well, go ahead and go!" When she reached both arms up to him, Dylon knelt down beside her and let out an exasperated, "Ah...Jeez!" While he pulled down her panties and held her over the pot. As he was standing up, she reached out both hands to him and made a face, saying, "Icky! Icky!" Shaking his head in frustration, he reached for a towel and wiped her hands off. "Now, do you think we can get back to sleep?" She gazed at him with her big soft eyes, her thumb back in place, and followed him to the rocking chair.

When he sat down, she tried to climb up on his lap. "No! No!" He whispered, gently pushing her away and pointing to the mat on the floor. "You go get back in your own bed." But the forlorn expression on her face pulled at his heartstring. "Ah...Jeez!" He uttered as he picked her up and set her on his lap.

When Chris awoke and reluctantly opened her eyes, she felt a moment of confusion and then embarrassment when the thought struck her that Mr. Clay must have carried her to the couch. Glancing around the cabin, she allowed her gaze to roam over the expensive furniture shoved haphazardly against the walls. The beautiful ornamental pieces were sitting on the table with no rhyme or reason. The floors and windows were bare, the only covering being a layer of dust. Oh! She thought dreamily, what a woman's touch would do for this place.

Settling her eyes on the huge man asleep in the rocking chair, she smiled when she saw Sarah snuggled deep in the crook of his arm, sucking at her thumb contentedly. As she pulled herself up from the couch, their faithful dog, Critter, came and stood beside her and whined. Patting his head, she went to the door and quietly let him out.

Dylon heard the squeak of the door and opened his eyes with a start. Gazing down at the baby sleeping in his arms, he felt a strange sensation in the pit of his stomach. He watched as the girl walked quietly into the bedroom and he couldn't help but to notice how her hair had fallen out of her braid and was hanging loosely around her shoulders. As he stood, he let out a painful groan as he felt his joints crack. Laying the baby on the mat, he walked into the bedroom and saw that the little girl had her eyes open and was drinking water from a cup Chris was holding to her mouth. She was covered with red spots.

Chris glanced up at him and spoke hesitantly. "She seems better today; she's not so hot and says she's hungry."

Dylon started a fire and filled the coffeepot. After setting it on the stove, he grabbed a towel from the peg on the wall and went out to the well to wash. The storm from last night had subsided sometime early in the morning. The sun was pushing its way from behind the mountains, spreading light and warmth throughout the meadow. Dylon gazed up at the clouds, and they reminded him of cotton balls dotting the clear blue sky. He felt a stab of loneliness creep through him, remembering how he and his brother would argue over the clouds different shapes and what sort of animals they looked like. The late April rain had washed away the rest of the grayness of winter; green grass and pungent wildflowers were beginning to dot the landscape.

Dylon inhaled the fresh air and felt the cleanness down to his bones. He loved this land. It was his and he would die here. Putting his clean shirt on over his hard work-worn muscles, he tucked it into his Levi's and went back into the cabin.

The girl was sitting at the table and he couldn't help but to notice the shine of her hair and the pink of her cheeks. He enjoyed looking at her and felt a twinge in the region of his heart that he hadn't felt in years. He pulled his eyes from her, at the same time thinking, this is getting too involved. I need to get this bunch out of here. He poured a cup of coffee and placed some of the bacon leftover from last night, between two slices of bread. Then he sat down across from her. "Is the child asleep?" He stated rather gruffly as he took a large bite of the sandwich.

Chris gazed up at him with eyes that held too much sorrow for someone so young. "I'm sorry Mr. Clay, here we've taken over your home and you don't even know our names."

She nodded toward the bedroom. "That's Karen in there. She's five and the baby Sarah. She'll soon be three." She threw him a half-hearted smile. "My name's Chris." The big black dog had rushed past Dylon when he came in from washing and was now sitting with his head on her lap. "And this big, old-loveable dog's name is Critter."

Gulping down the last of his coffee, he stood. "Yeah, we met." He said, avoiding her eyes. "Well, I'll ride for the doctor. The sooner he gets here, the sooner we can get you home."

***

Doctor Matthews looked relieved. "We were wondering what became of them. Ed Smith said he went out there a couple of times to tell them they had to move. He knew Clara had died and wanted to see what had happened to her family. When he saw they were gone, he put the place up for rent."

Dylon had tied his big bay on the back of Doctor Matthew's buggy and was sitting next to him. "What's going to happen to them, Doc?"

Doctor Matthews glanced at Dylon, shaking his head. He had always admired Clara Perkins for taking in the young girl. He had watched with fear as Chris grew into womanhood, knowing that Slade would soon force her into working in his saloon. In his years as a doctor, he had treated more cases than he wanted to count, of women who were brutalized by the men that were supposed to be their protectors. The injustice dealt out to women, and children for that matter galled him. He had seen men hung for stealing a horse, and yet, not a word said about a man beating his wife and allowing his family to go hungry. He was old, and the fight was about out of him. He knew he should have retired years ago, but he was the only doctor within a hundred miles. So, he just kept going. What little hair he did have was gray, and his brown eyes were usually bloodshot from not enough sleep. He was tall and way too thin. And he worked too hard and cared for people too deeply. "Don't know what's going to happen to them?" He answered. "The younguns will probably go to the county orphanage. The girl... well, that's Jack Slade's problem."

"Why would Slade have anything to do with her? She was living with Clara Perkins?"

The doctor pulled a match from his vest pocket and flicked it with his fingernail. Then he lit the corncob pipe hanging from his mouth. It had been his constant companion for more years than he could remember. He sucked in a deep draw, coughed a little, and then continued. "After Chris's mother died Clara made some kind of a deal with Slade so as to get the girl out of his clutches."

"Still don't get it, Doc?" Dylon asked, puzzled. "Is Slade her father or something?"

"Hell, Dylon!" Doc glanced over at him, perplexed. "Where you been? He owns the contract on the girl."

Chapter 2

Although Mr. Clay hadn't offered them breakfast, Chris found some mush in the cupboard and fixed a bowl for her and the girls. Karen ate a little and went back to sleep. Sarah ate greedily and after she was cleaned up, Chris set her on the floor to play with some wooden spoons and tin cups she found in the cupboard. Then she scraped the rest of the mush in a bowl and set it on the floor for Critter. She quickly braided her hair, washed her hands and face, and cleaned the kitchen.

The cabin was small, with only one bedroom. A beautiful rock fireplace covering almost the entire inside wall separated the spacious kitchen, front-room combination. The gun rack being the only thing hanging on the other wall further confirmed the absence of a female touch. She noticed that dust was the only thing that lay on the heavy oak mantle of the fireplace. Chris resisted the urge to set the floral vase and the blue china teapot on it. A homemade sawbuck table and benches in the kitchen looked out of place next to the huge Boston Rocker and the plush gold Victorian couch that was sitting in front of the fireplace. For a moment, Chris allowed herself to imagine this was her own home. In her dream, her husband was a wealthy farmer who loved her and adored Karen and Sarah.

She visualized yellow checked curtains on the window above the sturdily crafted kitchen cabinets and soft gold drapes for the large window in the front room. Shaking herself out of her fantasy, she began to sweep the floor, remembering the way Mr. Clay had treated her this morning. She realized they were unwanted guests. He would not even look at her and had barely spoken to her before he left this morning. Last night, he seemed so kind and caring. She had totally forgotten about the scars, and Sarah wasn't frightened of him at all. Smiling, she thought of Sarah asleep in his huge arms; then a strange excitement flowed through her as the thought struck her that those same arms carried her to the couch last night.

***

"Quarantined! Jeez, Doc, what are you talking about? Quarantined!"

"Now just settle down, boy! It's chickenpox, it looks like it's not a real bad case, but we just had a bad bout with influenza and I'm not up to having another epidemic sweep the town. It's only for fourteen days."

"Fourteen days!" Dylon exploded. "Fourteen days! Well...We'll just pack 'em up and take 'em back to their house. I'll even pay the rent."

"No, you won't! You won't leave this place." Nailing a big quarantine sign to the door, Doc yelled back. "You know what the law says; no one goes in or comes out for fourteen days. Besides, they don't have a house to go back to."

Dylon slapped his weather-beaten hat against his thigh and through clenched teeth gritted. "This house ain't big enough for all of us."

Climbing into the buggy, Doc grabbed the reins and glared at Dylon. "Well, you'll just have to make do. I'll be out every few days."

Furious, Dylon stomped off to the barn, not hearing Doc's old buggy roll out of the yard. After he cooled down, Dylon went back to the house. He would sleep in the barn, but it was his home and he would come and go as he pleased.

When he entered the cabin, he noticed Karen was lying on the

19

couch. Glaring at Chris with a fixed stare, he barked. "What's she doing on the couch?"

Chris glanced at him with fear in her eyes and ventured cautiously. "I thought you would want your bed back, so I brought her out here." Hurriedly, she continued. "But if you want, she can sleep on the floor."

"Put her back in bed now!" He growled, pointing toward the bedroom.

Chris quickly picked up Karen. "Don't worry, we won't be no trouble. I'll...I'll even sleep in the barn if you want me to." She stuttered as she carried the little girl to the bedroom.

Dylon cringed at the look of fear he saw in her eyes. "You'll stay in here and take care of the child. Do you hear me, girl?" He caught her eyes and waited for her nod. Then he turned and slammed out the door. Not wanting to admit that, he saw a look of fear in the girl's eyes.

The next few days were exhausting for Chris. Karen complained about itching, Sarah whined and hung on Chris's skirt, and Dylon sulked. Doc came out every few days to bring them supplies and check on Karen.

"Chris, you look exhausted," Doc told Chris one day about a week later. "You need to get some rest. Karen is doing better. Let her sit outside on the porch in the sun every day for a while, and you sit with her."

Dylon treated Chris with awkward politeness, and she stayed away from him as much as possible. But his relationship with Karen and Sarah was growing daily. The days grew into a routine, he would come in for his meals, play awhile with the girls, then leave.

One morning while Chris was serving breakfast, Dylon noticed a deep scratch on her arm. Grabbing it in his big, calloused hand, he asked her sternly. "What's this?"

"Oh, it's nothing." She replied, pulling her arm free from his grasp.

Karen was sitting on the floor playing with Critter. She glanced up at Dylon and answered for Chris. "She cut it trying to fix the chicken house."

Dylon's eyes narrowed as he threw Chris a questioning glare. "What's she talking about?"

"The coop was falling down." She answered, trying to shake off the warm feel of his hand on her skin. "And I was trying to fix it. A board with a nail fell on my arm." Shrugging her shoulders nonchalantly, she continued, "Really, it's nothing."

Dylon went to the cupboard and grabbed some ointment. "Did you clean it good?" He asked with a hint of irritation in his voice.

"Yes," she answered back, puzzled by his reaction, her own irritation showing through.

He gently began rubbing the lotion on her arm. "You don't need to go fixing things on this farm." He berated. "You just leave things alone. Ya, hear me, girl?"

"Well, I was just trying to help." She interjected, confused by the unexplained emotions flowing through her from his nearness.

"Well, I don't need or want your help!" He roared as he dropped her arm, threw the ointment on the table, turned, and started walking out the door.

"Sissy!" Karen squealed excitedly as her face lit up in puzzlement. "Why did you make a face and stick out your tongue at Mr. Dylon?"

Dylon stopped as he heard the surprising statement from the little girl, turning in time to see Chris's crimson face as she was hushing Karen.

Wide-eyed, Karen gawked at her, then she said in bewilderment. "You said it's not nice to make faces at people, Sissy." Chris, who was totally humiliated, glanced at Dylon. Their eyes met, held for an instant, and then he turned and walked out the door.

Standing on the porch, he rocked back on his heels as he felt the laughter rumble in his stomach. All that afternoon, while Dylon plowed the field, he thought about what had happened. Then he would chuckle at the shocked expression on Chris's face when Karen caught her in an act of rebellion. He had to admit he was a little embarrassed by the way he had been treating her. She had only been trying to help; even by bringing the girls here, she was trying to do something good for them.

Remembering the first day and how she had shouted at him that they should get hitched, he shook his head and chuckled. What a sorry lot they were. But maybe, he thought, getting married isn't such a bad idea. He was thirty, and he didn't figure her to be much older than eighteen. But age didn't seem to be a factor, or his appearance, for that matter. He knew she was just looking for someone to take care of her and the girls. She was at least honest about that. He smiled again, thinking of Karen and Sarah. There was no doubt they liked him, and he sure did like them. He had never been around children, and these two young ones were amazing. He had always wanted to marry and have a family, but after the accident, with his scarred face, he figured it would never happen. With this land and a house full of nice things, at least, he had something to offer a woman. There was no doubt that he liked the way Chris looked. Many a night he had gone to sleep thinking about her plump breasts pushed up against that old brown dress and her well-rounded bottom sticking up as she reached down for the baby.

He pulled the reins, bringing the plow horse to a stop. "That's it for today, Moses." He grinned as he slapped the horse's rump.

"I'm going to get me a wife."

As Dylon came around the barn and headed toward the cabin, he noticed three riders coming down the road. Chris was standing by the porch, holding the baby. He walked over and stood next to her.

Chris's face went pale. "It's Jack Slade." She whispered, with a fearful tremor in her voice.

Dylon watched as Slade and his two henchmen rode up to them.

"Well, Clay!" Slade sneered down at them as he leaned casually on the pommel of his saddle. "Hear you have somethin' that belongs to me."

Jack Slade was a handsome man, tall and lean with thick black hair, straight white teeth, and eyes the color of emeralds. He was a mean, powerful man. He took what he wanted and let no one stand in his way. Although Dylon frequented his saloon, a few times, he had little use for the likes of a man like Jack Slade.

"What do you want, Slade?" Dylon spoke with contempt.

"Just came to get what's mine." Slade's glance strayed toward Chris. "Come here, girl!" He snarled.

Chris looked anxiously at Dylon, then to Slade.

Slade's cold, calculating eyes narrowed. "You better not have ruined her for me, Clay." Riding closer, he motioned to her. "I said get over here!"

Chris handed the baby to Dylon and sauntered toward him.

"Is that Clara's kid?" Slade asked Dylon, watching the transaction from atop his horse.

Dylon nodded.

Slade gazed for another moment at the child, memories of

the only woman he had ever loved flooding his mind. Then he turned his attentions toward Chris. Reaching down, he grabbed her chin roughly. "Did Clay have his way with you, girl?" Chris jerked away in a defiant motion, only to have Slade backhand her, knocking her to the ground.

In an instant, Dylon sat the baby down and started toward him. When he heard the sound of metal leave leather, he knew there were two guns pointing at him.

Slade sneered at Chris menacingly. "I was right; you did open your legs for him. Damn you, Clay!" A black scowl clouded his face as he flung his finger at Dylon. "You lost me a lot of money. I could of gotten a high price for a virgin!"

He thrust his arm down to Chris, who was sitting on the ground with blood dripping from her mouth. "Come on, girl!" He demanded. "Get up here. You've had a free ride long enough!" Grabbing her arm, he pulled her roughly up and set her behind him.

"All right, Slade." Dylon met Slade's eyes and his voice remained calm. "What do you want for the girl?" Jack grinned, "Well, hell, Clay, come to my place of business and for a price you can have her anytime you want. But then you should know you been there a time or two. Haven't you?" Throwing his head back, he let out a lurid chuckle. Then he and his men turned and rode away. Slade rode a few feet, stopped, and surveyed the area, then shot back. "I always liked this property, Clay, and your cabin, too." Shrugging his shoulders in a matter-of-fact manner, he turned to Dylon and concurred. "That's my price."

Dylon snatched up Sarah, who was holding on to his leg, whining fearfully, and shouted with contempt. "You're a piece of scum, Slade!" Then he turned and walked into the cabin.

Jack shot Chris an evil grin. "Well, girl, you must not have pleasured him enough. Seems he likes his land better than you." Snickering, he turned his horse to leave.

Dylon quickly set Sarah on the floor in the bedroom where Karen had just awoken from a nap. He told both girls, sternly, to stay right where they were. Then he threw the cabin door open and stepped out onto the porch. "The land's yours, Slade!" He hollered. "Let the girl go!"

Jack Slade had never been surprised by much and usually trusted no man. He had known Clay for a few years and had heard he was a man of his word. Turning his horse around, he rode to where Dylon was standing. "Did I hear you right?" His voice held a note of surprise.

"You heard me right!" Dylon's voice held firm. Slade's piercing eyes narrowed, and he asked. "Where's the deed?"

"Let the girl go and I'll ride into town and we'll do it all legal," Dylon answered, his eyes never leaving Slade's.

Slade chewed on the idea for a few minutes, then he reached back and grabbed Chris around the waist. "Don't know which one of us got the better deal." He mocked as he lowered her to the ground. Throwing Dylon an evil grin, he tipped his hat and shouted, "See you in town!" Then he and his men rode off.

The moment Chris's legs touched the earth, they buckled, and she fell. Dylon exhaled a deep breath and slumped against the porch railing.

Watching as Chris tried to rise; he rushed over to her, grasped her by the arm, and pulled her to a standing position. Trembling, she leaned against him for support, and he stiffened. "Come into the house and get yourself cleaned up." Chris heard the anger in Dylon's voice, jerked away from him, and started walking extremely shakily, wiping the blood from her nose with her forearm.

Karen and Sarah rushed to them when they entered the cabin. Both were crying and shaking with fear. Dylon watched as Chris fell to her knees and enfolded them in her arms, soothing them with her calm voice. He noticed her nose was still bleeding, so he grabbed the bucket and stomped back out to get some water.

As he approached the well, he heard a horse and buggy drive into the yard. Sitting in the buggy was a wizened little man with a hunched back. His pasty skin was wrinkled and yellow. The suit he had on looked like a wad of dirty wrinkles and his greasy brown hair hung from under a faded bowler hat.

Dylon strode to the buggy and glared at him. "What do you want?"

Showing a mouth full of yellow rotted teeth, the man replied in a nervous twitter. "Oh...My, are you Mr. Clay?"

"Yeah, and I said, what do you want?"

"Well, sir, I'm Mr. Brande from the county orphanage. I understand you have Mrs. Perkin's two children here."

"Yeah... So?"

"Oh dear, oh dear." Mr. Brande stuttered. His fear of the huge scar-faced man standing before him was obvious.

"Well...Well, yo...you see, I have a paper here and I have to take them with me. I understand they have no relatives living. Are they in the house?" Glancing toward the cabin, he exclaimed nervously. "May I see them?"

Dylon nodded toward the cabin and started walking. Mr. Brande climbed down from the wagon and began walking-then half running to keep up.

Chris had washed her hands and face and had gone into the bedroom with the girls to change her torn dress. When she heard Dylon call her name, she lay the girls on the bed and told them to rest awhile. Both girls clung to her. "Listen darlings." She said, holding them close. "You lay here and be real quiet because Mr. Clay wants to talk to me. If you're real good, we will make some cookies this afternoon."

"You don't have to go anywhere, do you, Sissy?" Karen cried as she wiped her tear-filled eyes with the blanket Chris used to cover them with.

Chris heard Dylon impatiently call her again; so she kissed Karen's forehead. "Don't worry honey." She said, as she put her finger to her mouth in a shushing gesture. "You be real quiet now and I'll be back in a few minutes."

When Chris came into the room, Dylon's anger rose as he noticed the bruise forming on Chris's face. He introduced Mr. Brande and explained to her who he was. Then they all sat at the table to talk.

"What's all the fuss?" Dylon asked brusquely. "Why can't the girl take them? They've been with her since their mother died."

"Well, you see now, Mr. Clay, you just don't seem to understand." He looked toward Chris and pretended not to notice the mean bruise across her mouth. "I mean no offense, Miss Spencer, but with your background, no one in this town will hire you, and what would happen to you and those poor little ones? No!" Shaking his head, he stated flatly. "No! We just can't have that." Then, wiping his brow with the filthy rag he pulled out of his coat pocket, he complained. "Heaven knows, we don't need more mouths to feed at the orphanage, but it seems the only way."

Glancing at Dylon, he thought a moment, then sputtered excitedly. "Unless...Yes, Mr. Clay, you...you could take them. Of course, that would be the answer." He continued emphatically. "I hate to see us have to stuff two more children in that place, and girls, girls just don't have a chance." His eyes moving to Chris, he waited for a nod of support.

"Me!" Dylon yelled, shoving away from the table, not happy at all with the way this conversation was going, and definitely not liking this dirty little man with the nervous tic. "Look, mister, I just lost my house and land." Raking his hand through his hair, he expelled a loud sigh. "I don't even know what I'm going to do."

"Yes, well, I certainly understand, but still, it won't be hard for you to find work." Mr. Brande urged. "And they would be much better off with you." Pushing his chair back and standing, he placed his hat over his greasy hair. "Of course, if you don't see fit," heaving another sigh as if he were bored with the whole situation, he continued. "Then I'll just have to take them with me now." Glancing around the cabin, then back at Chris, he asked. "Where are they?"

Chris jumped up and frantically grabbed Mr. Brande's arm. "Please!" She pleaded. "Don't take them. I'm sure I can find some kind of work. Oh, please, I'll take good care of them."

Mr. Brande spoke sternly, as he patted her hand condescendingly. "Now, now dear, it can't be helped. You know, because of who your mother was, and your dealings with Mr. Slade, there's no future for you here, or anywhere else for that matter."

Dylon turned as he heard the bedroom door open and saw Karen and Sarah, so vulnerable, watching Chris. Tears were streaming down their faces. The muscles in his jaw clenched as he ran his hand through his hair. "Ah...Jeez!" He expelled an exasperated sigh. Then, glaring at Mr. Brande, he gritted. "What do I have to do to get them?"

Chris's head jerked up, and she stared at Dylon, stunned. "Oh... would you?" She exhaled a relieved sigh.

Dylon glanced at Chris and nodded toward the girls. "Take them into the bedroom." He commanded.

She quickly went and herded them into the bedroom. Stifling a sob, she hugged them close and whispered. "Shh...Don't cry. Everything's going to be fine."

After Dylon agreed to meet Mr. Brande in town the next day, he got on his horse and rode off without saying a word. Chris watched for him to come home, but he stayed away all night.

Chris understood how mad he was and how much he must hate her. The one thing she couldn't understand was why did he give up all that he owned for her? She felt unworthy and would someway pay him back, no matter what it took. He was a good man and would be a good father to the girls. She was determined to work hard for him and if he asked for more, then she would give him that, too. He owned her contract, and now she belonged to him. Thinking of Slade and what would have happened to her had she been forced to go with him, she breathed a sigh of relief. She was much better off with Dylon Clay, even though at times he was a big sulking oaf.

***

Dylon tied his horse to the hitching post in front of the law office of Herb Lavine. He had told Mr. Brande to meet him there at one o'clock. After the necessary papers were signed and Mr. Brande left; Dylon explained to the lawyer the situation he was in with Jack Slade. Herb told him he would draw up the change of deed papers and together they could go over to Slade's saloon. He would witness the necessary signatures for the deed and also for the change of ownership of Miss Spencer's contract. "I don't want to sign any papers for her," Dylon replied with irritation. "I'll just rip the ones up he gives me and she'll be free."

"If you care about the girl at all, it's best you go ahead and sign the papers and become her legal owner, then do what you want. Otherwise, she'll be open game for any man that knows her situation." Herb threw the papers on the desk and studied Dylon for a minute. "You know." He said. "This whole thing about bondservants is as unlawful as hell."

"What do you mean?" Dylon questioned.

"What do you think this country was at war with itself for?" Herb pushed back from his desk and angrily continued. "The Negro got their freedom, but the women, white, black, any color for that matter, are treated like property. I've seen some men treat their horses better than their women. And I can't do one thing about it."

"You said this whole thing was against the law. So why can't you do anything about it?"

Herb stood up and walked to the window, leaned against the frame, and stared out. "I have a wife and four daughters, so if anyone wants to see women treated fairly, it's me. But I got to make a living. It would take time and money along with the change of attitude in a whole lot of men." He turned around and glared at Dylon. "And the problem is, I'm talking about judges and lawyers. A girl like Chris, and believe me, there's a lot of them like her, doesn't have the money or the backing they would need to come against men like that."

Herb and Dylon were silent as they walked across the street to Slades Saloon. Dylon barged through the door of Jack's office without knocking. Herb Lavine was behind him and Slade's two gunmen right on their heels.

"Was wondering when you'd get here, Clay," Slade said as he stood and walked around his desk. "Thought maybe you changed your mind."

"Let's get this over with!" Dylon ground out.

"Why? Can't wait to get back to your new little whore?"

Dylon heard the snickers from his two henchmen and stepped closer to Slade. "Wonder how brave you'd be." He exploded as he motioned to the two men behind him. "Without your babysitters, always backin' ya up?"

Slade moved closer, and they stood sneering, inches from

each other, fire and hatred shooting from their eyes. "Anytime Clay, anytime!"

Herb Lavine, a big man himself and able to hold his own in a fight, instantly shoved his huge frame between them. "That's enough!" He ordered. "Let's get this thing over with!"

They signed the papers in silence, then Herb handed each of them their documents. Dylon grabbed it and turned to leave.

"Hey, Clay!" Jack called after him. "When you get tired of her, I'll take her off your hands, cheap!"

Dylon stiffened and turned around, but Herb Lavine shoved him out the door.

The next morning, as Chris was cleaning up after breakfast, she heard the rumble of a wagon out in the yard. Glancing out the window, she saw Dylon sitting in the wagon behind the reins, his horse tied to the back. The old man sitting next to him was a stranger to her. She picked up Sarah, grabbed Karen's hand, and led them out the door. The moment Karen saw him, she squealed. "Hey, Mr. Dylon, we missed you!"

Dylon jumped down from the wagon, grinned, and sauntered over to the porch. He grabbed Karen, chuckling, as he picked her up and swung her around. "Well, I missed you too, little girl." Sarah began jumping into Chris's arms. "Me too, me too!" She yelled. Dylon's eye's swept over Chris's face, and he noticed the ugly bruise forming on her cheek. He clenched his teeth in anger and regretted the fact that Herb Lavine stopped him from knocking Slade senseless. As he grabbed Sarah from her, his hand accidentally brushed across her breast. They both pulled back as their eyes met in both feeling a shocking embarrassment. With Dylon's hand still feeling warm from her touch and both girls in his massive arms; he walked over to the old man standing by the wagon. "Ned." He grinned proudly. "I'd like you to meet Karen and Sarah."

Ned Wilson was a small, wiry man. His head was bald except for a pure white halo that started behind one ear and ended behind the other. His deep-brown eyes were set under shaggy white brows. But his best feature was his smile; it showed off a set of straight white teeth, and would reach from ear to ear, deepening every line in his weatherworn, craggy face.

Ned was dead drunk the first time Dylon had seen him. He had just started working on a ranch back east. When he came out of the bunkhouse one day and saw that a couple of troublemakers had a drunken Ned held down in the horse trough. Dylon politely asked them to let him go, and when they refused, he knocked their heads together. From then on, he and Ned were partners. Dylon didn't mind; he liked Ned. He stuck to his own business, and only preached at Dylon when he would go on one of his drunken benders.

Ned gazed at the girls for a silent moment and with tears streaming down his face, he fell to his knees. "Thank ya Jesus! Thank ya, Jesus!" He began shouting with both arms raised in the air. Gazing at each of the girls and then toward the sky, he whooped. "Now mine eyes have seen salvation!"

Both girls nestled closer to Dylon, and Sarah started sucking her thumb profusely.

"Ned!" Dylon spoke sharply. "Unhitch the horses and take them to the barn!"

Ned jumped up and literally skipped to the horses, arms raised, laughing and shouting, "Praise ya, Jesus! Thank ya Lord."

Dylon glanced over at Chris and noticed she was glued to the porch in utter dismay. He arched his eyebrows and nodded toward Ned. "Old Ned was a circuit preacher. One day, after riding his circuit for a month, he came home and found that Indians had slaughtered his wife and two little girls. He went a little crazy after that, does some drinking, but won't hurt ya." Then he reached into the wagon, lifted out a large wooden trunk, and carried it to the porch. "Except for what we need to use daily, pack what you can in this. We'll take the rocking chair. I'm sellin' all of the other furniture. Mind you, pack it so nothing breaks; it's all I have left." Then he turned on his heels and strode to the barn.

When the men came in for lunch that afternoon, it didn't take long for Ned to grab the rapt attention of the girls. Even Chris caught herself smiling at his antics.

As Ned pushed himself from the table, Dylon noticed the tears in his eyes as the old man spoke to him. "Boy, we've been together since we worked at the Lewis ranch back east, and there are plenty of times this old carcass would be dead if it 'twarn't for you. I love you like ya was my own son." His gaze fastened on the two girls, and he swiped at his eyes with his sleeve. "Now these two little ones make us a complete family." Grabbing his wadded handkerchief from his pocket, he loudly blew his nose and rushed out the door.

Dylon said nothing, and he took no notice of Chris. He just patted the girls' heads, put his hat on, and left.

Her whole life, Chris had been neglected and constantly subjected to physical and verbal abuse. She was learning what love and family meant, but then the death of Clara Perkins took that from her.

Now she felt overjoyed for the girls. They would never have to feel unloved and unwanted. The mere look on these two lonely men's faces glowed with the love and care they would lavish on them. And who knows, Chris thought, maybe someday if I work hard for them, they would want me as part of the family too.

Chris washed the lunch dishes and put the girls down for their naps, then went and dragged the enormous trunk in from the porch. The two porcelain figurines, the small ornate clock, and the brass lamp would be the first things she would pack.

Remembering Dylon's harsh words to her about packing them right, she decided to go to the barn and get some fresh hay to lie in the barrel to protect the fragile pieces.

Ned was leaning on a shovel, watching as Dylon pitched hay in what seemed like a fevered frenzy. "Look, boy, you got to put this behind you. You have a lot more than you think you have. You're letting your anger take over. It wasn't that young woman's fault! She was doing what she thought was best for those babies. Shoot! I'll bet if you ask her, she'd probably even marry ya."

Dylon stopped and angrily stabbed the pitchfork in the hay. Then he pushed his hat back on his forehead, grabbed his handkerchief from his back pocket and swiped at his brow; then threw Ned a scornful smirk. Was it only two days ago that he had left his plowing to come and ask her to marry him? That was when he had something to offer her. It was bad enough that a woman would have to put up with his grotesque face. But now that he had nothing material to offer her, she wouldn't want the likes of him. He felt a surge of frustrated anger burst forth. "That doesn't make a whole lot of sense, Ned!" He yelled. "If it hadn't been for her, I wouldn't have lost everything I own. And I sure don't need an added burden, especially her!"

Chris was just coming into the barn when she heard what Dylon was shouting. Turning quickly before being seen, she ran back to the house. She quietly shut the door and leaned heavily against it. Wrapping her arms tightly around her waist, she moaned. "Oh, God, why, why?" Then she slowly sank to the floor. Why couldn't she just disappear? She thought as she quietly sobbed and rocked herself back and forth. Would she ever find some place to belong and to be loved and wanted? The pain she felt burned deep in her stomach and pushed up to her throat. Biting her bottom lip, she tasted blood as she stifled the urge to scream.

She was sitting on the floor by the trunk when Ned came in. The girls were awake from their naps, but she just didn't seem to have the energy to go get them. Ned noticed how tired she looked. "Listen here, little lady," he said. "I thought that maybe I could take those two young'uns off your hands for a while and take them down by the river. So's ya can finish up this here packin'."

Chris pushed herself up from the floor, nodded and gave Ned a weak smile. Then she went into the bedroom to get the girls ready.

She watched from the window as they walked down the path toward the river. The girls were laughing and playing as they ran ahead of Ned. Karen and Sarah seemed so happy. She knew that if Dylon raised these girls, they would be safe and well cared for. She also knew what she had to do. Going to the corner of the bedroom where she kept her few belongings, she wrapped them in her scarf. Then she walked to the kitchen and glanced around one last time. Her head held high and her shoulders squared; she walked out of the door and up the narrow dirt road, which she and the two little girls had walked down three weeks earlier.

Chapter 3

Dylon was coming out of the barn when he met Ned and the girls walking back from the river. Karen ran ahead of Ned with Sarah waddling after her. "Mr. Dylon!" she squealed excitedly. "We saw fishes!"

"You did, huh! Ya better be careful or those big fish might bite your finger off." Crouching down on his haunches, he waited for Karen to run into his arms. Grasping her small hand in his, he pretended to bite her fingers, savoring the sound of her squealing and the smell of her dirty little hands. When Sarah toddled up and threw herself at him, Dylon lost his balance and they fell to the ground. All three were laughing. Standing up, he placed Sarah on his shoulders and grabbed Karen's hand. "Come on!" He grinned at Ned. "Let's go get us some dinner."

The moment they entered the cabin, Dylon sensed something was wrong. He had gotten used to coming in from a hard day's work and finding a big meal on the table. He learned he liked the smell of fresh-baked bread coming from the oven in his kitchen, the feel of a clean, ironed shirt anytime he wanted one, and a tidy cabin. Most of all, he enjoyed seeing a plump little woman, with her face flushed from the heat of the cookstove, waiting for him. But tonight it was different. The house seemed empty. There was no aroma of food cooking, and no plump little woman waiting. And, the big empty trunk was sitting in the middle of the floor, with numerous articles scattered around it waiting to be packed.

Karen ran to the bedroom and, with a puzzled look, called. "Sissy, Where are you?"

Dylon set Sarah on the floor and glared at Ned with disgust. "Told ya, my money's gone. She has her freedom now, so she shucked her responsibilities on us and hightailed it out of here!"

Ned couldn't bring himself to answer Dylon. He had a strong feeling there was more to her leaving than met the eye.

After rustling up some dinner, Dylon made mats on the floor for two sad, tired little girls. Every time they asked where Chris was, both he and Ned cleverly changed the subject.

It was the first night Dylon slept in his bed in almost a month. Ned slept on the couch, just in case he was needed.

Dylon wasn't in bed long that night before Sarah wandered into the bedroom and tried to crawl in the bed. He ignored her, thinking if she couldn't climb up in the bed she would go back to her own mat. Watching and grinning at her determination, he finally gave in and picked her up, settling her next to him, only to have Karen a few minutes later tiptoe up to the bed and whisper. "Mr. Dylon, can I sleep with you?" He picked her up, tucked her next to Sarah, and wouldn't have been the least bit surprised had Ned and the dog tried to crawl in with him, too.

Watching them sleep, the responsibility that had been placed in his path overcame him. It even made him madder at the girl for leaving. Better she left now! It would have happened eventually, he thought, as he turned over in the small space left to him and tried to sleep.

The next morning, Dylon loaded the furniture that Doctor Matthews had bought from him on the wagon. Ned had agreed to stay with the children while he delivered it to the Doc's office in town. While the wagon jostled down the dirt road toward town, Dylon couldn't get Chris off his mind. What a drastic change his life had taken since the day she and those two little ones walked into his life. He had thought she loved the girls, but obviously, she had just wanted to be rid of them.

After the accident he had known a few women, most of them dance hall girls. They wanted money, and he wanted a night of release, no commitment for either of them, which was fine with him.

He had loved a woman once, or at least he thought he had. When he needed her, the most, she had left him. It was a big lesson learned. A woman would stick around as long as it would benefit her. Then she would bale out when there was nothing left to take. "I really misread this one." He muttered to himself. "She's like all the rest of them wants more than a man can give."

Ned slumped tiredly down in the rocking chair and watched as Karen and Sarah sat on the floor playing with some blocks. When Karen gazed up at Ned, he noticed the tears streaming from her big brown eyes. "Why did Sissy leave?" She asked as she got up and walked over to him.

"Well, now, honey." He answered. "I don't rightly know for sure."

"Doesn't she love us?" Her little face held a mask of puzzlement.

Ned's old brow furrowed as he reached down, picked her up, and set her on his lap. "Yes honey, I'm fairly sure she loves ya." When Sarah saw them, she toddled to the rocking chair and held her chubby little arms up to Ned. He lifted her up, and with a child on each knee, he started rocking. "Ya see, sometimes people kinda' get mixed up about things. I guess we're just gonna have to really pray about this." He could see by their bewildered expressions they had no idea what he was talking about. "Didn't your mama teach you how to pray?" He asked.

Both shook their heads no. Ned realized it had been a long time since he had prayed and also a long time since he had believed in a God that would answer prayer. When he had laid eyes on these two little babies just a few days ago, he knew that the 'Balm of Gilead' had healed his soul and cleared his mind. He was now ready to serve the God that he had so long been apart from. Pointing his work-worn hand upward, he explained. "Now let me tell ya, there's a God in the heavens that created us out of nothing but old dirt. Why he even gave us our hair and our eyes." He tugged at Sarah's thumb that was stuck in her mouth and his turned into a grin. "Why, He even made this here tiny, little thumb."

Karen gasped, Ned's face in her small hands, turned him to meet hers, and peered intently into his eyes. "Sissy said God took our Mama." A sharp pain stabbed at the pit of Ned's stomach, as a vision of Martha and his two little babies flashed through his mind. He held the girls a little closer, rocked a little faster, and forced himself to continue. "I lost someone that I loved very much too, and I was mighty mad for a long time." He expelled a deep sigh and tears rose in his eyes. "It still hurts, and I miss them a lot." He gulped as the unchecked tears rolled down his face. "I now know that God didn't take them away. It was the meanness of man that took them." With sureness in his voice, he continued. "But our God has them now. They're up in heaven along with your Mama, lookin' down here and wantin' us to do the best we know how."

"What does pray mean?" Karen asked with a curious squint.

"Well child, it's talkin' to God, just about like you and me are now, 'cept there's something real important."

Karen gazed at him quizzically and Sarah kept right on sucking her thumb.

"Ya gotta believe, child, ya gotta believe that God is who He says He is and He'll do what He says He'll do. And then when you ask for somethin' ya just gotta believe."

"We're going to ask God to bring Sissy back," Karen exclaimed with childish glee. "Aren't we, Sarah?"

After Dylon unloaded the furniture at the Doctor's office, Doc asked him to sit a spell. It surprised him when Dylon told him about Chris's abrupt departure. "It saddens me Dylon; I figured maybe she had finally found herself a place to belong."

"Yeah, well, you know how women are. Haven't met a one yet that's not fickle." Dylon spoke gruffly as he got up to leave.

Doctor Matthews watched as Dylon walked out of the door. He had known this man for a long time and considered him a friend. It disappointed him, as he had hoped Dylon had finally found a little happiness with his newfound family.

When Dylon left Doc's office, he went to the mercantile to pick up supplies. As he was out loading the wagon, Flossy, one of Slade's saloon girls, sidled up to him and wrapped her arm around his waist. Dylon angrily shoved it away. "Not now Flossy, I'm busy!"

"Tend like yer interested." She whispered as she put her arms around his neck and pulled him close, "I got somethin' to tell ya."

Dylon turned his face away, repelled by the smell of cigarette and whisky breath.

Throwing him a snide grin; Flossy showed a mouth full of rotting teeth. "Owning that little innocent made ya turn off the likes of me, huh?" She met his eyes and her voice held a note of concern. "Listen, Megan Spencer's kid came into the saloon last night." She glanced around nervously as she continued. "She told Jack that if he would give you back your land, she would work for him for as long as he wanted."

Dylon was taken aback. Grabbing Flossy by the shoulders, he held her away from him. "What did Slade say?"

"He told her to go back to you, 'cause he got your land, and that's what he wanted." Flossy reached into the bust of her low-cut gown and withdrew a cigarette. Dylon grabbed the match, struck it against the wagon, and lit it for her.

"Some of the men got a little rough with her." She continued as she inhaled a long drag of the cigarette and let the smoke trail out of her mouth. "Slade yelled at them to leave her alone, cause if you caught them messing with your property you'd kill 'em."

"Where is she now?" He bristled.

"I gave her what money I had and let her spend the night in my room. She headed East this morning, walkin' to the next town, gonna see about gettin' a job. Sure hope she makes it. She ain't never done no harm to nobody." Flossy shook her head sadly as she dropped the cigarette and ground it under her foot. "She's a nice kid. I'd like to see her get a fair shake."

Dylon finished loading the wagon, climbed in, grabbed the reins, and headed out. But instead of turning the wagon toward home, he headed East.

He hadn't gone far before he saw her. Pulling the wagon up a few feet in front, he got down and walked toward her.

Never imagining Dylon would come for her, Chris's first thoughts were of Karen and Sarah. "Are the girls all right?" She blurted as she ran to him with a worried frown.

"They're fine," shoving his hat back as he wiped his brow with his forearm, he spoke roughly. "Flossy told me what you did." His eyes narrowed as he watched her. "Why did you go to Slade?"

Her chin tilted proudly as she lifted her head and met his eyes and spoke firmly. "Because I didn't want to be a burden to you!"

The flash of her golden-brown eyes and the flush of her creamy cheeks didn't go unnoticed as Dylon threw his head back and laughed sarcastically. "Jeez!" He roared. "That's a little like closing the barn door after the horse got out, ain't it?"

Piercing him with an irate glare, Chris pushed past him and

started walking down the road.

His gaze followed her for a moment, taking in the sway of her nicely rounded bottom. Then he bellowed. "Girl...you get back here!"

She ignored him and quickened her pace. Dylon caught up to her in a few easy strides and grabbed her by the arm. "Wait a minute," he said. "I got an idea and it'll help us both out." His voice sounded calmer. "You wanna listen?"

She jerked her arm free from his grasp. "Go ahead!" She replied tersely, folding her arms and avoiding his gaze.

"Got a friend that owns a gold mine in Montana." He explained. "I'm sure he'll give me work. There's a wagon train a few days ahead of us we can hook up with." He pulled his hat down further on his forehead to block the sun and watched her expression as he continued. "You can take care of the girls for me. Figure nobody knows who you are in Montana."

Chris experienced an overwhelming surge of relief, a place to go, and a chance to be with the girls again. Her unfortunate birth gave her the stigma 'daughter of a whore. If Dylon was ashamed of her, well that was just too bad, she hadn't done anything wrong. Maybe he was right, she thought, there were bound to be decent people somewhere who would accept her for who she was not how she was born. No matter what Dylon's reasons were, she could at least be with Karen and Sarah for a while longer. Lifting her eyes and meeting his gaze, she calmly stated. "All right!"

Dylon breathed a sigh of relief and followed her as she started walking toward the wagon. He almost tripped over her when she came to a sudden stop and turned to meet his gaze. "I'd like to get something straight, Mr. Clay!" Dylon noticed the flush rise to her cheeks and with an amused grin, stated, "Go ahead!"

With her hands on her hips, and her eyes narrowed, she

spoke calmly and deliberately. "My name isn't 'girl', it's Chris, and I'd suggest you start calling me that!"

Turning swiftly, she climbed on the wagon, only to have Dylon grab her around the waist and lift her easily into the seat. A smile was curving the corners of his mouth.

That night, as Chris was preparing the girls for bed, Karen told her how they had prayed for her to come back. "Ned told us all about God and how if we really believed, then He would hear us." Wrapping her small arms around Chris's neck, she gazed at her seriously, "Oh! Sissy-I prayed, and I did believe!"

Dylon told them they would be leaving in a couple of days. He had heard the wagon train stopped and rested on Saturday and Sundays. If they left by Tuesday, they could easily catch up to it. So as not to overburden the wagon, Dylon told Chris to pack only the essentials. He figured, with luck, they could be in Montana in less than twelve weeks. Chris carefully packed the trunk, making sure Dylon's treasures had enough padding around them. This was all that he had left, and she wanted to make sure they got to their destination in one piece. As they carried it out to the wagon, Dylon yelled at Ned. "Careful, this is all I got left!" He tossed Chris a scowling glance over his shoulder. "Hope it's packed good." They tied the trunk to the outside of the wagon. Then Dylon put a box in the corner for the clothes. He also placed an old black metal container with his personal papers in the box under the clothes. Then he laid a big mattress in the wagon and set the crate with the food and cookware close to the gate for easy access.

He and Ned were securing the water barrel on the outside of the wagon the evening before they were to leave, when Karen came running out the door. "Papa! Papa! Can we go to the river to take a bath?"

Dylon's eye's lit up. "Papa?" He asked, his face showing surprise.

"Sissy said, you're our new papa now and we're going to a new home," Karen answered excitedly as she threw herself into his arms.

Not wanting to be left out, Sarah toddled toward him. "Pow! Pow!" she squealed, her arms lifted high.

An overwhelming feeling of joy flowed through him as he laughed, picked up Sarah, and glanced at Chris.

"I thought I'd take them to the river for a bath since we're leaving in the morning." She said as her eyes darted shyly from his face to the ground.

Dylon handed Sarah to her and ordered bluntly. "O.K., but make sure you watch them close."

Chris could feel the blush rise to her face as she took the girls by the hand and turned toward the river. Would he ever be nice to her, she wondered, or trust her? Sticking her nose in the air, she puckered her face and mimicked silently. "Make sure you watch them close." Then she angrily walked away from the massive figure working on the wagon.

When Ned and Dylon finished loading the wagon, Ned said he was tired and headed toward the barn with his Bible in hand. "I'm turning in boy, we got a big day tomorrow. Goodnight."

Dylon decided to walk to the river and check on the girls. He felt fear in the pit of his stomach when he thought about the trip ahead of him. He had a few dollars saved up. So money wouldn't be too much of a problem.

When Karen had called him Papa, it made him realize even more the responsibility that had been thrown on him. He was glad the girl had decided to come back and help take care of Karen and Sarah. Even though he hated to admit it, he liked having her around. He had heard her mumbling to herself when she had grabbed the girl's hands and started walking to the river. If he knew her like he thought he did, it was definitely something derogatory about him. She was a feisty little thing, he thought, chuckling to himself.

The river was a short way from the cabin, down a small knoll, and through a clump of maple trees. Dylon heard the rustle of the leaves from the warm summer wind. He inhaled deeply and smelled the fresh, clean air, feeling sick at heart to think that he would be leaving this place. He had worked hard to have a home, and now it was all gone. The night was warm and bright from the full moon. He heard them laughing and when he came around the corner; he stopped suddenly and stifled a gasp. Chris was emerging from the water; she stepped carefully on the bank, her small foot finding sure ground. Her wet, sheer bodice and bloomers were clinging to her. Her rich-brown hair was pinned to the top of her head with long tendrils escaping and sliding down, clinging to her cheeks. Dylon stared mesmerized as she reached to brush the stray locks from her face. Her jutting breasts and ample figure silhouetted against the full moon made him realize the tightening in his loins. He stood silent, watching for a wanting moment. Then, hearing their laughter again, he pulled his eyes from her and headed back toward the cabin. When he entered the barn and flopped down on his makeshift bed. Ned, who had noticed the tension between him and Chris, threw Dylon a knowing smile and commented. "The good book said it's better to marry than burn, son."

"Ah, Shut-up!" Dylon retorted as he fell into a fitful sleep.

Chapter 4

It took two days to catch up to the wagon train that was camped on the other side of a river. The river looked wide, deep, and angry, so Dylon rode across on his horse and talk to the wagon master. He came back across the river a couple of hours later and told them he and the wagon master had formed a plan. Dylon would take Chris and the girls across the river one by one on horseback. Then Ned would drive the wagon across while he led the team on his horse.

Chris held on to the dog as Dylon safely got her and the girls across the river. They were standing on the bank with a crowd that had gathered to watch Ned and Dylon. The wagon was over halfway across when one of the wheels got stuck in a hole. Dylon pulled on the horses and Ned cracked his whip over their rumps. As the wagon rolled out with a great jerk, the rope on the big trunk broke and the trunk went crashing into the roaring river. Chris saw what happened and, without thinking, quickly jumped in after it. The turbulence swiftly picked her up and jostled her through the water. When Dylon pulled the wagon onto the bank, he saw people running down the river, shouting. The wagon-master rushed up to him and yelled. "Something fell out of your wagon and your missus jumped in after it."

Ned went to look for the girls and Dylon started running downstream. He stopped when he saw Critter barking loudly. Glancing out into the water, he noticed a dead tree secured between two rocks. Chris had a firm hold on the stump with one arm, and the big trunk was held securely in the other hand. Dylon knew that the current was too strong to jump in after her;

it would just carry them both away. He yelled for a rope while shouting at Chris to let go of the trunk. Some of the men tied a rope around Dylon's waist. And as he crawled onto the log, he called out to her, "Hold on! I'm coming!" He could see the water was pulling her under and the trunk was smashing her against the log.

"Let the trunk go!" He yelled as he crawled closer to her.

Chris gasped. "Take the trunk...Quick!" Choking and sputtering, she tried to pull it closer to him.

"Let it go!" He shouted again.

"No! No!" she yelled frantically. "Grab it!"

Dylon jumped in the water, throwing one strong arm around the tree branch and the other around her waist. "Let it go, Chris!" He ordered as he moved his foot up and gave the trunk a swift kick. The trunk tore out of her hand, and she let out a loud moan as she tried to pull out of his arm to go after it. He held her tightly and with his face close to her ear, he whispered. "It's too late!"

"But it's all that you own." She whimpered as he lifted her to the log and helped her crawl back to shore.

A plump little gray-haired lady helped Chris off the log. "Goodness, child," she admonished. "What were you trying to do out there?"

Chris gazed at her in a confused manner. "But it's all that he owns." She muttered.

"Well now, child." She said as she smiled kindly. "It appears to me with you and those young'uns; he's got a lot more than most." Then she grasped her gently by the arm. "Come on darlin', let's get you dried off." Chris shivered with fear and exhaustion as she allowed herself to be led away by this kind stranger.

Dylon watched as the kindly lady led Chris away, feeling

stirred by a mixture of frustration and relief. Chris brought out feelings in him he thought were long buried. Clenching his fists, he turned and strode to the wagon.

After Dylon changed his wet clothes, he climbed out of the wagon and began inspecting it for damage. He glanced up as a tall, handsome, young man approached him. "'Scuse me, Mr. Clay, but Miz Watts asked me to come and get a set of dry clothes for yer missus."

Dylon threw the man an annoyed glance. "She's not my Missus." Then he asked the stranger curtly. "Is she all right?"

"Yes, sir." The young man answered, puzzled. "A little scratched up, but Miz Watts says she'll be fine." Shoving his hand out toward Dylon, the stranger grinned. "Name's Ken Drew."

"Howdy!" Dylon answered, as he reached out and grabbed his hand in a firm shake.

"Me and my brother Sam are traveling with the Watts. We got us some land in Montana, plannin' on doing some ranchin'." He nodded toward the wagon and asked. "Where are you headin'?"

"Going to do some mining, Butte." Dylon returned. "Thanks for coming by, but I want to fetch my little girls. So I'll bring the clothes on over."

As Dylon searched through the few tattered clothes Chris owned, he felt his face redden when he saw her much mended under-things and his body tensed as the picture of her in the moonlight flashed through his mind. Fear mingled with anger coursed through him as the thought struck him she might have drowned today. "What was she trying to prove?" He muttered to himself as he wrapped her things in a dress, jumped out of the wagon, and stomped toward the Watts camp.

Marie Watts and her husband, Tim, left a married daughter in Kentucky. Then, with their other three daughters, Anna and nine-year-old twins, Katy and Jordan, they headed west to find their dream. Tim had heard about Montana and decided to try his luck at homesteading.

Tim was as tall and thin, as Marie was short and plump. Except for her cheerful disposition and his thick head of black hair, they wouldn't be considered comely people. But they had produced four beautiful daughters. Seventeen years old, Anna's slight frame, luxuriant auburn hair, and flashing gold eyes turned the heads of even the happiest of married men. She was a kind, happy young woman and totally unaware of her effect on people.

As Dylon entered the Watts campsite, he saw Ned and the girls sitting by the campfire. Karen ran to him. "Papa, Sissy's all right, she almost drownded!"

He reached down and picked her up, then saw Mrs. Watts come from around the wagon. She threw him a friendly grin. "Howdy there, young man." Looking him square in the face she asked. "Did ya bring the clothes?"

"Yes Mam," he answered, liking her instantly when he realized she hadn't flinched at the sight of his scarred face.

"Dylon Clay, I thought that was you. I can't believe after all these years we meet up like this." Dylon quickly did an about-face as he heard the soft, familiar southern voice. Abruptly setting Karen to the ground, he gazed at the beautiful, tall, slender woman sauntering toward him. From her dark eyes and olive complexion, it was easy to see she was of Mexican descent. A thick, black braid was wrapped neatly around her head in a coronet. The cut of her elegant clothes and regal appearance spoke of money and breeding.

Dylon shot her an uncertain look, "Rita...Rita Lewis?" Nodding his head in a bewildered manner, he started toward her. "What are you doing way out here?"

"It's been a long time, hasn't it?" She exclaimed as she flew to him. Then she wrapped her arms around his neck and gave him a lingering kiss.

Chris had just changed and was coming around the Watts wagon when she saw a strange woman wrapped around Dylon kissing him. Dylon seemed to be cooperating fully in the act.

Karen giggled as she watched them. "Look at Papa kissing the pretty lady!"

When Dylon heard Karen's excited squeal, he quickly put Rita at arm's length. Then he glanced over to where Chris was standing and noticed her pale face and puzzled expression. Shoving his hat back on his head, he stared at the beauty in front of him. "Rita Lewis," his mouth forming into a grin. "Well, I'll be."

Rita's face lit up with a smile. "Oh, Dylon, I've thought of you so often these past years and what we had together." She stepped closer to him, grabbed his hand, and hugged it to her heart. "And now here we are again."

Dylon pulled away from her and threw Chris a sheepish glance. It was then he noticed everyone else around the campfire staring at them. Placing his arm around Rita's shoulder, he steered her toward the group. "Ah…!" He hesitated for a moment and then said. "Let me introduce you to the Watts family."

"Why, Dylon," she chuckled. "I've been traveling with the Watts since we left Kentucky." Then Rita glanced toward Ned and spoke with an unexpected edge in her voice. "Hello Ned, see, you and Dylon are still a twosome." Glancing down at the little girls standing next to Ned, she smiled. "And who are these two pretty young ladies?"

Dylon grinned proudly. "They're my daughters."

The disappointment covering her face didn't go unnoticed by Chris as Rita glanced at her. "Oh… then, this must be your wife?"

"Ah…no…She's…ah, Ned's daughter." Sheepishly glancing at Ned, he rushed on. "She's helpin' take care of my girls."

"Well, Ned, that's a surprise." Rita cast them all a relieved smile. "I didn't know you had children."

Ned got up from the log stump he was sitting on and walked over to where Chris was standing. He flashed Rita a disgusting glare. "Didn't figure you were interested." Then he grabbed Chris by the arm and nodded to Karen and Sarah. "Come on, let's go set up camp."

Chris couldn't help herself. "O.K. Pa," she answered with a drawl. The sound of her sarcasm didn't go unnoticed by Dylon.

After Chris thanked the Watts for their kindness, they took the girls and walked toward the wagon. Glancing over her shoulder at what she thought to be the most exquisite woman she had ever seen, Chris whispered. "Who is she, Ned?"

Ned's voice was full of concern as he explained. "I met up with Dylon at the Lewis ranch; it wasn't long after his accident. We was workin' as cowhands." He nodded back toward the Watts camp. "She was married to old man Lewis; he became completely bedridden from a stroke. She was a lot younger than him and had roving eyes." Ned rubbed his work-worn hand over his face in a tired gesture and continued bitterly. "The boy was easy prey for her with him all scarred up. He was hurtin' a lot on the inside, too. Bein' he had just lost his brother in the fire that messed up his face. And then the gal he was gonna marry took off on him."

Chris had never really known the full story of how Dylon received his scars. Now she was beginning to understand why he acted so harsh at times. Glimpsing back again at the woman, she asked. "She appears to be older than Dylon. Is she?"

"Probably by a good ten years," Ned stated flatly.

Chris paused, shocked, and grabbed Ned by the arm, stopping

him in his tracks. "Then she took advantage of him, Ned."

He shook his head and grinned at this naïve child. Then he patted her hand and spoke with a tinge of irony in his voice. "Well now, girl, I can't say, as I have much use for the lady. In fact, I wouldn't trust her as far as I could throw her. But I figure they both did some takin' advantage of. Dylon didn't feel real good about the whole thing, her being married and all. That's why we up and left and came out to Colorado."

"Why do you suppose he introduced me as your daughter?"

"I don't know his reasonin', but I'm glad he did it. Saves us some tall explainin'."

That evening, after Chris had finished fixing dinner and was sitting down resting, Dylon came back to camp. He walked over to where she was sitting, at a makeshift table, and sat down next to her. She could feel his steel-blue eyes on her but refused to meet what she knew to be a penetrating gaze. "Would you like to explain to me what that stunt was all about this afternoon?" He gritted through clenched teeth.

His anger surprised her, hoping he would understand. "I thought I could save it." She answered sadly, finally meeting his gaze. "I know how much those things meant to you."

He glared at her through embittered eyes, noticing the tired lines and defeated look on her face. "You don't know nothin' about me, girl." He shot back.

She threw him a glance of disbelief without bothering to answer. She got up, went and fixed his plate, then she slammed it down in front of him. He reached out and snaked his hand around her arm and saw pain shoot across her face. Pushing up her sleeve, he saw bruises and scratches on her hand and arm. With a pained expression covering his face, he let out an explosive sigh. "Jeez, girl! You could have gotten both of us killed."

Chris jerked her arm away, tired of being constantly chastised by him. "I don't recall asking you to jump in after me."

"Good. Maybe next time you decide to do something stupid, I won't be there to pull you out." He snarled as he grabbed his fork and started to eat.

After he ate, Dylon did some repairs on the wagon and then took a walk down by the river. He needed to clear his head. Since the girl came barreling into his yard a few weeks ago, yelling they needed to get hitched, his life had been in total turmoil. She brought feelings out in him that he couldn't understand. She made him boil with anger. Yet at the same time, he felt the need to protect and care for her. He realized he had to bury those feelings. She was young and pretty and needed more than he could ever give her, especially now when he had nothing to offer her.

He heard her sobs before he saw her. She was sitting next to a tree, rubbing her arm. Dylon caught a glimpse of her face framed in the moonlight, tears streaming down her cheeks. She watched hesitantly as he approached her, then he knelt before her and grasped her arm gently. "What's wrong Chris, does your arm hurt?" He asked kindly.

Sobbing, she cast her eyes downward. "My...huh...huh ar...arm. N...no."

He grasped her chin in his big, calloused hand and lifted her face to meet his. "What is it then?" With a confused expression, he urged. "What happened?"

Dylon's gaze roamed over her forlorn face, and his heart ached. Their eyes met, and he fought the urge to pull her to him. He wanted to tell her everything would be all right. But he owned nothing, and he had very little money. Now he had two children to support. And he had absolutely no idea what the future held. She would want and need more than he could ever offer her.

He knew how afraid and alone she must feel. She had been through so much in her short life. Yet he didn't know what to do for her. The hurts of the world had so embittered him that he was afraid to give any more of himself. So he just knelt there, gently massaging her arm.

Chris felt so afraid. She never remembered a time when she felt safe. Except maybe the time she was with Clara Perkins. But then the threat of Jack Slade coming for her was always hanging over her head. Although Clara did care for Chris and the girls, she didn't know how to show it in the physical sense. Now, Chris felt she was nothing but an added burden to this kind, gentleman.

Two scared, lonely people who had so much to give. Yet, the injustice of this world that had been heaped on them deadened their hearts and made them feel worthless. Had it not been for two little orphan girls, their lives would be closed in their own world of hate and mistrust.

Dylon stood, pulling her up with him. He grabbed a handkerchief from his pocket and handed it to her. She noticed the look of wariness on his face as he drug his gaze from her and expelled a sigh. "Here, wipe your eyes and go on back to camp."

Dylon saw the helpless expression on her face as she turned and walked away from him without uttering a word. Then he headed toward Rita's wagon, failing to notice Chris turn back to watch him with fresh tears rolling down her cheeks.

Chris and the girls slept in the wagon, and the men slept under it. Dylon hadn't come back to their camp when she went to bed. She hated that he'd caught her crying. The last thing she wanted to be was more of a burden. Because of her, he had lost everything. Chris felt a deep shame when she realized that this time, because of her, he had almost lost his life.

He wasn't in camp when she got up the next morning. Ned

seemed worried when she asked about him. He told her that Dylon didn't get back until real late and was gone again at first light.

The wagon train took Saturdays and Sundays off to rest the animals and do repairs. Chris had her chores done early since they had only been on the trail for two days. She took the girls and walked around the train to meet everyone and to offer her help. When she stopped by the Watts' to visit for a few minutes; she felt as if she had known this family forever. Anna was a real joy to be around. She was younger than Chris, but Chris hoped they would become good friends.

As Chris and the girls approached one wagon, Karen saw him first. "Papa!" She squealed gleefully. "Look Sis, it's Papa." He was sitting on a wood barrel with a towel wrapped around his shoulders. An old Mexican man was cutting his hair, and it looked like his beard had already been neatly trimmed. Rita was lounging on a chair nearby, watching. As Chris started to turn and leave, she heard him holler. "Girl! Bring my children here!"

Chris stiffened her shoulders and placed Sarah on the ground. "Run to Papa," she told them. Then she turned and hastily walked away without a backward glance.

Much later she was bending over the fire frying ham when she heard Ned exclaim. "Well, I'll be!"

"Look Sissy," Karen squealed, running to her. "Doesn't Papa look nice? Miss Rita said he's handsome."

Chris wouldn't say he was actually handsome, but he looked nice. His golden blonde hair waved back from his face and hung just to the edge of his collar. His beard also was neatly trimmed. Chris had really forgotten about his scarred face and only noticed it now from the blush on his cheeks. It was obvious he was uncomfortable with the various comments on his looks. Since she had been with him, she saw his clothes were always cleaned and ironed. Even though he infuriated her at times, after his kindness the first night when he found them in the barn, she had never really been frightened of him, much less thought that he wasn't good-looking. She knew she was falling in love with him but also held the bitter knowledge in her heart, not to expect anything in return.

"Yeah," Dylon exclaimed. "Rita said I was looking pretty ragged." Walking to the cook fire he looked in the heavy kettle hanging from a makeshift teepee-style frame and threw Chris an embarrassed glance. "What's to eat? I'm hungry."

They all gathered around the table and as Chris leaned around to serve him his food, she spoke in a low voice. "I think you look very nice." He nodded, and she thought she saw a blush rise to his face.

The next few weeks went by quickly. They started traveling at sunup and stopped at about an hour before sunset in order to set up camp. Dylon ate his meals with them and in the evening after supper, he and Ned would check the rig and make any needed repairs. Then he would spend some time playing with the girls. After helping Chris get them ready for bed, he would leave. Most nights Chris didn't think he even came back to camp to sleep. She was sure of it one day when she heard Dylon and Ned arguing. "Listen, boy!" Ned growled. "Your gonna get yourself in the same mess as before."

"Her husband's dead, Ned," Dylon argued. "It's not the same at all."

"Don't care what you say! She's trouble; trust an old man's instincts."

"It's my life, Ned, let me live it!" Dylon bellowed as he stomped off and stayed away the rest of the night.

They set up camp early Friday and as Chris was preparing supper, Anna came over to visit. She had a dress draped over her arm. "Chris." She asked. "You are going to the dance tonight, aren't you?"

"Well, really I hadn't thought about it." Then, remembering she had nothing to wear, Chris sighed. "No, I don't think so. Besides, Sarah's not feeling too good."

"Oh please, Chris, it'll be so much fun." Then she remembered the dress on her arm. "My mother wants to know if you'd like this dress. It was my sister's, but she outgrew it when she started having babies." Anna held the dress up to her tiny figure and giggled. "And it would take me forever to grow into it."

Chris gazed longingly at the dress. The skirt was dark blue, with tiny yellow flowers. The bodice was a much lighter blue and had soft yellow lace around the short puff sleeves. A row of small bone buttons ran up the bodice of the modestly low-cut neck. "It's beautiful!" Chris exclaimed, taking the dress and holding it up to her.

"It looks like it'll fit too and I've got some yellow ribbon you can borrow for your hair." Anna rambled on excitedly. "Come on, Chris, let's go. It'll be so much fun."

A few minutes later, when Anna saw Ned come into the camp, she ran to him. "Oh...Mr. Wilson, please tell Chris it's all right to go to the dance tonight."

Ned saw the glow on Chris's face as she held the dress up to her. "Why not? It'd be good for you to go." Then he threw her a wink. "And besides, that dress looks like it's lookin' for someone to wear it."

"Oh, Ne... Pa, you really think it would be all right?"

"Sure honey, I'll stay with the girls. You go and have a good time." Ned liked the feeling he got when she called him Pa. Chris was a good girl, and he wished Dylon would take the blinders off when it came to her.

The dress fit as if I made it for her. She wore the yellow ribbon braided into her thick, brown hair and wrapped the braid around her head. Her bangs fell softly on her forehead and sun-streaked curls shaded her cheeks.

Dylon and Rita were at the dance talking to Ken and Sam Drew when Dylon saw Ken's eyes widen. He glanced around and saw young Anna Watts. He realized she was what caught the young man's attention. Ken politely excused himself, and Dylon continued talking to Rita and Sam. When the music began, Dylon turned back to watch the young people dance. He noticed Anna Watts standing alone and saw that Ken was talking to some other woman. He couldn't tell who she was as Ken was blocking his view. But, when Ken stepped aside and reached out his arm to her, Dylon realized who it was. He watched Ken lead Chris to the dance floor and when she smiled up at him, Dylon felt as if someone had tied his stomach into knots.

Rita placed her hand on his arm. "Isn't that Ned's daughter?" She asked. "I thought she was plain, but she's a very pretty young lady."

"Come on, Dylon," she coaxed, pulling him to the dance floor. "I'm sure you haven't forgotten how to dance."

Reluctantly, he followed her. All the while wondering what was wrong with him? Here he had the most beautiful woman on the wagon train in his arms, and couldn't take his eyes off the young woman in Ken's arms. Especially when she smiled. When another young man came and cut in on a reluctant Ken, Chris even smiled at him. Jeez, he thought. What's she trying to prove?

Dylon didn't feel much like dancing. He was worried about Sarah; he knew she had been sick most of the day. He made his excuses to Rita. She didn't seem to mind, and he headed back to the wagon. The vision of Chris dancing with Ken Drew shot through him like a flash. His body went rigid when he remembered what she looked like, with the yellow ribbon in her hair and the blue dress framing her plump body so perfectly.

What was wrong with him? He wondered. He sure wasn't in need of a woman. It seemed like Rita couldn't get enough of him. Although, he did figure there was a catch to that relationship somewhere down the road. "Ah Jeez!" He muttered, "This is going to be a long trip. Guess I had better apologize to the girl about the way I've been treating her. Best we be on speaking terms," he thought.

Rita watched Dylon until he got out of sight and then grabbed Sam's arm and, with her prettiest smile cooed. "Come on, Sam. Dance with me."

Sam led her to the dance floor, all the while wishing Clay hadn't left him stuck with this woman. She had been like an albatross around his neck since his little brother talked him into joining up with this wagon train. She was beautiful, no doubt about that. But he'd had his share of beautiful women. Mary was beautiful and look what she did to him. They weren't married much over a year when she decided farm life wasn't what she wanted. One day, he came home, and she was gone. She ran off with some gambler. Sam got a headache just thinking about the drunk he went on. After about a week, his brother Ken came and threatened to kick him up one side and down the other if he didn't straighten up. Then he talked him into this trek to Montana.

"What's the matter, Sam? You seem awfully quiet tonight."

Sam threw her a half-hearted grin. "I'm fine, just tired." Rita gazed up at this man and her heart leaped. He was one of the most handsome men she had ever seen. He was at least a head taller than she was. His thick, black hair was unconventionally long, and he wore it neatly tied back with a piece of leather. His eyes were the color of the expensive brandy her husband used to drink and shaded in thick, black brows and long lashes. His nose was straight and set in the middle of high cheekbones. When he smiled, he showed a set of gleaming white teeth. She loved the feel of his hard taut body next to hers as they were dancing.

She had plied all of her feminine wiles to get him to share her bed. He was a bit closer to her age, too. But he did everything he could to avoid her, although he wasn't what she could call rude. When the dance was over, Sam led her to where the Watts was standing. "I'm riding out with the hunting party tomorrow and we're leaving at first light," he told them. "So, I'm going to call it a night."

Ken, Anna, and a couple of the other young people walked Chris back to the camp after the dance. Dylon was in the wagon, checking on Sarah and Karen. Chris stood by the fire for a few minutes, thinking about how much she had enjoyed this evening. She could see that Ned was fast asleep under the wagon, so felt reassured that the girls were all right. She reached up and unbuttoned the top front buttons of her dress, feeling free from the tight bond. She realized that she would have a busy day tomorrow and needed her sleep, although she hated to see this night end. She unwound her braid and dreamily pulled it over her shoulder and started combing it with her fingers, carefully pulling the yellow ribbon out of her hair. Waving the ribbon in the air, she began humming a familiar tune while swaying and whirling herself toward the opening of the wagon. Dylon came around the corner, and she smacked right into him. "Oh, I'm sorry!" She gazed up at him, startled, wondering if he could hear her heart pounding with the nearness of him. "I...I thought you were at the dance."

Dylon steadied her, put her at arm's length, studied her disarray, and then let her go. He glanced around the camp sight trying to see who she had been with. Then, glaring at her, he hissed. "And I'm sorry I ruined your evening." He stomped off without another word.

The next morning, Dylon didn't show up for breakfast and Ned muttered a nasty remark about the Lewis woman under his breath. Chris spent most of the morning hauling water to fill the wash tubs for washing. Ned had helped her and now was sitting at the table mending bridles.

When Dylon walked into the camp, Ned threw him an angry glance. "Good, just the person I wanted to see. Come over here, boy." He ordered. "And help me get some of this work done."

Chris was bending over the washtub scrubbing one of Dylon's shirts when Karen came running up to her with the Watts twins not far behind. Dylon glanced up from his work. "Sissy, can I spend the night with the girls?" Karen asked. "Mrs. Watts said since Sarah didn't feel good, it would be O.K.

"I'll come and talk to Mrs. Watts about it later. You run on and play now," Chris said, still bent over the washtub.

"You mean Sarah's still sick?" His eyes narrowing on Chris, Dylon snarled. "Maybe instead of you running off partying all night, you should of been here where you belonged." Standing up and charging toward her, he continued angrily, "I thought you came on this trip so as to make a new reputation for yourself. You sure ain't startin' out too good...!" Just then, a wet, soapy shirt hit him smack in the face, slid down his chest, and hung on his arm. "What...The?" He gasped in shock.

Chris stormed over to him, red-faced and fists in a ball. Then she began poking at his enormous chest. Her eyes were blazing as she spoke through gritted teeth. "My mother was the whore, Mr. Clay, not me! And it just so happens that I'm not the one that stays out all night sleeping in someone else's wagon!" She poked him again, this time a little harder. He backed up and almost lost his balance from the sheer shock of what she was doing. With tears streaming down her face, she yelled. "You...You, big oaf! You, leave me alone!" Angrily, she poked him again. "You hear me? Just leave me alone!" She yelled as she brushed past him and ran toward the creek.

"Who in the blazes does she think she's talkin' to?" Dylon spat out as he threw the shirt in the washtub and started after her.

"That's all right, boy." Ned chuckled, handing Dylon a towel. "I'll go after her, you go ahead and wipe the egg…er…I mean soap off yer face."

Dylon was changing out of his wet shirt when Ned came back. "Where'd she go?" He asked, concern covering his face.

"Saw her down by the creek with that Drew feller. Figured I'd let em' be."

Dylon tossed the towel on the table and, with an unintelligible curse, stomped off in the other direction.

Ned glanced up toward heaven, knowing that true enough, Chris was at the creek, but it was Anna Watts she was with. "Well now, Lord," he whispered. "I'm mighty sorry for that little white lie, but I figure we got to get some jealousy a-brewin, or we're never going to get your will accomplished here."

Dylon came back to camp early that night. As he rolled under the wagon onto his bedroll, Ned reached over and patted his arm. "Night, son."

"Night," Dylon returned as he lay under the shelter of the wagon. It was comfortably cool out and the sky was full of twinkling stars. The night was quiet except for the scattering sounds of people around the camp closing up their day. Weariness seeped through his bones, yet he couldn't find sleep. When he closed his eyes, a picture popped into his mind of Chris, down by the creek, sobbing on Ken Drew's shoulder and telling him how horrible the scar-faced man she works for treating her. When he heard Sarah crying, he looked up through the cracks of the floorboard and saw the dim glow of the lantern. Quietly easing out from under the wagon, he went and opened the flap and climbed in. He was caught off-guard, when he saw Chris sitting cross-legged, with her rich-brown hair cascading over one shoulder. She was wearing nothing but one of his old shirts that barely came to her knees, holding the crying baby in her lap. Feeling his cheeks redden, he lowered his eyes and backed out of the wagon. But then Sarah saw him and started crying harder, "Pow! Pow!" she wailed, reaching her arms out to him. He climbed in the wagon, closed the flap, and crawled over to her. "What is it, baby?" He whispered in a soothing voice as he reached out for her. "You don't feel good?" As he lifted her from Chris's arms, he noticed the button of the shirt had come undone and the top of Chris's breast was in full view. Chris also noticed and with cheeks blazing she reached up to button it, at the same time pulling a blanket over her bare legs.

Dylon pulled his gaze from her, glanced apprehensively at the baby, then back at Chris. "What's wrong with her?" He asked in a worried whisper.

"She has a cold and can't sleep. I really don't think it's anything to worry about. She just doesn't feel good." Chris reached over to take Sarah back. But Sarah whined and snuggled deeper in his arm. "No, Sissy." She pouted. "Pow, Pow."

"Where's Karen?" He asked, glancing around the wagon.

"Mrs. Watt thought it would be better for Karen to stay with them, just in case Sarah didn't sleep again tonight."

Dylon noticed the dark circles under Chris's eyes while trying to avoid the other things about her he wanted to notice. "You mean she hasn't been sleeping?"

Chris stifled a yawn. "Oh, just off and on for the last couple of nights."

Brushing back the baby's fine black hair with his hand, he glanced at Chris. "Go ahead and go to sleep. I'll stay with her for a while."

Chris was so tired she felt numb. She lay back on the mattress, watching Dylon's huge hand gently brushing the baby's hair. Feeling her body crave for the slightest attention from him. She closed her eyes, imagining his powerful arms around her, and drifted into a dream-filled sleep.

Dylon let his gaze roam over Chris's sleeping face. She was beautiful, not like the austere, classic features of Rita. Chris's beauty called out to him in her soft round curves; in the delicate scent of lilacs that would fill the surrounding air when she would walk by. He wanted to kiss each freckle on her creamy smooth complexion, and when she looked at him with her golden-brown eyes; he felt his breath leave him. She had taken over a part of his being and it scared him. He refused to let himself want her because he knew he couldn't stand losing her. She deserved a handsome man with something more to offer her than the mere pittance that he had. Besides, she was involved with that Drew fellow, which was just as well. He was young, good-looking,, and seemed nice enough. Dylon lay back with Sarah asleep in his arms and closed his eyes. The sooner she left, he thought, the better off they would all be.

Dylon woke with a start, forgetting for a moment where he was. When he felt a warm breath on his neck and the scent of Lilac fill his nostrils, he knew the body pressed up against his backside was Chris. He lay there for a moment, savoring the feeling of her warmth and imagining dreams far beyond his reach. Sarah was snuggled fast asleep in his arm, so he gently picked her up and moved her. When he turned over to face Chris, she rolled on her back, still in a deep slumber. The blanket fell away from her, again exposing the top mound of her ample breast. That stupid button, he muttered to himself. That's exactly why I threw the shirt in the rag box. He clenched his hand in a tight fist, willing himself not to touch her while trying to ignore the deep urge in his loins. Reaching for the blanket to cover her, he saw that her naked leg was tangled in it. Stifling a groan, he quickly climbed out of the wagon.

It was mid-morning, and Ned and Chris were sitting in the wagon as it jostled along the rutted trail. They were right amid the Rocky Mountains. Signs of many wagon trains before them well marked the trail. Chris loved the mountains. They gave her a sense of security, with their ever-present strength and beauty, never changing except for their dress in the season.

It was a beautiful day. The sun was shining and the soft white clouds streaked with gray sprinkled the blue sky. The baby's breath and the bright yellow dandelions filled the air with their pungent aroma. Dylon rode up alongside of them on his bay. He threw Chris a surly look and growled, "How's the baby?"

She averted her eyes, remembering the intimacy of last night, and felt her cheeks blaze. "She's a lot better today. She's sleeping now."

"You see to it you keep a close watch on her, you hear me, girl?" Glancing at Ned, he asserted flatly. "Goin' hunting-see you at camp tonight." Giving the horse a nudge with his heel, he galloped off.

Chris expelled an exasperated sigh as she watched Dylon ride away. "Oh...Ned, he really hates me."

Ned arched his brow worriedly, and then he reached over and patted her hand. "Now honey." He said. "That's just not true. In fact, I'd say the boy likes you a lot more than he'd care to admit."

"Don't be silly. He's got a beautiful woman like Mrs. Lewis chasing after him. What would he want with a fat, ugly girl like me?"

"Child, let me tell you a story. It happened to me a long time ago." Ned's face took on a far-away gaze. "I was going to Bible school back east when I got me a bad case of pneumonia. Didn't have no family to tend to me and no money to go to the hospital." He shook his head and let out a little chuckle. "So's I laid there in my bed thinkin' I was gonna die. One of the teachers at the school came by to visit me. Now I didn't even remember his name. The only thing I remembered was that we all called him the teacher with the ugly daughter. All my classmates and me, we'd see her at chapel every morning, and she sure weren't much to look at. She had bright red hair with a face full of freckles to match. She was big too, oh…not fat, mind you, just big-boned."

"Well now, this here teacher said that he was worried about me and that he would like for me to come and stay in his home while I was recuperatin'." Ned absentmindedly clicked his tongue at the horses as he flicked the reins to quicken their pace, then he continued with his story. "He explained to me that his wife died a few years ago, and it was just him and his daughter. I was mighty thankful when she greeted me at the door. I noticed her smile right away." Ned shook his head and grinned. "It was huge, why it lit up the room. And she had a set of the prettiest white teeth I ever did see. She helped her father carry me to the bedroom. I found out later she had given up her bedroom for me. She waited on me hand and foot and treated me as if I was someone real special. I learned that she was the most giving person I'd ever met. She was always taking food to someone that was sick or caring for people's youngun's, cleanin' the church or fixin' somethin' or another. The more I got to know her, the more beautiful she became."

Chris heard a sob rip from deep within his throat and when she looked at him, she could see tears streaming down his craggy face.

"You see child that was my Martha."

Slipping her arm through his, she laid her head on his shoulder as he continued. "She was so beautiful, always laughing and singing and she had a deep love for the Lord too. She never once doubted that she was made in the image and likeness of God. Why after we was married I'd wake up in the middle of the night just to look at her. I couldn't imagine that I ever thought her to be ugly."

"Oh Ned, I'm so sorry."

Ned reached for his handkerchief and mopped his tear-stained face. "Don't be a sorry child. I'm not, I spent too many years feeling sorry for myself, found out it's nothin' but a waste of time. Gonna spend the rest of my years doing what I learned from Martha, being happy with who I am." Ned patted her hand and grinned through his tears. "And I recon' it's time you do the same."

Dylon never spent the night away from camp again, and the rest of the trip was made under a silent truce.

The wagon train was two days out of Pony, Montana. A small mining community, that comprised about three hundred people. It was set in the midst of the Tobacco Root Mountains. In 1870, in a small mining camp called Strawberry, a man by the name of George Moreland found a load of ore so thick with gold it could be mashed out with a pestle. The ore was worth $20,000 to $100,000 a ton. The population soon grew to several hundred people and produced a post office, store, and the usual jerry-built saloons. The town of Pony took root in 1875 when the Mallory brothers built a five-stamp mill with huge four and half-foot fir blocks where the stamps were set. By 1876 Strawberry had become merely an outlying district, and Pony began growing by leaps and bounds. The Boss Tweed Mine, in Pony, had the largest system of untimbered stopes in the world, cut out of solid granite. It produced thousands of dollars a day of ore for the stamp mill to grind out. And, there was numerous small gold and silver mine claims around the area that were prosperous. The farm and ranch land was plentiful, and the earth produced wild strawberries, raspberries, and blueberries. There were acres of graze land and sturdy timber for the settlers to build warm cabins to protect them against the cold Montana winters.

Most of the people on the wagon train, including the Watts and the Drew brothers, were planning on settling in Pony. The main street had boardwalks on both sides. At one end of the street was Taft and Potter's Livery Stable. The jailhouse sat next to it. Right across the street from the jail was the community hall. In the center of town, Isdell's Mercantile held all that a person needed for daily life, work clothes, dress clothes, material, hats, tools, and numerous articles of canned goods and food supplies. But the talk of the town was the William H. Morris Drug Store. It was said that, while his new store was being built, the Vigilantes used an exposed beam to string up five dangerous outlaws. And of course, at the other end of MainStreet were the inevitable, Gilbert's Saloon and Duffy's Saloon and WhoreHouse.

That night in camp, after dinner, Dylon lingered over a second cup of coffee with Ned. Chris noticed the sound of apprehension in his voice when he spoke. "Girl...come and sit down. I want to talk to you and Ned." When Chris was seated, Dylon began. "Decided to settle in Pony, Rita owns a gold mine and a thousand acres of ranch land about twenty miles from the town." He gulped a swig of his coffee, then rubbed his hand tiredly across his face and stroked his beard. "She made me an offer. She wants me to run it for her and..well," he rushed on. "We're going to get married."

Chris quickly pushed away from the table, afraid they would hear the sound of her heartbreaking. "I hope you'll be very happy." She managed to say as she began clearing the dishes from the table.

"Wait, I'm not finished." He continued glancing at Chris. "I got an offer for you." Pausing, he waited anxiously as she sat back down.

"You see there's only a lean-to on the property, its fine for us to live in, but," he spoke hesitantly. "I can't expect the girls to live like that. There's an awful lot of work that needs done. And I'm going to build us a house. I...er...we was wonderin' if maybe you would stay on and tend to the girls for a little while longer." Dylon shot her a pleading glance, then quickly continued. "I'd rent you a place and pay ya."

The mistaken dreams and fantasies Chris had built up in her mind these last few months came crumbling down. Although, in reality, she knew all along that her life here would have to come to an end. Now he was giving her some reprieve and she could at least be with the girls a while longer. Just the thought that she would ever have to leave was unbearable. Chris would stay, she would stay under any conditions. She plastered a smile on her face and drew her eyes to meet his. "Yes, of course, I'll stay, as long as you need me."

Dylon exhaled a sigh of relief. He wasn't certain she would stay, and he wasn't sure how he felt about her leaving. He knew he didn't like the feeling he got when he thought about her not being a part of his life, and yet he knew he had no right to feel that way. Glancing toward Ned, he sheepishly grinned. "Me and Ned will come by and help with the chores."

"Not me, boy!" Ned declared with a tinge of disgust, frosting his voice. "I'm staying with Chris and the young'uns. They'll need a man around the house to look after 'em."

Dylon shot him a surprised expression, and then shrugged his shoulders. "Suit yourself." He declared indifferently.

Dylon rode to Pony, ahead of the wagon train. That way, he could find a place before Ned, Chris, and the girls arrived. Rita had also told him to hire some men to help rebuild the mine. She had inherited the mine when her husband died. Rita had hated the South, so when she found out about the gold mine and the huge amount of land she had inherited, she decided to sell the ranch and come out west.

The mine hadn't been worked in a few years. It was the end of October and they were running out of time. Winter wouldn't be long in coming.

Dylon couldn't help but think about last night's events. After their talk, he walked down by the river and Ned had followed. He had seen Ned in many different moods; drunk, sober, happy, and melancholy. But he could never, in all the years they had been together, remember him being so angry. "What do you think you're doing, boy?" Ned had yelled. "To even consider marryin' someone like that Lewis woman when you got a gal like Chris, tendin' to those young'uns, seein' you're always cleaned and pressed! Your bellies never been happier with the good food she always seems to rustle up. Sometimes, boy, I think you got pig manure for brains!"

"Come on, Ned!" Dylon yelled back, "Give me a break, I don't have nothin' to offer a girl like her. She's lived poor all her life. She's gonna want a lot more than I could ever offer her, besides I got those two little girls to think of."

"Oh!" Ned sputtered sarcastically. "And you think Rita Lewis can give those girls what they need?"

"Darn right, I do. That mine's going to make a lot of money, and I'm gonna be a part-owner." Dylon yanked his hat off and raked his fingers through his hair. "Besides," he said sheepishly. "That Drew feller's courtin' Chris."

Ned's shoulders drooped as he shook his head sadly. "The only thing I can do for you, boy, is to pray that the good Lord will help ya to see how wrong ya are."

Dylon hadn't seen Ned before he left the next morning. But Chris handed him a sack of food. As he was hugging the girls, she glanced up at him, smiled shyly, and told him to be careful. Their eyes had met, and Dylon noticed the sadness in hers, but she quickly pulled away from his gaze.

As he was riding out, he turned to wave to the girls. Chris was standing with Sarah in her arms and Karen next to her. But all he could see was Chris, with her thick auburn hair falling over one shoulder. The picture of her wearing his old shirt with the top button undone and her creamy breast exposed made him shake his head to clear his brain as he waved, turned, and rode.

Chapter 5

Dylon, Ned, Chris, and the girls were standing in the yard, looking at a small shabby cabin with a ramshackle barn and chicken coop both in need of much repair. As they climbed the stairs to the big porch, they could see the swing off the side dangling dangerously by one rope.

"It's a real dump, but it's all I could find." Dylon pushed the door open, and they walked into a large common room. They probably used the left part for the sitting room. It had a large window overlooking the front yard, with the only furniture being a plain wood bench pushed up against the wall. A small rock fireplace on the far wall helped to separate the sitting room and the kitchen. A big pine kitchen table with trestle leg benches to match sat on the rough plank floors. There was a long kitchen counter that ran under a gigantic window with a few bare shelves hanging on the wall. The cast-iron stove was black with grease, but Chris knew that with a good cleaning, it would work well.

They pushed through one of the two doors off of the kitchen and found a small bedroom. Although covered with grease and grime, the windows were all intact. While the others went and explored the bedroom next door, Chris wiped some grime off of the window and peered out. She gazed in awe at the sight. The majestic Tobacco Root Mountains towered around her. They gave her a peculiar sense of peace and security, with their tall snow-covered peaks of many shapes and sizes reaching toward the heavens.

The bright blue sky with a scattering of white clouds and the warmth of the sun shining through the window seemed to give her renewed strength. Watching the gold, crisp leaves falling from the trees, she could smell winter in the air. Sensing Dylon standing behind her, she trembled with delight at the touch of his breath on her cheek as he bent over her shoulder to peer through the small clearing in the dirty window.

"Well, at least the views good." he reached around Chris to clear some more grime away and gazed up toward the sky. "It looks like you can almost reach out and touch it. That must be why they call Montana the big sky country."

As he pulled himself to his full height, he glanced around the room in disgust. "Jeez!" He muttered. "This place is falling apart." Reaching over, he pulled a piece of loose chink from one of the logs. Chris grabbed it from him and pushed it back into place. "Don't worry." She said. "With a little work, it'll be fine."

Ned decided they should sleep in the wagon until he finished some work in the cabin. Dylon helped unload, and they stored what little there was in the barn. Then he checked the well and the privy and felt satisfied they were in good shape. When it was time for him to leave, there were teary farewells from Karen and Sarah. Ned talked the girls into walking down by the creek, so Chris and Dylon could have some time alone. Dylon handed Chris some money and watched her through narrowed eyes. "Here," He instructed. "Buy what you need to fix the place up! Best see that the girls are set for winter." Grasping the reins of his horse and mounting, he gazed down at her. "I probably won't be back for a few weeks."

Chris lifted her hand to her forehead, shielding her eyes from the sun. "We'll be fine." She smiled up at him. "Don't worry."

Dylon rode off, then stopped and turned in the saddle. "Oh...and girl," he yelled. "Get yourself some nightgowns." Grinning as he saw the blush rise to her cheeks, he put the spurs to his horse and galloped off.

After Chris and Ned spent two days cleaning and moving in, they took a day off and went to town. Ned kept teasing Chris about the money Dylon had given her. He said it would more than likely burn a hole in her pocket if she didn't hurry up and get it spent. The town was just two miles from the cabin. This was the first trip to town for both Chris and the girls. As they jostled along in the wagon, Chris listened to the girl's silly chatter. The glitter of the gold and yellow leaves in the trees and the smell of the cool, crisp air gave her a feeling of exhilaration. And again, a strange sense of belonging flowed through her

She was jarred from her thoughts as they rumbled into the main street of Pony. Ned pointed to Isdell's Mercantile. "I reckon that's where you three want to go."

Ned lifted Karen and Sarah out of the wagon and told Chris he would come back for them in about an hour. He needed to get some things done to the wagon at the livery stable. Before they entered the store, Chris told the girls if they were nice and polite she would let them have a peppermint stick; but only after they picked out their new coats and boots. The store was huge and exceptionally clean. It smelled of leather and smoke from the big wood stove that was setting like a warm welcome sign in the middle of the floor.

Chris liked Mrs. Isdell the moment she saw her. She greeted them with a big, toothy smile that came from a long, narrow, plain face. Her eyes were almost as black as the thick hair that was wrapped in a tight coil on top of her head. She was very tall and very thin. "Hello! Hello!" She smiled as she motioned to Chris and the girls. "Come on in here where it's warm. I'll bet you're one of the new families with the wagon train that pulled in a few days ago. Sure hope you're planning on staying."

Chris nodded and smiled back. "Yes, Mam, we rented a place a couple of miles from here."

Mrs. Isdell glanced over at the girls and wiped her hands on her apron. "I'll bet you're Dylon Clay's little girls?" She walked over to them and placed her hand on Karen's head… "Let's see now. Is it Sarah or Karen?"

"I'm Karen and she's Sarah." Karen giggled as she pointed to Sarah.

"Well, howdy!" She answered, reaching out for their hand. "I'm Rachel Isdell and I'm the one that rented that old house to your pa." Glancing at Chris, she apologized. "I'm afraid there just isn't much around here to live in right now."

"It's fine," Chris answered with a smile. "Ned and I are working now to fix it up."

"Ned?" she asked. "He's your father, right?" Mrs. Isdell glanced toward the back of the store and called. "TC, come on out here. I want you to meet somebody."

Rachel Isdell's nephew, TC, was a tall, handsome young man with the same black hair and dark eyes as his aunt. He was about the same age as Chris. He had traveled from Washington State to spend a few months helping out his widowed aunt. "These are the people that are tendin' to Mr. Clay's young'uns." Mrs. Isdell told him as she introduced them. "They're trying to fix up that old place I rented to them. Thought maybe we'd supply the paint and you could help with the labor."

"Did I hear someone say they'd supply paint and labor?" Ned called out as he entered the store and grinned over at Rachel.

After they made more introductions, TC quickly agreed to help them with any chores that needed to be done. Chris finished her shopping while Ned and TC gathered the supplies that were needed for the repairs.

As the men were loading the wagon, Rachel told Chris a little about the town of Pony. "It's a good town; most of the people are hard-working and mind their business." She nodded toward the jailhouse. "We got a fine man for a sheriff." Then she winked at Chris and grinned. "He's not married either, so he keeps all the old maids busy cooking and primping for him." Then she asked. "Are you church-going people? Because if you are, that's, to my regret, the only thing lacking in this town." Ned had just entered the store and heard Rachel's comment, and with a big grin, answered. "Well, Mrs. Isdell, we'll just have to do something to change that," Rachel answered, his grin with one of her own.

TC came out to the cabin the next afternoon to help with the painting. Mrs. Isdell came with him to supervise and ended up helping Chris fix supper. After they all ate, the four of them set about getting the cabin to look like a home. Rachel and Chris sewed new curtains and pillows for the chairs, and the men finished the painting. Chris liked TC, and it didn't take long for them to become friends.

"There's a barn-raising Saturday over at the Smith's place," Ned said a couple of days later as he came into the kitchen from doing his chores.

"I know," Chris replied. "TC asked me and the girls to go with him. He said there would be a picnic and dance after. They want to get the barn raised before the first snow."

Ned grabbed a mug from off of the shelf and poured himself some coffee. "Thought maybe I'd take Rachel."

Chris stopped what she was doing and turned to him. "Who?" She asked, raising her eyebrows and her mouth turning into a grin.

"Mrs. Isdell... and don't give me none of your silly grins."

"I think it's great, Ned. She's been widowed for quite a while now. It's time both of you have some fun."

Chris reached into the cabinet for some dishes. Ned came over and took them from her and started setting the table. "Same goes for you, little lady. That TC seems like a nice enough young man."

"Maybe so, but he's engaged to be married and is leaving in a few months, back to Washington. Besides, I'm not interested in finding anyone." Chris was stirring the pot of rabbit stew on the stove. She stopped for a moment and gazed out the window. Would this yearning for Dylon ever go away? She mentally shook herself, refusing to think anymore about it.

"You're thinking of Dylon, aren't ya, honey?" Ned asked as he went to her and placed his hand gently on her shoulder.

Tears sprang to Chris's eyes. "It hurts Ned. Will this feeling ever go away?"

"Not if you really love someone. All I can say is it gets a little easier with time." Ned's experience with love was different, and he knew it. His love for Martha had been returned. Dylon needed a good thrashing. He loved the boy and hated to see his life ruined with that Rita Lewis when he could have a pure love as this young girl had for him. Ned placed his hands on her shoulders and turned Chris to face him. "You know honey; the good book says that if you pray and believe, what you pray for shall be given to you."

Chris managed a smile through tear-filled eyes. She didn't know much about that sort of thing. She had never really heard about God or prayer. She wanted to believe. It would be nice to know that there was someone to love her the way Ned said that God did. It was hard to believe that the Son of God would die for the likes of her and her sins. She knew it could happen. Hadn't Dylon given up all that he had in this world to save her? Although, she couldn't, for the life of her, figure out why. She didn't think she could handle any more rejection. So maybe, for now, she would just let Ned handle the God thing.

Saturday morning burst upon them with a cool breeze and a warm, bright sun. TC came out to the cabin for Chris and the girls in the buggy. Ned drove the wagon into town to pick up Rachel. She had to deliver some supplies to the building site, and

Ned agreed to help her.

Chris had on the blue calico dress she had received from Mrs. Watts. She pulled her hair back and tied it with the yellow ribbon Anna had given her. It was the first time she wore the dress since the dance on the wagon train. She also put a couple of extra petticoats on under it to keep her warm. Not having a decent coat of her own, she borrowed one of Ned's old jackets to wear. Then, Chris bundled the girls up in their new coats and packed a bunch of ham sandwiches and some butter cookies she had baked for the occasion.

It was a long ride, about five miles from Pony, but TC kept them entertained with stories about Seattle. Karen and Sarah especially loved hearing about the ships that were bigger than their house and would float on top of the water.

A lot of people had already arrived and were milling around, greeting each other, sharing any local news, and setting up tables for the food. TC lifted the girls down from the buggy and was reaching in to help Chris when they heard Karen yelling. "Look it, Papa!" Chris grabbed TC's hand and stepped down from the buggy just as Dylon and Rita approached them. Dylon reached down and swooped up both of the girls, and gave them a big bear hug. "I didn't know you were coming." He grinned at them. "But I'm sure glad you did." Setting them to the ground, he turned them toward Rita. "Can you say hello to Mrs. Lewis?" Karen shot her a quick hello and then turned to Chris. "Katy and Jenny are over there. Can we go play?" "All right," Chris said. "But you stay right where I can see you." Karen reached for Sarah's hand, and they both ran off. Karen stopped and turned to Dylon, "Papa, we miss you. Can you come home?" Dylon walked over to her, scooted down on his haunches, and gathered both of them close to him. He whispered something in their ear and they giggled, kissed his cheek, and skipped away.

Rita gazed up at Dylon as he came over and stood next to her. "They are beautiful little girls." She said as she tucked her dainty leather gloved hand in the crook of his arm. Chris quickly stuck her red chapped hands in the pocket of Ned's old jacket, feeling so inferior next to this beautiful woman. Rita looked exquisite in a forest green coat with a rich brown fur collar. Her coal-black hair was falling in waves down her back and held in place by an ornate beaded comb. But Chris's eyes could hardly leave Dylon; he looked so handsome. She could see a blue flannel shirt under his sheepskin coat. They both looked new. His beard was neatly trimmed, and the sun had darkened his face to where the scars were hardly noticeable. His dark brown Stetson sat back on his head with a few stray locks of his blond hair hanging on his forehead. It made Chris's heart sad to see what a handsome couple he and Rita had made.

"Where's Ned?" Dylon asked, none too friendly, as he glanced at TC and then at Chris.

"He went into town to pick up my aunt. They should be here any minute." TC answered as he stuck his hand out to Dylon. "We haven't met, Mr. Clay. I'm TC Isdell. You rented the cabin from my Aunt Rachel." Dylon returned the handshake. They all turned as they heard a wagon roll-up. Ned saw Dylon and grinned. "Hey, boy, I didn't know you'd be here."

Dylon grinned back. "Thought I'd better, so the favor can be returned when we start building our place."

Chris quickly turned and began walking away, trying to stifle the hurt that was welling through her, at the thought of him and Rita building a home together. TC followed.

Dylon watched as the handsome young man ran after Chris and felt a rush of jealousy. For some reason, he always felt like a missing piece of him was put back when she was around. But today, she hardly spoke to him. Then he felt Rita's hand on his arm and realized he had no right to any feelings toward the girl at all.

"You're in love with him, aren't you, Chris?" TC asked as he caught up to her.

Chris let out a sarcastic laugh. "Is it really that obvious?"

TC slipped his arm through hers. "Naw! Come on, let's go see what we can do to help." He walked toward the men working at the barn, and she went to help the ladies prepare the food. Chris unwrapped the cookies and while she was placing the sandwiches, she made on the table, Rita walked over and picked up a cookie from off the plate. She ate it and grabbed another. "Your cookies are great." She purred sweetly to Chris. "Maybe I'll have you make some for our wedding."

"Sissy, will you take us to the river?" Karen, the Watts twins, and some of the other children were standing in front of her with pleading eyes.

"Go ahead and take them. I'll watch Sarah," Rachel said. Reaching down, she picked up Sarah and handed her a cookie as Chris and the children left.

Dylon had just picked up his tools and was heading toward the barn sight when he spotted Chris with a bunch of the children walking to the river. He stood and watched them until they drifted out of sight through a clump of Cotton-Wood trees.

"What's that out there?" Jenny Watts asked, pointing toward some big rocks in the middle of the river. Chris looked to where she was pointing and saw a gunny sack stuck on the rocks with three little wet kittens clinging to it, trying not to fall into the water. Chris could see the bottom of the river through the clear water. She realized though it would be cold, it wasn't very deep, and it only had a light-flowing current. "They're kittens," she exclaimed. Shrugging off Ned's jacket and throwing it on the ground, she hurriedly kicked her shoes off. "Someone must have tried to drown them and they got hung up on the rocks." She reached down and pulled the front part of her dress up and stuck it in the waistband of her underskirt. Then, she grabbed at the bottom of the petticoats, pulled them up through her legs, and stuck them also in the waistband. "I'm going to go get them. You stay right here." Her eyes narrowed as she spoke to the children seriously. "Do not come close to the water! Do you understand?" Not moving until she received an answer from each of them.

When she stepped into the water, Chris felt the bitter cold. Balancing herself carefully, she wadded out to the kittens.

"I'm going up to get TC," one boy yelled, as he headed to where the men were working at the barn.

Dylon was on the ladder just finishing a window frame when he noticed one child running up to TC. Then he saw TC drop his hammer and start running with the boy, in the river's direction. Dylon quickly climbed down the ladder and went to look for Chris and the girls. He saw Sarah with Rachel and, with icy dread in the pit of his stomach, he turned on his heels and dashed toward the river.

Chris grabbed the soggy little creatures and whispered to them as she wrapped them in the gunnysack. Then she held them securely in her arms as she started back toward the shore. Her feet were numb, and she was shivering. When she glanced at the shore, she noticed TC. He had rolled up his pant legs and waded out toward her. "Hand me the sack, Chris," he called, reaching out for it. He grabbed the kittens from her and threw them onshore. Then he reached out for Chris's hand. As she grasped hold of him, she slipped. He tried holding her up, and they both toppled into the ankle-deep water. He tried standing, pulling her with him, but they both fell again. TC glanced at Chris and when their eyes met, they both burst into laughter.

Dylon was standing on shore with the children. Growing agitation surged through him as he watched the two gigglings, shivering people crawl out of the water. Then he shouted, "What's going on here?",

"Papa, somebody tried to drown the kittens and Sissy went to get them." Karen pushed a wet furball in Dylon's hand. "Can we keep them?" Dylon handed the kitten back to Karen without looking at it and rushed toward Chris. She was sitting on the ground, shivering. He reached down and helped her up. Then he slipped out of his coat and wrapped it around her.

"Are you all right Chris?" TC asked through chattering teeth.

She threw him a shivering nod.

"G...Good, I...I'm going up and get some d...dry clothes on." He motioned to the children. "Come on l...let's go get those kittens dried off."

Chris was shivering so hard her teeth were rattling. Dylon grabbed at her petticoats and started yanking them down. She put her arm out to stop him. "Wh...wh, what are you doing?" She asked, her voice trembling.

"I'm trying to get these wet things off so you can get warm." He knelt in front of her, and she placed her hands on his shoulders as he pulled the petticoats off. Then he pulled the dress down over her damp pantaloons. She was trembling so hard he drew his coat more securely around her, picked her up, and carried her to a dry spot under the tree. He set her on the ground, then he went and got Ned's jacket, wrapped it around her legs, and started rubbing them. His jaw clenched in agitation as he gritted out. "You got to start acting more like a lady...girl!"

"What did you say?" She asked, feeling her anger rise.

"You heard me!"

His hands were still rubbing her legs, and she pushed them away and snapped at him. "If you want me to act more like a lady, quit calling me girl!"

"You and that TC acting like two little kids." He muttered, as he ignored her and concentrated on getting the circulation back in her legs.

"I'm so sorry!" She ground out, speaking to the top of his

head. "But where I grew up, there wasn't much time to learn how to be a lady!" Then she threw out sarcastically. "Maybe your future wife can teach me! That is, of course, after I finish making my famous cookies for your wedding!"

His head jerked up. "Maybe so!" He shot back with the same sarcastic tone. "And you don't need to have anything to do with my wedding." Dylon's eyes narrowed as he brought his face close to hers. "Do you hear me, girl?"

"Oh yes, I hear you loud and clear," she answered, glaring back at him. "Now tell your lady friend that!"

Dylon glared at Ned's old jacket. "Why didn't you buy a coat like I told you to? You look like some poor orphan, running around in that old thing."

Chris felt humiliated by his insulting remark. "You told me to buy the girls each a coat. You didn't say anything about me."

He glanced up at her in surprise. He figured she'd know that he meant for her to get herself prepared for winter.

When he watched her getting out of that buggy, in Ned's old jacket, he felt like some kind of a fool standing there in his new finery. "Don't you have any money left?" He asked.

"Well…I."

"Here, buy yourself a coat," he interrupted as he reached into his pocket and threw some money at her. "I owe you money for watching the girls. That's what you're supposed to be doing. Not running around in your underclothes with some man."

She grabbed the money and pushed herself up from the ground, and glared at him with eyes blazing, tired of his crude accusations. "It's too bad that I embarrassed you and you're fine, lady, but you can't tell me what to do. You don't own me!" She spun around to leave, but he grabbed her by the arm and pulled her close to him, and growled into her face. "You're absolutely right, girl, because of you I don't own nothin'!" Dylon heard Chris gasp as she placed her hands on his chest and pushed away from him. He watched her beautiful face pale, and he realized he had gone to far this time. He dropped her arm and stepped back. "Aw...Jeez, Chris," he pleaded, reaching out for her. "I'm sorry, I didn't mea..." But this time Chris interrupted, her voice shaking from anger. "No! No! You're right." She sobbed as she glanced down and noticed she still had the money. Chris reached out, grabbed his hand, and shoved it into his palm. "Here!" She yelled furiously. "Take this as a down payment for what I owe you." She swiped the tears from her eyes. "I'll not touch another penny of your precious money. And if you're so ashamed of me and what I wear, then...then just get someone else to watch the girls." She shrugged out of his jacket and threw it at him. "Maybe it's time for your future wife to do something with your children." Tears streaming down her face, she grabbed Ned's jacket, turned, and ran away.

Dylon watched her as she ran from him. Hating himself for what he had said to her. She played with emotions that he thought were long dead and buried. He hated the jealousy that totally engulfed him when he saw her with some other man. The fear that he experienced when he thought she or the girls were put in danger was almost uncontrollable. He felt himself shivering from the cold and slipped into his jacket. Noticing the money in his hand, he shoved it into his pocket. He had worked hard for that money, and he needed it to support the girls. He was going to get back what he lost. It didn't matter what he had to do to get it, that's what was most important, material things. With a little hard work, Rita's gold mine and ranch would supply everything he needed in life. He sure didn't need a girl like Chris in his life. His mind ground out, but his heart seemed to be saying something different.

When Ned saw the state Chris was in, Rachel told him she would go back to town with TC in the buggy and he could take Chris home in the wagon.

Ned helped Chris into the wagon, making sure she was securely wrapped in his jacket. Then, he went to gather the girls.

"Papa, can we keep one of the kittens?" Karen asked as Dylon approached the wagon with Chris's wet clothes. He placed them in the back of the wagon and pulled a blanket out that was lying on top of the picnic basket. Picking up Karen and the kitten, he went and sat them next to Chris. Then gathered Sarah in his arms and placed her there too. "We'd better ask Sissy, don't ya think?" He told Karen as he threw the blanket over Chris's wet legs. Trying in some way to show her how sorry he was for the way he had acted.

Chris shifted the baby onto her lap and muttered a bleak. "I don't care."

"Dylon, come on darling, I'm getting cold," Rita called out to him. "Ned can take care of your little family. I want to go home."

Chris kept her eyes straight ahead, as Dylon kissed Karen and Sarah and told them he would be home in a few days.

Ned made sure the girls were securely covered. Then he climbed into the wagon, snapped the reins, and started the long trip home.

Chris felt as empty as the echo of the wagon wheels that jostled along the rutted road. Dylon, as much as told her, was an embarrassment to him. Her cheeks blazed when she remembered the insinuation he had made about her running around in her underclothes in front of men. She wasn't like her mother. It didn't matter what he thought. She would never do the things her mother did. Never! Would there ever come a time in her life that someone would tell her they loved her or were proud of her? She heard the giggles of the girls playing in the back with the kitten and felt a tinge of guilt. She knew they loved her. Right now, at least for a while, they needed her. Dylon had given up so much for them, and she was determined that someday she would pay him back for the happiness he gave them. Even though he hated her, he was a good man and deserved the best that this world had to offer.

Chapter 6

Sam Drew could see the excitement on his brother Ken's face as they stood in front of a tumbled-down shack. "I know the cabin's in pretty bad shape," Ken exclaimed enthusiastically. "But after work, and on weekends, we can fix it up." As he swept his arm around the surrounding area, he continued, "Look at this, Sam! It's all ours, all five hundred acres."

Sam loved Ken; sometimes he felt more like a father to him than an older brother. Sam was grown and married when their parents died. Ken was still a teenager. They had come from a happy home, and the death of their parents devastated them both. Ken came to live on the farm with Sam and Mary. When Mary ran off, Ken was there to pull Sam out of a slump of depression.

Placing his arm around Ken's shoulder, he grinned. "All right, little brother, but it looks like we're going to be stuck in that rented room in town for a few months." He shook his head in awe as he took in the dilapidated old cabin. "Well, anyway." He laughed. "At least until we can see about a loan to fix up this shack. Then, when we get some livestock on the property, we can be weekend ranchers."

It was almost six weeks before Dylon could come home from the mine. He had hired a crew to help rebuild the sluice boxes and reconstruct the small shanty that was on the mine site. He was excited about this mining adventure, and they had already seen some gold. Dylon figured he could have a couple of the men he hired to finish the work at the mine. Then he would take the rest of the crew to the area where Rita wanted the house built.

It was prime land, and it would be good for raising cattle. Rita had given him total control, and then she had rented a house in town. Dylon was relieved about that turn of events! He realized he was eventually going to have to deal with the fact that he was marrying a woman he didn't love. It really didn't matter, he kept trying to tell himself. He would do anything he had to for Sarah and Karen. They were going to have the best things life had to offer. No matter what he had to do to get them!

Besides, he didn't think there really was such a thing as love. Although he loved the girls, there was no doubt about that. All that romantic stuff between a man and a woman was only one-sided. With the way he looked and what he owned, he would have to be the one who did the siding. Best to keep his heart closed, he thought, a whole lot safer that way. Dylon wasn't stupid. He knew Rita didn't love him. She was only using him to get what she wanted. That worked well for him. He didn't feel quite as guilty, because he was using her to get what he wanted as well. He wanted that land! If he had to put up with her roving ways, then so be it. It was good land and the men he hired had worked hard these last weeks to clear it. He was glad the weather was holding up. Here it was December, and they still hadn't really had a terrible snowstorm.

As he rode within sight of the cabin, he could feel the excitement surge through him. This had been the longest six weeks of his life. He thought he had known what loneliness felt like when he lost his brother, but this was a whole new feeling. They had become a part of his being, a part that he didn't realize he had. They made him feel warm, happy, and needed. The funny thing was when he thought of Karen and Sarah, Chris would always pop into that very same thought. He was glad there had been so much work to do at the mine. The days were full, but the nights were always the loneliest.

The last time he had seen Chris, they were at the barn raising, and she was furious with him. He couldn't blame her. He had said some stupid things. His gut ached just picturing the scene in his mind. Him shouting at her that she had ruined his life, then she yelled back that he didn't own her. He never believed in slavery of any kind, especially not putting women into servitude or prostitution. He felt a chill run through him when he remembered Jack Slade, and what could have happened to Chris and the girls. They were safe now and he would see that nothing would ever happen to them again.

He knew he needed to apologize to Chris for all the horrible things he had said to her. He also knew, deep down, it was only out of jealousy that he had said them.

He had asked around about TC Isdell and was told that Rachel Isdell's nephew was just staying in Pony for a few more weeks to help his aunt. Then he would move back to Washington State. It put Dylon to wondering if TC was planning on taking Chris back to Washington with him. They had seemed to really enjoy each other's company. Dylon had to admit to himself that he hated the idea of Chris being with anyone else.

As he neared the cabin, he glanced around and wondered if he had made a wrong turn. For a moment, he didn't think this was the right place. The dilapidated porch had been repaired, and the entire cabin had been whitewashed. The porch swing was hanging on new ropes and swaying in the breeze. There was a rock garden in the yard, ready for spring, and even some small trees and shrubbery had been planted. As he rode into the yard, he noticed new curtains hanging in the gleaming windows. He was just dismounting when Ned and the girls came out of the barn. When Karen and Sarah saw him, they started running toward him, squealing. "Oh! Papa! You're home, you're home!"

Dylon reached down and swooped them into his arms, laughing. "Boy, how I missed you two little monkeys." He declared, as he glanced over at Ned and grinned. "Did they run ya ragged, Ned?"

Ned stood back watching and smiled as he took in the touching scene. "Welcome homeboy, we missed ya."

Dylon eyed all the changes that had been made in the yard and in the cabin. "The place looks good." He told Ned. "See, you haven't been bored."

"Ya hungry? We was just gonna' get cleaned up for dinner." Ned put his finger to his mouth in a shushing motion and whispered to the girls, "Let's surprise Chris."

The smell of baked bread and apple pie teased his nostrils the moment he entered the cabin.

"Look who's come for dinner!" Ned exclaimed with a big grin.

Chris was bending over the oven when she heard Ned. She straightened up, with a pie in each hand, and turned. When their eyes met and she smiled, Dylon felt like his stomach was doing somersaults. Her cheeks were rosy from the heat of the oven. A ringlet of damp hair was dangling on her forehead, and she kept trying to blow it away with her bottom lip. His fingers tingled from wanting to brush it away for her.

Setting the pies on the table, she quickly brushed her hands over her hair, realizing the disarray she must be in. "You're just in time for dinner." She said with a smile as she glanced up, drinking in the sight of him. She had missed him so much and hated the fact that he was living with Mrs. Lewis, or she thought with dread, they might be married by now.

Dylon looked around the cabin and was amazed at the transformation. The walls were all whitewashed, and the window in the sitting room was covered with bright flowered curtains. The bare wood bench was made to look like a couch, with a pad on the seat and pillows on the back to match the curtains. His wooden rocking chair also had a bright pillow propped on it. The old kitchen stove was gleaming and the window above the sink had a yellow-checked valance with pots of green plants sitting on the sill. The table was covered with a white cloth and there was a glass fruit jar in the middle with pine and holly branches arranged in it.

Dylon ate so much supper that night, he thought he would burst. Then, while the girls played, he and Ned pushed back in their chairs and relaxed, while Chris poured them another cup of coffee.

"Has that mine of yours showed any color yet?" Ned asked Dylon.

"We salvaged a couple of sluice boxes, and I've got two men at work in the creek bed, gold washing. But we haven't seen much yet." A deep feeling of belonging that Dylon had never before experienced crept over him. He felt at home in this cozy little cabin. As he watched Chris going about her chores, he knew he wanted her to be a permanent part of his life.

He was shaken from his thoughts as Ned asked. "Was there much left to salvage?"

"Naw, the shack was pretty bad and there wasn't much left lying around. Rita sent out a bunch of supplies, so I got some of the men building new sluice boxes and a decent place for them to live. The creeks gonna freeze up soon, so we won't be workin' it much longer."

"What's the water supply?" Ned questioned, taking a swig from his coffee.

"Mill Creek, about twenty miles west of here. It runs to the Jefferson River." Dylon stood up and stretched, then glanced toward the sink where Chris was finishing up the dishes. "Fine meal, girl." He said, as his eyes drank in the sight of her. Then he went and settled down in his rocking chair. He folded his hands in his lap and stretched his long legs as far as they would go. Glancing over at Ned, he shot him a slow, comfortable grin. "You ought to see the ranch land, Ned. It's prime land, over 500 acres. Enough trees on that land to build a whole town. We're gonna build the house at the base of the mountain. It's really going to be somethin'"

"Papa, will you read to us like Ned does?" Karen interrupted as she pulled herself up on Dylon's lap. He reached down and picked up Sarah and placed her in the crook of his other arm. "Tell ya what; I'll hold ya and we'll let Ned do the reading."

Dylon realized Chris had hardly said a word the whole evening. While Ned was reading, he watched as Chris set up the ironing board and placed the irons on the stove. She then brought a basket of clothes out and started to wet them down. They were men's clothes, and he didn't recognize any of them to be his or Ned's. He kept silent until after the girls were in bed, and Ned had said goodnight and gone to his room. Walking over to where she was ironing, and picking up a shirt, he asked quizzically. "Whose is this?"

Chris glanced at the shirt. "Oh, that one is Ken Drew's." She answered as she continued her ironing. Dylon dropped the shirt back on the pile and picked another one up that was much larger. "Whose is this?" His voice rose an octave.

"I don't know!" She glanced at it and replied with a note of irritation. "I suppose one of the men who works with Ken."

"What are you doing their ironing for?" He yelled, looming over her. "I suppose you're doing TCs too?" His voice reeked of sarcasm.

Chris glanced up at him, startled, and answered. "Well, I...wanted to make some money for Christma..."

Dylon threw the shirt down and interrupted loudly. "I don't care what you need the money for." Shaking his finger in her face, he continued yelling. "You don't need to do other people's laundry. If you need money, you come to me," bringing his face close to hers, he snarled. "You hear me, girl?" He could see the tears forming in her eyes as she brushed past him and ran out the door.

"Papa, I don't like you!" Dylon turned, surprised to see Karen standing at the door, tears streaming down her face. "You never talk to Sissy nice. You always make her cry." Ned came out of the bedroom, walked over to Karen, and rested his hand on her shoulder. Then he looked at Dylon in disgust, "Boy, sometimes I don't think you have a brain in your head. She's working for extra money for Christmas."

Dylon cringed as he grabbed the back of his neck and started rubbing. "Oh! Yeah! ...Christmas!" He responded with a look of chagrin.

"That's right!" Ned's disgruntled reply made Dylon cringe even more. "You and me never bothered with Christmas, but she knows with these two little girls somethin' needs to be done. And you've been so busy with your rich lady, building your mansion, we ain't seen hide nor hair of ya." Ned's voice was a little more than a whisper, but Dylon knew he was angry. "And another thing, boy, why did ya bring TC up to her like that? He's been a good friend. And even though you have no right to be jealous, you can let it go. He's engaged to be married and he'll be going back to Washington soon." Ned shook his head in disgust as he started for the door to go after Chris.

"Wait, Ned!" Dylon urged as he reached for his coat. "Let me go, I'll talk to her."

Chris was standing by the well with her arms wrapped around her. It was cold, and she realized she had done a foolish thing by running out. Listening to Dylon talk about Rita and their plans to build their house really hurt her. She had thought she was more prepared for his marriage. Actually, she figured he might already be married. She had felt his presence even before she turned from the stove this afternoon. And when their eyes met, she knew she would never be prepared to lose him. Dylon had become so much a part of her very being. Every thought she had, it seemed he was right in the middle of it. Why couldn't she just accept this situation and go on with her life? He had given her a new start. She needed to take it, and the sooner the better. Maybe tomorrow she would go to town and talk to Mrs. Isdell about working in the store. TC would go back to Washington in January and she thought Rachel would probably need the help. The sooner she leaves here, the better. He had made it very clear how he felt about her at the barn raising. And now, by the violent reaction that just took place, she figured it would be better for everyone if she leaves. Hearing someone come up behind her; she turned to see Dylon.

"Ya better come on in, girl. It's cold out here."

Chris swiped at her eyes with the back of her hand and started around him. He reached out and grasped her arm, pulled her close, and slipped the coat around her shoulders. "Look," He began with tenderness in his voice. "I'm sorry, I yelled at you. Ned told me what you're trying to do." Placing his hands on her shoulders and turning her around to face him, he gazed down at her. With a slight smile forming his lips, he spoke softly. "You got enough to do with taking care of Ned and the girls." He ran his hands down her arms and entwined his fingers in hers, feeling a wave of relief knowing that she wouldn't be leaving with that TC fellow. "I got some money, don't worry. We'll have Christmas. And, what I said to you at the barn raising about you not being a lady and all that other stuff, I'm really sorry. I had no right to say those things." Then he turned with her hand still in his and led her back to the cabin.

Ned was sitting in the rocker with Karen asleep in his arms. She opened her eyes when Dylon picked her up. Wrapping her arms around his neck, she whispered with a drowsy plea. "Papa, please don't be mean to Sissy anymore."

Dylon grinned as he nuzzled her cheek. "Will you like me again if I'm nice to her?"

Karen snuggled into his arms and sighed sleepily. "Oh, yes Papa. If you're nice to her, maybe she won't want to leave us."

Dylon raised a questioning eyebrow toward Chris, who was back ironing and hadn't heard Karen.

After he put Karen back in bed, and Ned said goodnight again, Dylon sat in the rocking chair and watched Chris finish up the ironing. She must be thinking of leaving. Maybe it's her and that Ken Drew fellow? He wished he could say he didn't care, but she was always on his mind. Sort of like an aching tooth, he thought, as he drifted off to sleep.

Chris noticed Dylon sleeping in his chair, so she very quietly folded and put the ironing board away. She grabbed the quilt from off her bed and covered him with it. While gazing down lovingly at his sleeping face, she realized how much she had missed him these last few weeks. Then she grabbed her sewing basket and wearily sat down to work on the Christmas presents she was making. The knitted hats, mittens, and scarves for the girls were finished. She just had to finish up some slippers for Ned. Then she could start working on Dylon's gift. She had bought some white silk material and had taken one of his old shirts to use for a pattern. With the bone buttons she had bought, running up the front of the shirt and the black string tie she would make, Chris could picture how handsome he would look.

She realized that he and that Lewis woman hadn't married yet. This is one thing she wanted to do for him before she had to leave. She had been trying to prepare the girls for her evident departure. She told them about their nice new house that Papa was building. And she would try to say good things about Mrs. Lewis.

She hated the thought of leaving Ned and the girls. She loved them. They were the only good thing that had ever happened to her. Gazing at the selfless giant sleeping in the rocking chair, her heart ached knowing that she loved this man and could not be a part of his life.

Dylon opened his eyes and noticed the quilt thrown over him. His nostrils caught the scent of lilac, and he realized the quilt must be from Chris's bed. He watched Chris sitting at the table, knitting. He loved looking at her, but her face held an air of haunting sadness. He remembered the night of the wagon train dance when she smiled at Ken Drew while they were dancing together, and his gut ached with the selfish desire for that same smile from her.

Chris glanced up and right into Dylon's eyes, giving him a shy smile as she whispered. "You must be tired; I made up the other cot in Ned's room for you. You can stay awhile, can't you?"

Standing, he stretched, his long arms touching the ceiling. "Yeah, I can stay tonight, but I got to go to town tomorrow. Rita wants me to go to some kind of a meeting to discuss the growth of Pony." Walking past her toward the bedroom, he reached down and picked up one of the knitted hats from the table. "What we got, about three weeks before Christmas?" He asked as he placed the hat back on the table.

"No, two weeks." She answered.

"Yeah, well... good night."

Dylon left right after breakfast the next morning but said he would stop back on his way from town. Karen and Sarah began crying when he started to leave, but he hugged them both, telling them he would be home in time for Christmas and spend a couple of weeks with them.

That same afternoon, Chris was working on Dylon's shirt,

when she heard a horse and buggy pulled up in the yard. She looked out and saw it was Anna Watts. Running out the door, she called out happily. "Oh, Anna! It's so good to see you."

"Hurry Chris and get ready," Anna said, giving her an excited smile. "You're going to town with me. There's a town social meeting and Ken wants me to meet him there. But Chris," she continued pleadingly. "Mama said I couldn't go unless you went with me."

Chris knew that Anna and Ken were falling in love and she was thrilled for them. After checking with Ned about watching the girls, she hurriedly dressed, looking forward to an afternoon in town with Anna.

Dylon and Rita were talking to Sheriff Gallen in the community hall when Rita saw Chris. "Isn't that Ned's daughter?" She asked Dylon.

Dylon turned around to see Chris, Anna, Ken, and Sam Drew standing in the corner, talking. He felt a stirring of agitation when she started laughing at something Ken had said.

"Dylon! Sheriff Gallen is talking to you. My goodness, you act as if you were a hundred miles away." Rita placed her hand on the sheriff's arm and gazed at him in a flirtatious manner. "Go ahead Jim, I'm listening."

"Chris," Anna whispered. "I've gotta go to the privy. Go with me."

Chris was waiting for Anna in front of the outhouse when she heard a woman scream. Anna came out and glanced around. "What was that?" She asked, frightened.

"I don't know!" Running toward the fence that led to the alley, Chris shouted. "Come on, it's over here."

As they came around the fence into the alley, they saw two men in a vacant field, viciously beating on a young woman.

Chris picked up a big board that was lying on the ground and started running toward them. "Anna, go get help!" She yelled back over her shoulder.

Dylon was just coming down the porch stairs of the community hall. He had to get out of there. It was embarrassing the way Rita was throwing herself at the sheriff.

He saw Anna running toward him. "Mr. Clay...Help! It's Chris...She needs help!" Pointing toward the alley, she stopped to catch her breath, and then she exploded. "It's Chris...Two men, help!"

Dylon started running, fear engulfing him. As he came around the fence, he saw Chris standing in front of a woman who was propped up against a tree. Chris was holding onto a big board with both hands and wielding it at two men. They appeared to be drunk. "Come on girly!" One of the men slurred. "She sells it. We were just trying to get a sample before we buy." Staggering closer, he reached out to grab her. "But you look pretty tasty; maybe I'll get a sample from you." Chris swung the board, smacking him on his side. Letting out a yelp, the man fell to his knees, spitting out a string of curses. When the other drunk saw what happened to his partner, he shouted out, "I'll get you!" He stumbled toward her, just as Dylon reached out and grabbed him by the back of the neck. When the wounded man saw it was Dylon, he yelled. "Damn, it's scar-face; let's get the hell out of here!" Limping off, he ran head-on into Sheriff Gallen and Sam Drew. When Chris saw Dylon, she dropped the board, then ran and knelt by the girl, who was bleeding from the mouth. A crowd of people had gathered to watch, so she called for someone to come and help, but no one moved.

Dylon was talking to the sheriff when he heard Chris screaming. "You bunch of self-righteous hypocrites!" He turned and watched Chris help the girl up, then he followed Sam over to assist her. Someone from the crowd yelled. "She don't need no help! She's nothin' but a whore." Chris grabbed the board and rushed toward the male voice. Dylon quickly snaked his arm out and wrapped it around her waist, pulling her off the ground and up against him, with her screaming and kicking. "She's a human being, which is more than I can say for the likes of you!"

Dylon pulled her closer. "Settle down, Chris," he commanded.

"Let me go... Just let me go!" She raged through clenched teeth as she squirmed from his arms and ran to where the girl and Sam were standing. "Are you all right?" She said gently as she put her arm around the injured girl. "Yes!" was the girl's whispered answer as they started walking toward the saloon.

Sheriff Gallen told everyone to break it up and go back to the community hall. Dylon heard some man in the crowd chuckle. "Whoever gets that fiery little lady is gonna have a job breakin' her."

He ignored the statement and started following Chris. But his irritation became stronger when Ken ran up next to him and shouted. "Hang on, Chris. I'll get my horse and give you a ride home."

"Forget it!" Dylon snapped over his shoulder as he went for his horse. "I'll take her home." Then he shot Chris an unrelenting glare and ordered her not to go into the Saloon.

"He's right, Chris, you don't need to go in there," Sam said as he took the girl's arm from Chris. "I'll help her."

Chris glanced worriedly over her shoulder at Dylon, who was riding down the street toward her. Then she looked back at the girl with concern in her eyes. "Are you going to be all right?"

The girl nodded and gave her a wan smile. "Thanks. You've been real kind to me. But you better go on now. Your mister looks mad." Then the girl detached herself from Sam's grasp, pulled herself to a proud stance, lifted her head and walked, by herself, through the saloon doors.

Dylon reached down, grabbed Chris by the arm, and pulled her on the back of his horse. "Jeez!" He mumbled to himself. "I spend most of my time getting this girl out of some sort of trouble."

They had only ridden a little way when he turned in his saddle, his face just inches from hers. "You know, don't ya, girl?" he said with a hint of a smile on his face. "You can be a real pain in the neck."

Reaching up with a balled fist, Chris punched him in the shoulder.

"Ouch! What did ya do that for?"

"Don't call me girl!" She countered, lifting her chin defiantly.

He chuckled and rode the rest of the way home in silence, enjoying her plump little body pressed up against his.

When they reached the cabin, Dylon eased her down off of the horse and told her he would be back in time for Christmas. As Chris started up the steps of the porch, Dylon yelled. "Girl!"

She stiffened her shoulders, turned, and, with a resigned sigh, answered. "What?"

"Stay out of trouble until I get back." He grinned, tipped his hat, and rode off.

Chris was fuming when she told Ned what had happened. "They're terrible people; I don't care if I ever go to that town again. You know why the girl was there? She was trying to see how refined people act. She sure got a good lesson, didn't she? They claim to be Christians, well if that's what a Christian is, I don't want nothing to do with God!"

Ned was sitting at the table drinking coffee, watching Chris knitting with a fury. "Listen here, young lady, you can't go blamin' God for the mistakes people make. We're all made with a free will, because of God's goodness and love for us. If we decide to do mean things, that's our fault, not God's."

Chris lay her knitting down and gazed at Ned, her eyes brimming with tears. "But Ned, they were so cruel. Christians shouldn't act that way."

"You're right, honey, they shouldn't. But the only difference between a Christian and someone else is the Christian is saved and has a right to ask God for forgiveness." He reached across the table, where his Bible was laying, and pulled it in front of him, then he placed his hand on top of it. "You don't automatically sprout wings when you start servin' the Lord. You're just like anybody else trying to make it day by day. The only difference, I'm a guessin', is that you have a helper in the good Lord? That is if you'll let Him."

Chapter 7

Sam Drew couldn't get the young prostitute off his mind. She seemed so young and defeated. Yet, he had to smile in admiration when she pulled from him and walked into that saloon. She had held herself with more dignity than anyone he had ever seen.

He had just gotten off work, and Ken was over at Anna's, so he decided to take a walk over to Duffy's Saloon and have a beer. Thought maybe he could get to know her a little better. Walking by the jail, he saw Sheriff Gallen sitting on the porch. "Evenin', Sheriff. What's going on at the Community Hall? Notice a bunch of people going in?"

Sheriff Gallen nodded toward Sam. "Travelin' preacher's in town. Gonna give a service. You a church-going man?"

Sam gave a chuckle. "Not me, Sheriff. Reckon they'd have to put in extra beams to hold the roof up if I ever walked into a church." Just then, Sam saw the young woman from Duffy's Saloon sneaking around the back of the Community Hall.

"Night, Sheriff," he called over his shoulder as he headed toward the Hall. He quietly followed her and watched as she found a window. It was too high for her to look in, so she grabbed the ledge and tried to pull herself up. Her feet couldn't find anything to grasp, so she began looking around for something to stand on.

"It'd be a lot simpler to go through the front door. Wouldn't it?" Sam asked as he leaned up against a tree, his arms folded and a grin forming at the corners of his mouth.

She swirled around, a shocked look on her face, and slapped a hand at her heart. "Goodness, you scared me!" Then her eyes narrowed, and she started backing away. "What do you want? I ain't done nothin'!"

Sam backed off, his hands held high. "I'm not going to hurt you. Just wonderin' why you won't go inside?"

She glared at him with weary eyes and shot out a scornful laugh. "Oh yes, I'm sure they'd welcome the likes of me with open arms."

Sam glanced up at a tree by the side of the building. "You afraid of heights?" He asked.

She followed his gaze. "No, I reckon not."

He went and stood by the tree, bent over, and cupped his hands. Then he motioned to her. "Well, come on, before you miss something."

The indecision on her face was evident, but finally, the desire to see the church service convinced her. She carefully placed her small foot in his hands and their eyes met and held for an instant. Then he boosted her up on the tree branch.

She threw her leg over the branch and modestly pulled her dress down to cover her exposed leg. Then she peered intently through the window.

Sam leaned up against an opposite tree, lit a cigarette, and watched her. She was little, and not very old either, he thought. She wore the usual saloon girl costume, red satin with black lace, but it looked faded and old and too big for her. A tattered gray wool cape was wrapped around her. He wondered if she wasn't cold as he felt the chill of the winter night through his heavy jacket. Her long straight hair was the color of clean ocean shore sand. It was pulled tightly back from her face and tied with a faded ribbon. Her complexion was smooth, except for the bruises from the beating she had received the other day from the two drunks. Her large, sad eyes caught his attention; he had never seen eyes that blue. They reminded him of the midnight sky and they seemed to change color with her moods.

He didn't think she even realized he was there, because she was so intent on what was going on inside. The muscles in his jaw clenched in irritation when he saw her fold her hands, bow her head and close her eyes. "Damn it!" He raged to himself, as he watched her move her lips in prayer. Her vulnerability stabbed at his heart and he found himself hoping for her sake there was a God.

When the service was over, he watched for a second as she tried climbing down the tree. Shaking his head at her stubbornness, he moved forward and held his arms up to her. Their eyes met again, his with a hint of a smile, hers with distrust.

"Well, come on." He urged with a grin. "Unless you want to get stuck up there. You better let me help ya." He could feel her body stiffen as he lifted her from the tree.

She mumbled a quick thank you and started moving away from him. "Hey, wait a minute," Sam called after her. "What's your name?"

"Holly," she replied, as she quickly scurried away.

Sam went to Duffy's Saloon every night for the next week just so he could see her. Watching her at work, he realized she wasn't like any saloon girl he had ever met. When he came into the saloon, she would throw him a shy smile, but for the most part, she avoided him. In fact, she avoided everyone. She waited tables, served drinks and put up with the men pawing her. But she never laughed or flirted with the customers. He was relieved when he realized he had never seen her go upstairs with a man. Sam couldn't figure out why he was so taken with this girl. She really wasn't much to look at. He was at least fifteen years older than she was. And most of the time, she acted like he didn't even exist. Except for one night when Rose, one of the other saloon girls, started calling him dream man. He thought he saw a trace of anger on Holly's face. Rose just laughed and chucked her under the chin. "You're right Holly; he sure does look like a dream man."

Duffy yelled at Rose to leave her alone and to get back to work. Sam felt a chill run down his spine when he watched Duffy put his arm around Holly, whisper in her ear and pat her hind-end as she started up the stairs. Now he was beginning to understand why she never went upstairs with any other man. A feeling of disgust ran through him as he thought that she might belong to that old geezer.

Sam took a good look at Duffy. He was tall, skinny, and old enough to be her grandfather. He had thinning yellow-gray hair and his big nose was covered with swollen purple veins. What few teeth he had were rotten. He was a friendly sort and seemed to treat his whores right, although Sam could tell by their dress and the look of the place the business wasn't very prosperous.

"Hey, dream man, no sense in thinking about going after her. She's as stiff as a board." Rose sidled up to the bar and was rubbing up against Sam seductively. "You want to know something?" She chortled as she glanced over at Holly. "The few times she had a customer, they complained so much, Duffy had to give one of us to them so he could keep the money." She threw him a suggestive glance. "Although, sweetie, with what she's always saying about you and your looks, you might be her first success." Throwing back her head and laughing, she teased. "You know she calls you her dream, man." As Rose rubbed her hand seductively over his buttocks, her lips, thick with red rouge, formed into a pout. "But if she doesn't want ya, baby, come to me. I'll give you somethin' to dream about."

Duffy placed a fresh beer in front of Sam and motioned for

Rose to leave. "Hope you're not plannin' ongoing up after Holly," he said bluntly.

Sam pushed the beer away. "Why?" He countered. "Is she your personal property?"

Duffy leaned across the bar, and by the glare on his face, Sam thought he was in for a fight. "Look, boy!" Duffy growled. "That little girl was born right up those stairs. She was born on Christmas day. And I'm the one that named her." He backed off a little and expelled a sigh. "If I would of had an ounce of sense at the time, I would of realized she could have been my daughter." Sam saw the deep sadness in his face and felt a tinge of pity for the old man. "But." Duffy went on. "I was too busy drownin' myself in the bottle. I never paid her one lick of attention."

He caught Sam's eyes with his own and continued. "Her mother died when she was just a little tyke. She was a good girl and pretty much stayed out of everybody's way." Duffy dropped his eyes and fixed his stare on the mug of beer before him. "When she was about fifteen, a drover offered me big bucks to spend the night with her said he never broke a virgin before." Duffy's face grew pale. "She just laid there, the drover said, never moved or made a sound. He thought she was dead. Had to give him one of the other girls for free, so's he wouldn't cause trouble." Duffy began wiping the bar with the rag he was holding, then glanced at Sam and sighed. "Thought it would be easier for her after that." He shook his head sadly. "But it was always the same. She doesn't have the heart of a whore. None of the regular customers would bother with her, but every now and then we would get a stranger who would want to try her out. Like those two bums, she ran across the other day." Duffy tossed the rag down and leaned heavily against the bar, emitting a deep groan. "I was too busy hidin' my head in the bottle to see that she was dyin' bit by bit." Sam was surprised to see tears forming in Duffy's eyes. "Then," Duffy continued. "A couple a years ago she was with a customer that beat her real bad. Holly never made a sound, but luckily Rose's room was right next door and she heard the creep cussin' and screamin' and ran and told me. I got the sheriff, and we threw the guy in jail. When we came back to help Holly, she was gone."

"What do ya mean, gone?" Sam finally interjected.

"Just what I said, gone. Oh, I knew where she was. Ya see she found herself a hiding place years ago. There's an old cabin on some property for sale a few miles out of town. She calls it her dream house. That's where I found her, and when she asked me to leave her there alone, 'cause she didn't want to live anymore." Duffy stopped, mopped the streaming tears from his face and continued. "Right then, somethin' changed in me. I picked that little girl up and brought her home. I ain't had a drink since and she ain't been with a customer since."

Sam shifted on his stool uncomfortably.

Duffy grabbed Sam's empty beer mug and refilled it. "Suppose you're wondering why I'm telling you this?" He asked as he set the filled mug before Sam.

"It crossed my mind."

"Well, ya see, for some strange reason, she thinks you're her Knight in Shining Armor. She's been happy since she met you."

Sam raised his eyebrow and stared at Duffy. "We've hardly talked." The tone in his voice sounded puzzled.

"You must have done something to attract her attention. Holly's always wanted a home and family. That's why she goes to that beat-up old shack all the time. She pretends her husband and children live there. You and that Chris woman are the only people outside of this saloon that have been good to her."

Duffy nodded toward the stairs and then glared at Sam. "If you go up those stairs, it would have to be over my dead body. I ain't about ready to let you take away her dream and what little desire she has left to live."

Sam glanced toward the stairs, finished his beer, and went back to his room.

Dylon didn't get home until the morning of the twenty-third. There had been a heavy snowstorm the day before, but now the sky was crystal blue and the day was warm and sunny. As he came within sight of the cabin, he could feel the excitement growing. Home! This dumpy little cabin felt more like home to him than any place he had ever been. When he lost his land in Colorado, he thought he had lost something of value. Now he realized Ned was right all along. Your values come from how you feel about yourself and your treatment of other people.

He could see them in the yard, the three of them, they were building a snowman. He let out a whistle and heard Karen scream. "Papa!" Then she started running to him, with Chris and Sarah not far behind. He swung down from his horse and stood watching them. "We missed you, Papa!" Karen squealed as she threw her arms up to him.

"I missed you too, little girl." Grinning, he reached down and picked her up, savoring the feel of her little arms wrapped around his neck. He returned her hug and then lifted her onto the horse. Grabbing the reins, he led them toward Chris and the baby. He swung Sarah up in his arms and laughed as he received a hug and a wet kiss from her. His glance strayed to Chris, and he noticed her cheeks were pink from the cold. Excitement rippled through him as he saw the gentle radiance of her golden-brown eyes. She smiled up at him, and it was hard to pull away from her when Ned called out a greeting from the porch. Lord...It was good to be home.

They entered the warm cabin, stomping off the snow Dylon had playfully thrown that on them. The girls were giggling, while the three adults grinned from ear to ear.

The smell of cinnamon and fresh pine wafted through the air.

Dylon shrugged out of his heavy jacket and hung it on the peg by the door. He felt a twinge of guilt as he noticed Ned's old jacket. Remembering how he had reacted at the barn raising, he silently made a vow. He would try not to go off half-cocked when it came to this girl. His life had held little meaning until she had barged in and changed it so significantly.

"Can we get the tree today, Papa? Sissy said we had to wait for you." Karen and Sarah were both hopping up and down excitedly. "Can we...Huh?"

"We sure can, sugar, but I'm hungry." He glanced at Chris and their eyes met, then he threw Karen a wink and grinned. "Do ya think Sissy will fix me somethin' ta eat?"

Chapter 8

Holly breathed a sigh of relief when she saw there was no smoke coming from the cabin. She had felt a real sense of loss when she heard the place had been sold. She had hoped the new owners would wait until after the holidays to move in. Snuggling deeper into her cape for more warmth from the brittle cold day, she shifted the heavy pack she was carrying to the other arm. The cabin door squeaked and except for the one rusty hinge holding the door in place, it would have fallen off. Holly righted it with her shoulder as she entered the cabin. She could see the room was as she had left it, except for the neglected dust that had settled in her absence. She felt reassured that no one would bother her for the next few days. Setting her pack down on the table, she went back outside to gather some wood. If she built a small fire, it would take some of the chill off and, hopefully, no one would see the smoke. After she got the fire going and found the old broom in the corner where she had left it, she began sweeping. The cabin comprised one small room, which served as the kitchen and living area. The fireplace was used both as a source of heat and also for cooking. There was a crane in the fireplace with a pothook to hang the iron kettle on. The old table had one leg partially broken, but Holly had propped it up years ago with a tree stump, and it served its purpose. The only two chairs in the cabin were in fairly good shape. There was a bed frame in the corner with no mattress, but Holly always slept on the floor by the fireplace.

After wiping the table off with a rag she had stored in the small cupboard hanging on the wall, she opened her pack and took out her meager supplies. There was a blanket, a loaf of bread, some crackers, and two sausages. When she brought out the three hard-boiled eggs, she smiled, remembering the look on Duffy's face when he gave them to her. "Here," he said. "The kids can share one, and you and your husband can eat the other two." Ever since that night two years ago, when he picked her aching body up off of the cabin floor and carried her back to the saloon on his buckboard, he was a changed man. He hadn't had a drink since that night. He then reassured her she would never have to be with a customer unless she wanted to. Best of all, he understood her dream. Holly smiled, realizing she finally had a face to put to her dream. She could never visualize the face of her fantasy man before until Sam. She had asked Rose to find out who he was and learned that he worked with his brother at the stamp mill. Rose told her that Sam and his brother Ken had come in on the wagon train a few weeks back. Holly thought Sam was one of the most handsome men she had ever seen. He was the only man other than Duffy that had been kind to her without wanting something from her in return.

With the table dusted, she laid her scarf over it, and then she went to the empty cupboard and got her two pretend dishes out, and set the table. "Children, it's time to get ready for dinner." She called out cheerfully, imagining three happy children playing around here. "Your daddy will be home any time from work at the stamp mill." Holly pictured the stranger named Sam coming home from a hard day's work and swooping her in his arms, giving her a kiss, and then laughingly playing with the children while she got dinner ready. "Your daddy said, after we eat, you can put the Christmas tree up. Come on now, boys." She scolded. "Bobby, you take little Sammy into the bedroom and get some clean clothes on."

***

Sam was in no mood to celebrate the holidays. The stamp mill, where he and Ken worked, was closed until after the New Year. So Sam went to the cabin and did some cleaning and fixing up. The Watts had invited him over to spend Christmas with them, but he politely declined, much to Ken's anger. His horse was weighed down with the goodies that Marie Watts insisted he take a fruitcake, a jar of peach preserves, a loaf of fresh bread, and a cured ham. With the groceries, he had bought and with the food given him, he could be snowed in for a month and gain ten pounds.

He had even splurged and bought himself two new flannel shirts. He and Ken had brought a wagonload of supplies and stored them in the barn a few days ago, so he would have plenty of work to keep him busy. They had to meet with a banker in Helena about buying some stock. But that wasn't until the 29th, so with no interruptions, he could get some much-needed repairs done.

Sam liked his job at the stamp mill; actually, he liked the whole aspect of mining. The mill he worked in was only a five-stamper. He had heard that there were one hundred stamper mills being built. He chuckled to himself, remembering how Ken had explained what a five-stamp mill was to Anna and the twins. He had told them the machine looked like a horse with five legs stamping on a bunch of rocks in order to get the gold out. But instead of feeding the machine oats and hay, like you would feed a horse, you would feed the machine steam.

Sam had never enjoyed working the land. The only reason he farmed after he and Mary had married was because of Ken. Then when she left, they sold the farm and Ken wanted to come to Montana to try his hand at ranching. If Sam had his way, he'd travel and do some mining. It looked like Ken was interested in Anna Watts, so maybe someday he would be free to pursue his dream.

As he rode into view of the cabin, he thought he saw a small stream of smoke coming from the chimney. Nudging his horse into a grove of trees out of sight of the cabin, he looked around for horses or any other signs of life. Seeing nothing out of the ordinary, he whipped his gun from the holster and cautiously crept to the door. As he got closer, Sam heard a woman's voice inside the cabin. "Little Sammy, I'm going to have to tell your father when he gets home."

Sam quietly reached for the latch and shoved on the wobbly door with his shoulder. Holly heard the door fall open and let out a startled yelp as she saw the frame of a man, with a gun in his hand, standing in the glare of the bright winter day. "Who are you? What do you want?" She shrieked as she rushed to the corner and picked up the broom in self-defense.

Sam watched as Holly cowered in the corner with the broom held in front of her. Then he remembered the story Duffy had told him about Holly and her dream house and he realized it was this little shack. He quickly holstered his gun, stepped in, and pushed the door shut. As the light from the sun faded, Holly recognized Sam. "You!" She cried out, throwing her hands to her mouth in a horrified gasp. "What are you doing here?"

"I guess I have a right to be on my own property." He spoke casually as he walked to the fireplace, bent down, and added more wood to the fire. "It's freezing in here. Do you want little Sammy to catch a cold?" He asked teasingly.

Holly felt her face redden and was mortified. Duffy or Rose must have told him about her fantasies and now he was making fun of her. She quickly grabbed her pack and started shoving her belongings in it. Sam watched and saw the anguish on her face and felt appalled that he caused it. He went to her and laid his hand gently on her arm. "Holly, I'm sorry. I was just teasing you."

She jerked away as if she had been burned. Then she grabbed up her cape, threw her pack over her shoulder, and, without a backward glance, rushed to the door.

"Holly! Wait!" Regret was seeping from his voice.

She stopped and in a few easy strides, Sam was beside her.

"Please...don't leave, stay here." He urged. "Spend Christmas with me."

She stood as if her feet were nailed to the floor. She didn't want to walk out that door; she wanted to stay. But she was afraid...so terribly afraid.

He reached out, took the pack from her, and led her to the fireplace. He placed his hands on her shoulders and turned her to him. Then he gently grasped her by the chin and lifted her face so their eyes met. "I won't ever hurt you." He whispered softly. "I promise."

***

Chris had fixed Dylon a big lunch of ham, fried potatoes, green beans, and fresh cornbread with gingerbread cookies for dessert.

She bowed out of the tree-hunting trip, because she told the girls teasingly, "there is some Christmas surprises that have to be finished."

When Dylon, Ned, and the children came back from the woods, Chris could hear their laughing and the stamping of feet on the porch. Throwing open the door, she saw Dylon holding a large pine tree. "How in the world are you going to get that big tree in here?" She wondered.

Dylon threw her a big grin and a wink and then teased. "I don't know." Then he glanced at Ned. "What do ya think, Ned? Are we going to have to cut a hole in the roof?"

Ned chuckled. "Maybe so, boy, maybe so!"

Ned had already made a tree stand, and with a little chopping and sawing, the tree fit perfectly into the corner of the sitting room.

Bouncing up and down and clapping joyfully, Karen's small voice rang out. "Oh Papa, can we trim it now?"

"Not until tomorrow," Dylon answered. "It's got to have some time to thaw so the branches can fall out."

Dinner that evening was a festive occasion. Ned kept them entertained with tales of his Christmas pasts. Even Dylon hadn't heard some of the tall tales he was spinning. He caught himself more than once watching Chris's face as she laughed at Ned's stories. A deep sense of peace crept through him, as he realized he was responsible for these people, and that they were his family. "Family..." He thought to himself. "Yeah! This is my family."

Sarah was so tired that she almost fell asleep at the table. Ned told Chris he would get the girls ready for bed, but Dylon interjected. "Go ahead and get Sarah ready, Ned." Then he threw Chris a quick glance and looked at Karen. "But as for you, little girl, it's time you pulled some of your weight around here." He shoved away from the table, grasped her by the hand, and grinned at Chris. "You and I are going to help Sissy wash the dishes."

Chris enjoyed watching as Dylon showed Karen how to scrape the dishes. When she heard Ned in the bedroom, saying something to make Sarah giggle, she glanced around the room, caught a whiff of the pine from the huge tree standing in the corner, and suddenly felt an overwhelming sense of belonging. She quickly stifled the fear as it pushed up to her heart. This would not be her family for much longer, she sadly realized. Throwing that thought to the back of her mind, she determined to make this a time that she could hold on to, during the lonely years that lay ahead of her.

Dylon lay in bed that night, listening to Ned's snoring, and thought about the day's events. He had never celebrated Christmas with family. When his brother Dan was alive, they would usually drink the night away at some saloon. After Dan's death, Christmas was like any other day. Now the void he had felt for all those years was being filled with a snoring old man, two little girls, and a golden-brown-eyed, pink-cheeked, brown-haired, plump bundle of dynamite.

When he heard a noise in the setting room, he slipped into his pants, not bothering to put his shirt on. As he entered the room, he saw Chris sitting on the floor by the tree. His jaw clenched at the intimate sight of her flannel gown peeking out of the blanket she was wrapped in. The dim glow of the lantern hallowed her long chestnut-brown hair, flowing in soft waves around her shoulders. He walked over and knelt down next to her, and felt intoxicated by the scent of her. "What's the matter?" He whispered. "Couldn't you sleep?"

She lifted her eyes to meet his. "Isn't the tree beautiful?" She said. "If I ever have my own home, I'd like to have a pine tree growing in the corner of my sitting room." Placing her hands over her mouth, she stifled a giggle. "I know that sounds silly, but this is the first real Christmas I've ever had."

Dylon recognized he knew very little about this girl, even though he spent a good bit of his time getting her out of one kind of scrape after another. "Didn't the girl's mother give them a Christmas?" He asked her.

Chris's gaze ran up his broad, sun-bronzed chest covered with golden curls and she had to clench her fist because of the desire to run her hand over the rippling muscles on his shoulders and arms. Her cheeks blazed when she realized the enjoyment she got from just looking at him. "You couldn't have asked for a better person." She answered as she pulled her eyes from his naked chest. "She loved the girls very much. And I think she loved me, too." Snuggling deeper into the blanket, she continued, holding no judgment in her voice. "But her life had been hard. She never had the money or the time to give them things like birthdays or Christmas." Chris drew her legs up and wrapped her arms around them, then rested her chin on her knees, and stared at the tree. "The family I lived with before celebrated Christmas." This time Dylon detected bitterness in her voice as she went on. "But I was nothing more to them than a servant, and they felt the season was just for their family. So, I would stay in the bedroom on Christmas Eve and Christmas Day. When my mother was still alive, she would come and get me, and if the weather was nice, we would go for a long walk. On cold days, she would sneak me past Jack and we would go and spend the day in her room."

Dylon watched the tears brimming in her eyes. He reached out, as if it were the natural thing to do, and grasped a lock of her silky hair, entwining it gently through his fingers. Chris shivered with excitement at the feel of his touch, then smiled slightly and gazed at the tree. "My mother would always have some little gift for me, a piece of ribbon or handkerchief and always a peppermint stick. She wasn't a bad woman, she really wasn't." A tear crept out and rolled down her cheek. Dylon let the lock of her hair fall and with the back of his callused hand caressed her cheek, wiping the tear away. She turned to him, their faces inches from each other, and Chris sighed grievously as she gazed at him. "I know that I was the cause of you losing everything, and I'm sorry about that. And someday I really do hope to pay you back. But I'll never regret bringing the girls to you." She repeated emphatically. "Never!

You and Ned are the best thing that ever happened to those two little girls."

The sound, sight, and smell of her overwhelmed Dylon. "What about you?" He asked huskily. "Aren't you happy with us?" She gazed searchingly into his eyes, and he brought his face close to hers. Then he reached his hand to the back of her neck, gently pulling her to him, touching his mouth to hers. He suddenly pulled away and gave a throaty chuckle. Her eyes were squeezed shut and her lips were pursed as if she had just sucked a lemon. "You've never been kissed before, have you?"

She opened her eyes, shrugged her shoulders, and gave him

an embarrassed grin. "This is the first time."

Dylon's eyes narrowed. "What about Ken Drew?"

Her hand touched his bare chest and the mat of hair tickled her fingers as she felt a torrent of heat vibrate through her body. "He's my friend." She gazed at him, mesmerized by the feelings he was arousing in her. "But he's in love with Anna Watts."

"Does that bother you?" Dylon choked out, afraid to hear the answer.

"Not at all. I'm happy for them both."

A wave of relief flowed through him. "Well, then, shall we try this again?" He grasped her chin in his hand and brought his lips close to hers. He had to smile as she again closed her eyes tight and puckered her lips. Dylon brought his thumb to her mouth and gently caressed it. "Chris, are you afraid of me?"

Her eyes flew open in shock. "Afraid of you. Oh, no, never!"

Her words touched his heart with pure pleasure. "I'm glad Chris, cause I'd never want to hurt you." He ran his thumb across her lips again and whispered urgently. "Open your mouth, honey."

With a puzzled gaze, she did as he commanded and opened her mouth wide. "Not quite so wide," he chuckled. She closed her mouth and as he watched her nervously lick her lips, he let out a groan and took her mouth into his. The blanket fell from her as she wrapped her arms around his neck. He pulled her closer and as he pressed her up against his naked chest, he felt instant anger at the flannel gown for barring him from the feel of her soft warm breasts. Chris wondered if she shouldn't feel fear at the emotions that he was arousing in her. But all that mattered was she was in his arms and drowning in his scent. She knew this was where she wanted to be. This is where she belonged. The kiss deepened and their desire intensified. Their whispered moans intertwined as he laid her back on the floor, half-covering her with his body, his hand roaming to the buttons of her gown.

"Papa! What'cha doing? Is it Christmas yet?"

"Ah...Jeez!" Dylon uttered as he pulled away from Chris. "No, sugar, not yet," he answered with a trembling voice, as he watched Karen walk toward them, rubbing her eyes sleepily.

Chapter 9

Holly cleaned the cabin from top to bottom, while Sam did some much-needed repairs. The first thing he did was fix the old weather-beaten door. They were both famished from all the work, so Holly set out the eggs, sausage, and bread and Sam made a pot of coffee. There was only one cup and as he gave her a drink of the strong black liquid, he noticed the grimace on her face. He wished he had some sugar for her. She was so young and had missed out on so much. He wished he could do more for her.

She seemed to be more relaxed around him. Her smiles were coming a little more often, and she was even beginning to converse in more than one or two-word sentences.

After they ate, they decided to tackle the lean-to off the side of the cabin. There were three large boxes set up on the shelf and as Sam took them down, he called out. "Look, Holly, they all have something in them."

She clapped her hands together and laughed excitedly. "I know."

"What do you mean, you know?"

"Oh, they've been there for years. The last owners must have left them."

"And you've never bothered to open them?"

Holly threw him a surprised expression. "Well, no, they're not mine." Then she smiled. "But I guess now since you're the new owner, they belong to you."

Sam noticed the eager excitement on her face when he asked her to help him carry the boxes to the cabin. They sat them on the table, but before they started to open them, Sam got an idea. "Wait, a minute; let's go find us a Christmas tree."

Holly glanced at him disappointedly. "Can't we open the boxes first?"

He grabbed her cape and wrapped it around her. "Come on!" He said excitedly as he held the door open for her. "You can pick the tree out and I'll chop it down." Noticing her look longingly at the boxes, he pushed her out the door.

She chose a pretty little pine tree not far from the cabin. Sam chopped the tree down with a few easy strokes and carried it into the cabin. He stuck it in a bucket of wet sand in the corner of the room, then rubbing his hands together he eagerly exclaimed; "Now... we can open the boxes."

Sweeping his arm in front of him and bowing, he mimicked a southern drawl. "Ma'am, if you would be so kind as to do the honors."

The first box contained books. "Look, this one's a Bible, isn't it?" Holly's face glowed as she handed the book to Sam.

Sam studied her for a moment and then gently asked, "Holly, don't you know how to read?"

Her face flushed with embarrassment. "The teachers didn't want my kind at school." Her chin lifted defiantly, and then she smiled. "Except for one, Miss McDowell, she spent extra time with me and taught me to read a little bit." A sad expression crossed her face as she continued. "Then she up and got married. And the new teacher said there was no way he would let my kind in his school."

You might know it would be a man, Sam thought as he shook his head in disgust. "Wow!" He grinned as he started searching through the box. "These people really left a gold mine behind." He excitedly pulled out more books. "They not only left the Bible but look at this! 'Little Women,' 'Black Beauty' and James Cooper's 'The Last of the Mohicans.'"

Holly watched as a look of sheer joy washed over Sam's face. "You can read?" She asked hesitantly.

"One of my favorite pastimes." He answered, thumbing through the leather-bound copy of 'Black Beauty.

"Oh, Sam, will you read to me?"

"Sure...Well, will ya looky here?" He pulled out a magazine and handed it to Holly. "A Ladies' Home Journal it's a few years old, but it has a lot of pictures in it. Here," he said, handing her another box. "Open this one."

Holly carefully laid the magazine on the table, then opened the next box. It held a set of dishes, with gold trim around the edges and a cluster of bright yellow flowers in the middle. There was a small wooden box containing silverware and also a lovely white lace tablecloth with a beautiful crystal vase wrapped in it. Sterling silver salt and pepper shakers were wrapped in the matching napkins.

"Bet there was one unhappy lady when she found out these things were missing," Sam said. But he couldn't bring himself to feel sorry for the owner of these treasures when he saw Holly's radiant face before him. "Here, open this one." Grinning, he pushed the last box in front of her.

She carefully opened the box, peeked in, and then threw Sam a beaming smile. "Oh, Sam, you peeked." The box held a silver Christmas star. She carefully pulled the yellowed tissue off and laid the star on the table. As Holly began digging deeper into the box, her eyes widened. "They're Christmas ornaments!" She pointed out gleefully, as she unwrapped them and carefully set them on the table next to the silver Christmas star. Then she pressed and folded the wrapping paper and laid it back in the box. Glancing at Sam, she asked. "Can we trim the tree now?"

Sam watched the excitement on Holly's face. She had been through so much and yet she still held the innocence of a child. "We sure can, honey." He grinned. "But I get to put the star on."

They trimmed the tree, with Holly constantly changing ornaments from one branch to another, explaining that each branch of the tree was special and had to have its very own ornament. Sam topped it off with the star, and they both agreed that it was the prettiest Christmas tree they had ever seen.

Sam went outside and drew water from the well, and then they washed the dishes and set the table with their new find. They finished off the sausage and bread and had a piece of Mrs. Watt's fruitcake. This time, Sam poured Holly's coffee into one of the fancy cups and added a little water so it wouldn't be so strong. When they finished eating and cleaning up, Holly persuaded Sam to read to her from the Bible. As he read, she interrupted him with numerous questions. "What does God look like?" She asked. Before waiting for the answer, she continued with child-like excitement. "Is there really a heaven and did the angels sing the night Jesus was born?"

"Look, Holly," Sam said uneasily. "I don't know a lot about this kind of stuff." He noticed the disappointment wash over her face. "I'll tell ya what, I'll read 'Little Women' to you, and tomorrow we'll take a ride over to your friend Chris's place. They don't live far from here and her pa can answer these questions for you."

"No, I don't think that's a good idea. They wouldn't want my kind at their house."

"Awe, Holly, that's not true. They're good people and Ned's a Christian. He'll answer your questions."

She threw him a hesitant glance, but Sam wasn't about to

back off. Besides, there was something he wanted to borrow from Chris.

It was late, so Sam went out to the barn to get some fresh hay. Then he made beds for them. Holly's was on one side of the room and his was on the other. He read to her late into the night and only stopped when she asked what a word meant.

"That's it for tonight." He yawned as he laid the book on the table. "We had best get some sleep. We got a busy day tomorrow." Crawling into his bed, he turned his back to her and called out. "Night, Holly."

Sam woke to her whimpers and realized she was crying in her sleep. Quietly rolling out of the bed, he went and knelt before her. Her small body was curled in a fetal position, and his gut wrenched when he watched her child-like face form into a painful grimace. Not wanting to scare her more, he laid his hand on her shoulder and stroked it gently. "Holly," he whispered. "Wake up, darlin'." Her eyes flew open, and she lay unmoving, in a state of fear. "Don't be afraid." He soothed. "It's me, Sam."

Holly slowly sat up, pushed the hair from her face, and rubbed her eyes. "I'm sorry." She said sleepily. "I guess I should of told you. All the girls at the saloon are used to it." She wadded the edge of the blanket, held it close to her, and shyly met Sam's eyes. "They say I cry in my sleep."

Sam reached over and brushed a stray lock of hair from her face. "Bad dreams?" He probed, his voice soft and soothing.

She chewed on her bottom lip, her eyes filled with tears, and then she nodded her head.

Sam stood up, went and stoked the fire, then grabbed his blanket. He came and stood before her. "Move over." He ordered.

When she did as she was told, Sam lay next to her and then spread the blanket over them, making sure she was securely tucked in. He tucked his arm under her and pulled her over so her head was lying on his chest. Turning a little on his side, he pressed a kiss on each eyelid. "Now darlin'." He whispered. "You go to sleep. I'll chase the bad dreams away." She wrapped her arm around his waist as she molded herself to him. Holly felt safe, and for once, the fear that always lingered in the pit of her stomach was gone. Closing her eyes, she let this new feeling drift throughout her body and soon found a secure sleep in the smell and the feel of this kind, gentle man.

Holly awoke to the smell of coffee in the air. She stretched her small body, feeling rested, and thought for a moment she was dreaming. Sam was down on his haunches in front of the fireplace, holding a pan of sizzling, thick slices of bacon. The sweet aroma of the bacon and coffee awakened in her stomach a hunger that she hadn't felt in years. She gazed at Sam and noticed he had just washed; his wet hair was dangling loosely around his shoulders in coal, black ringlets. His new flannel shirt was hanging open and showed his broad, hardened chest with a light spattering of curly black hair. His jeans fit smoothly over his hips and down his long legs, making her fully aware of how tall and powerful he was. She knew his strength and what he could do to her and wondered why she held no fear of him. Her body quivered at the thought of him holding her all night. She could still feel his warmth on her, and the lingering scent of his body filled her nostrils. He'd never tried to touch her in any shameful way, and she felt it strange that she completely trusted him. For a moment, she wondered what it would be like to have him touch her in her most private places.

"Ya awake?" Sam asked as he scraped the bacon on a plate. "Up and at em', darlin', we got a busy day ahead of us." He grabbed the toast off the grate in the fireplace and quietly cursed under his breath. "Damn! Hot! Hot!" As he quickly juggled it to the plate. Then, wiping his hands on his jeans, he tossed Holly a grin. "Come on, lazy-bones, I'm hungry and we're going visiting."

Holly sat up and sighed reluctantly. "Do we have to go?"

"Yep, it's Christmas Eve and people visit on Christmas Eve." Sam wrapped a piece of bacon in toast and before shoving it in his mouth, he glanced at her. "And besides," he remembered. "You need to ask Ned those questions about the Bible."

Holly began rummaging through her pack. Sam noticed the look of displeasure on her face as she pulled out her faded red silk dress. "There's a new flannel shirt on the chair," he told her. "It'll be a little long, but if you put it on over that dress, it should keep ya nice and warm." Sam caught the relieved look on her face as she started to get up from the comfortable bed of hay.

"Hurry up." He teased. "We slept away most of the day. There's wash water for you on the table." He grabbed his coat from the peg on the wall and walked to the door. "I'll see about my horse while you get yourself washed and dressed."

Holly was glad Sam gave her some privacy, although she wouldn't have been embarrassed if he had stayed. For some reason, she felt as if she had known him for a lifetime. She felt safe with him, and that kind of feeling was strange for her.

Holly ate the bacon and toast with great enjoyment and surprised herself by asking for more, which was also quickly consumed.

Sam grunted as he lifted Holly onto the horse. As he climbed on behind her, he chuckled. "Gonna have to get a team of horses if you keep eating like you did this morning."

Holly giggled as she leaned back into him for more warmth. Sam had offered her his jacket, but she refused, saying that the cape and flannel shirt was more than enough. He pulled her closer into his opened jacket, hoping that his body heat would help keep her warm.

As he wrapped his arms around her and grabbed the reins, he thought to himself. This slip of a girl was really getting to him.

***

Christmas Eve was a flurry of excitement. Ned and Dylon went outside with the girls to finish building the snowman, while Chris completed the preparations for the Christmas dinner. After lunch, they put the girls down for a nap with the promise of a tree-trimming party when they awoke. Ned went out to the barn to finish his surprises and Dylon rode into town for some last-minute shopping.

Chris saw Sam and Holly through the window as they rode into the yard and ran out to the porch to greet them. "Holly, Sam, what a pleasant surprise!" She called out with a welcoming smile. "Come on in. You must be freezing!"

Sam could feel the reluctance in Holly as he eased her from the horse, then climbed down after her.

"Sam," Chris said, wrapping her arm around Holly. "Ned's in the barn. Why don't you go get him? Holly and I will fix some hot chocolate and cookies."

Chris told them that Dylon had ridden to town, and the girls were sleeping. Sam had to admit, he was a little relieved. He wasn't sure what kind of reception Dylon would give Holly. Although Sam liked him, he appeared to be a hard man. He didn't like the way he treated Chris. He could never figure out what Dylon saw in Rita Lewis when a woman like Chris was living right under his roof. Remembering the smell of Christmas cookies and the promise of hot chocolate made him quicken his pace, as he headed toward the barn to get Ned.

They all sat around the table enjoying the delicious snacks. Sam was delighted to hear Holly's cheerful voice speaking excitingly about the boxes they had found and the Christmas tree they had decorated. When she started telling them about the story Sam read to her, Ned interrupted. "Sam says you want to ask me some questions about the Bible? I'd be glad to answer what I can for ya."

Chris glanced out the window when they heard someone ride up. Sam noticed the glow on her face and heard the delighted note in her voice when she announced it was Dylon. The door flew open, and he walked into the house with an armload of packages. Surprise showed on his face when he saw who his company was. Sam breathed a sigh of relief when he gave them both a friendly greeting. Although, sadly, Sam watched Holly shrink back and could see her guard go up.

Ned and Holly were at the table in deep conversation, and the girls were awake from their naps, so Chris excused herself to go and tend to them. Dylon and Sam walked outside to replenish the wood box.

"How's the work at the stamp mill?" Dylon asked Sam as he picked up the ax and threw a log on the chopping block.

"I like it. In fact, I find I really like mining," Sam answered as he started stacking the wood Dylon was chopping. "What's going on with the Lewis mine? Is it working or did you have to shut it down for the winter?"

"We shut it down. The creek froze up." Dylon answered as he finished chopping the last piece of wood and leaned on the axe, watching Sam finish stacking the wood. "Noticed your land as I was riding back from town. Looks like some good grazing land."

Sam leaned up against a tree and reached for a cigarette from his shirt pocket. He lit it, then took a deep drag and let the smoke trail from his mouth. With little enthusiasm in his voice, he answered. "Yeah, Ken sure seems satisfied. But I don't know if ranchin' is for me."

"Reckon I was cut out for ranchin' or farmin,'" Dylon said as he leaned over and started piling the wood in his arms. "Seems like it's in the blood."

Sam flipped the half-smoked cigarette down and ground it under his boot. "We better be heading out," He said, glancing toward the sky. "I want to get back before dark."

When they entered the cabin, both with a pile of firewood in their arms, Sam noticed Holly sitting on the floor in front of the Christmas tree. The baby was on her lap and Karen was sitting next to her, playing with the kitten. It made his heart leap for joy when he heard her laugh at one of the baby's antics. "Come on, Holly, it's getting late." He told her reluctantly. "We need to go."

Chris turned from the stove with a look of disappointment on her face. "Can't you stay for dinner?" She glanced at Dylon for a nod of support, but both Sam and Chris could see that he wasn't too thrilled with the idea.

"No, thanks." He answered. "I'd like to get back before dark." Sam appreciated the genuine look of disappointment on Chris's face.

"Come in the bedroom Holly," Chris said as she grabbed her by the hand. "I made a Christmas present for you."

When Holly walked out of the room, her face held a look of sheer delight. "Look, Sam!" She exclaimed excitedly while showing him the bright green scarf and mittens. "Chris made them. Ain't they beautiful?"

While Chris wrapped some Christmas cookies, Holly said goodbye to the girls and Ned. It surprised Sam when Dylon smiled at her and wished her a Merry Christmas.

The crunch of the horse's hoofs in the recently fallen snow broke the silence as Sam gazed at the full moon and the stars sparkling in a blue-black sky. He breathed the crisp air and a wave of homesickness engulfed him, as he smelled Christmas pasts. He had come from a loving family. His mother and father, long dead now, cared deeply for each other and raised their two sons in a home full of love and happy memories. When Sam married, he wanted the same kind of life but realized too late that he had picked the wrong woman. When his parents died and his marriage broke up, he thought he knew what it was like to have your life torn apart. That is until he met Holly, the child-woman, who had no life at all. Sam felt her snuggle deeper into him, so he tightened his hold on her. "Seem like a good bunch of people." He said, feeling the wisps of her hairbrush against his face. "Sure nice of Chris to make you the scarf and mittens, wasn't it?" Sam placed his mouth to her ear, kissed it, and whispered. "What's wrong darlin'? You seem mighty quiet."

"Chris really loves Mr. Clay." She answered. "But she told me he was going to marry another lady." Sam could hear the sorrow in her voice. Then he heard the sudden change to anger. "I don't know why she loves him, anyway. He doesn't seem nice."

"Why, Holly, because of the way he looks or acts?"

Holly half-turned in the saddle and glanced at him indignantly. "I don't care how he looks." Then she sighed, remembering the angry look on his scarred face the day the two drunks beat her, and Chris wanted to help her go into the saloon. "But when he's mad he does look scary, doesn't he? Whatcha' think happened to his face?"

"Don't know," Sam replied.

"Those little girls sure seem to love him. He's different around them, ain't he?"

"You like kids, don't you?" Sam asked as he nuzzled her ear. "Does little Sammy have any brothers or sisters?" Holly sat rigid for a moment, then realized he was teasing her. "Yes, two brothers, Danny and Tommy."

"How come no little girls?"

"Because I don't want any, that's why. Besides, it's too hard for girls to live in this world."

"Yeah, maybe so, but she'll have a father who loves her and three brothers to protect her."

"It's all pretend, anyway! It ain't true!"

He detected the bitterness in her voice and felt her body tense as she tried to shrug away from him. He pulled her back, so she nestled closer to him and whispered in her ear. "It could be darlin', it could be." They rode the rest of the way home in silence, the scent of pine and wood smoke filling the night air.

"I'm starved!" Sam said as he entered the cabin. He went to the fireplace, stoked the smoldering embers, and added more wood as he watched Holly. She carefully folded her new scarf and lay her mittens on the table. Then she stroked them gently and gazed at Sam. "She made them just for me!" She exclaimed, a faint smile parting her lips.

They were pleasantly surprised when they opened the pack and found that Chris had made them sandwiches to go along with the cookies. There was also a jar of pickles and fresh cranberry sauce. Sam smacked his lips together when he saw the cranberries. "This will go great with the ham; we're having for our Christmas dinner."

While they ate their sandwiches, Holly entertained Sam with the stories that Ned told her about the Bible. "Ned said God is a bright light and when we get to heaven, his son Jesus is going to be the only light we'll need." She scrunched her nose as she continued. "We won't need no smelly oil or candles. And Sam, the angels really do sing and they are here to protect us and he said that Mary was real young when she became the mother of the baby Jesus." Holly stopped a minute, took a breath, and rushed on. "I like the name Mary, don't you? It's such a nice name."

Sam thought of his ex-wife Mary and how selfish she was. "It's the person that makes the name, Holly. Not the name that makes the person." Going over to where she was sitting crossed-legged in front of the Christmas tree, he knelt down, placed his rough hands on the sides of her face, and pulled her to meet his gaze. "Holly is a good name because you make it a good name."

She held his gaze and shyly smiled at him while he brought his lips to hers and gently kissed her. Feeling her body tense, Sam stood up and pulled her with him. "Come on, it's late. Let's go to bed." He lay down next to her. She turned her body to him and brought her face close to his. "I liked it when you kissed me." He could see the worry in her eyes as she spoke. "But Sam... I don't want to be like the girls at the saloon." Her face reddened, and she looked away. "They seem to like it when all kinds of men touch them." Shivering, she glanced back at him. "I don't want to be like that."

Sam knew her life held too much sadness for one so young. He realized he not only needed to but also wanted to make her feel safe. He brought his hand up and began caressing her cheek, and brushed a light kiss on her nose. "Darlin', when a man and woman care for each other, they have something very special. They belong to each other and they're supposed to like kissing and being close together. That's why people marry and have kids, and spend the rest of their lives together." He kissed her again gently; this time on the lips, then pressed her head to his chest. "Go to sleep now, little one. It's getting late."

Sam heard her steady breathing, and while she slept in his arms, he studied her. She reminded him of one of that expensive dainty porcelain, lady-figurines he would see in the shop windows. Long, straight sand-colored hair framed her face and was silky to the touch. Her tawny complexion was clear with no freckles, except for one right at the corner of her mouth. Thick dark lashes framed her blue eyes, which would light up like the sky in the early morning sunrise when she was happy. That didn't happen often, Sam sadly thought. Since he had met her, he had spent a lot of time wondering how he really felt about her. Although it excited him at the thought of making love to Holly, he held no great lust for her, and he had been known to be a man with a lusty appetite. He was willing for it to happen between them. But he realized that for her sake, the time had to be right.

That night after Sam and Holly left, Ned persuaded Chris to pop the popcorn, so they could string it and put it on the tree. Dylon was helping Karen make paper ornaments while trying to discourage Sarah from eating the flour and water glue Chris had made. Ned had carved them a wooden star, and Karen giggled in delight as Dylon lifted her on his shoulder to place it on top of the tree. Going to a sack that he had laid in the corner, Dylon opened it and took out a box. "Ned, I'd like for you to open your gift now."

"Now boy, it twarnt necessary for ya to get me nothin'." As he opened the box, he grinned up at them. "Well, will ya look at this?" Reaching into the box, he took out a wooden barn. Setting it on the table, he pulled out the statues of Mary, Joseph, and the baby Jesus, along with the three kings, the shepherds, sheep, and even a cow and a donkey.

"What is it, Ned?" Karen asked as she and Sarah went to look closer.

"Why it's a nativity scene, child, it's to remind us of the night the baby Jesus was born. Remember, I told you why we celebrate Christmas. It's Jesus' birthday." He tossed Dylon a cheerful grin. "Thank you, boy. It's a real fine gift."

The nativity scene was set in a prominent place on a table beside the tree. Karen grabbed Sarah by the hand and they scurried to the bedroom, running out a few minutes later, giggling. "Look, Papa, what we have!" Karen held up three gifts that looked like they had been wrapped by tiny little hands. Dylon reached out as if to grab one. "Where's mine-I'll open it now!" He teased as they ran from him giggling and excitedly laying the gifts under the tree.

While Ned and Dylon got the two sleepy babies ready for bed, Chris fixed hot chocolate and they all had more gingerbread cookies. Dylon tucked the girls in bed, but they insisted he lay with them while Ned read them a bedtime story. Chris stuffed the turkey and put it in the oven. The pumpkin and mincemeat pies had been made and were setting on the table covered in a clean cloth. She prepared the cranberries for the table by canning them. The only thing left to do was peel the potatoes and that could be done in the morning.

Chris felt disappointed that Holly and Sam wouldn't stay for dinner. She hoped they hadn't seen the look on Dylon's face when she had asked them. It was obvious he hadn't liked the idea. A blush of embarrassment crept onto her cheeks as she wondered if she would ever be able to please him. Remembering how kind and gentle he was with her last night, when they kissed under the Christmas tree, made her whole body still tingle with excitement. She couldn't help but wonder what would have happened had Karen not interrupted them. Was this a dream she was in? Maybe she should pinch herself. No! She thought because if it was a dream she sure didn't want to wake up.

"I think I'll turn in," Ned yawned, as he headed toward his room. "Those little ones run me ragged today." But both Chris and Dylon saw the contented smile on his face.

Chris was standing by the kitchen table taking her apron off when Dylon handed her a box. "Here, I want you to open this now."

The box was wrapped in crisp white paper and had a red bow tied to it. Chris sat down on the bench and laid the box on the table. Dylon sat down next to her and watched her carefully untie the ribbon as if she were savoring every moment. When she finally opened the box, he heard her gasp in surprise, and then she gave him the look that he had hoped for. Taking out a royal blue robe with satin ribbon ties, she held it up to her and saw that the sleeves were also cuffed in satin. "It's beautiful!" She exclaimed as she held it against her cheek.

Dylon felt like a clumsy schoolboy. "There's a piece of ribbon in there for your hair, too. I...I hope ya like it." Standing up, he hesitated for a moment as if he had something else to say, then changed his mind. "Well... Night," He mumbled, as he walked to the bedroom.

The next morning Dylon awoke to the smell of bacon frying. Feeling fully relaxed, he lie on his bed for a moment and listened to the girls jabbering in the bedroom next door. When he heard Chris's soothing voice, he had to grit his teeth to control the emotions that he was feeling for her.

"Morning, Ned! Bacon sure smells good." Dylon greeted as he came out of the bedroom. "Merry Christmas!"

"Same to you, boy." Ned returned with a cheerful grin. "Ya best get washed up for breakfast before those young'uns get out here and want to tear into their packages."

They both glanced up when they heard the bedroom door open. "Well, will ya look at that?" Ned gave a low wolf whistle. "You look like a regular princess."

"Isn't she pretty?" Karen exclaimed as she followed Chris out of the bedroom. "Papa gave it to her last night."

Dylon went stone still as he gazed at Chris. She really was beautiful, he thought. He noticed her hair was brushed to a velvety shine and held back with the satin ribbon, and her cheeks glowed with a soft red blush. It made Dylon's heart thump as he watched her. He realized that it was the first time he had ever seen her aglow with happiness. "Yeah...You look mighty fine." Dylon choked out, trying to swallow the lump in his throat.

"Oh! Ned-I should be doing that." Chris frowned as she rushed to the stove where Ned was frying the bacon.

"No!" Dylon broke in. "You and the girls sit at the table, and let

Ned and me cook breakfast this morning." Throwing a wink at the girls, Dylon teased. "Then we'll open the presents."

A leisurely breakfast was out of the question this morning. Karen and Sarah were so excited when they saw the new brightly covered surprises under the tree. The adults decided that it was best to set breakfast aside until after the gift-giving.

After they all had gathered around the Christmas tree, Karen told Ned and Dylon to open the gifts from her and Sarah first. So with many ohs and ahs', they opened the girl's packages. "I made them all by myself, and Sarah helped me wrap them." Karen's face was beaming with pride as she watched while they opened the long, red crochet chains she had made. "Sis taught me how to make them."

Ned and Dylon, with grand ceremony, tied the chains around their necks. Then Dylon whispered something in Karen's ear, and she ran to his bedroom and brought out a big box and sat it on Chris's lap. "This is from us, Sissy, for taking such good care of me and Sarah for Papa."

When Chris opened the box and saw the lovely reddish, brown cloak with a lighter brown cape and hood attached to it, her eyes immediately shot up too Dylon. He just grinned back at her, knowing she couldn't refuse a gift from the girls.

"Now, that was a real good gift to give her," Ned spoke up with a satisfying grin.

"Try it on Sissy; Papa said it would look real pretty on you." Both Ned and Chris glanced at Dylon and watched his face turn a beet red.

Chris wrapped the cloak around her shoulders. "It's beautiful," she said, gazing into Dylon's eyes. For the first time in her life, she felt really warm inside and realized it was not from the warmth of the cloak.

Then the girls started ripping excitedly into their presents.

They put on their scarves and hats that Chris had made them, and then they ran and gave her a big hug. When they saw the cradle Ned had made for the dolls Dylon had bought them, they scurried into the bedroom for some towels to wrap their new babies in. Next, they emptied their stockings and found oranges, apples, and also some candy and nuts. Karen squealed for joy when she saw a book filled with children's stories fall out of her stocking. Sarah dumped her blocks on the floor plopped down with her thumb firmly in place and started piling one on top of the other.

The three lonely adults, who at one time thought the hurts heaped upon them by the world would destroy them, now grinned. As they watched lovingly, these two little girls play contentedly in front of the Christmas tree.

"I'm next," Ned said as he rushed into his bedroom and brought out Chris's gift. It was a varnished cherry-wood sewing box he had made, with a lid that was slanted and hinges on each side. Her name was neatly carved in it, and alongside her name were two-hand prints, one smaller than the other. "Oh, Ned!" Chris exclaimed joyfully, rubbing her hand over the box. "It's beautiful! Thank you!"

"Well, you can see the girls helped." He grinned back at her. "They sure did like the part of gettin' to put their hand in the paint."

Next came Dylon's gift from Ned. Again he went to the bedroom and this time it was a smaller wood box, with hinges on the lid, and the initials D.C. carved in it. There were two-tiny footprints again, one smaller than the other, on each side of the initials. "Figured you could use this for your boot polish," Ned explained as he set the box before Dylon.

Dylon felt overwhelmed as he picked the box up and examined it carefully. "Can't remember gettin' many gifts, Ned." He glanced over at Ned and grinned. "But I sure will get a lot of good use out of this. Thanks! ”

Next came Chris's gifts. She handed them both neatly wrapped packages, with bright red bows and fresh holly tied to them. Ned opened his and raved about the slippers, scarf, and hat she had made for him. "Go ahead, boy," Ned said, pointing to Dylon's gift. "Open yours; she worked mighty hard on it."

Dylon became tongue-tied when he opened his gift. He had never owned a silk shirt. He knew by the neat, even stitches and the bone buttons that matched the precise buttonholes all the work that she had put into it. He held the black string tied up to admire, knowing that it was also her handiwork. Watching him as he picked the shirt up, with his big, calloused hands, Chris ventured shyly. "I hope it fits. I used one of your work shirts for a pattern."

Not taking his eyes from the treasured shirt, his mouth formed a huge grin. "It's mighty fine... mighty fine!"

There was still one small package left. Dylon got up and retrieved it from under the tree. When he laid it on Chris's lap, their eyes met as he spoke. "Saw this in town yesterday and thought you might like it."

Chris threw him a puzzled glance as she opened the elegantly wrapped package. But when she saw the small crystal box with a pine tree engraved on it, she smiled at him knowingly.

"Lift the lid." He told her.

She did, and the soft tinkle of Silent Night flowed from the music box.

The glowing smile and delighted gasp from Chris pleased Dylon. "Thought that might be easier to set in the corner than a real tree." He teased in an unsteady voice.

"But the cloak, the robe, and now this, it must have cost you a fortune."

Dylon stood up and glared down at her. "Don't you like it? If not, just tell me!"

Chris gnawed on her bottom lip nervously. Should she tell him how she truly felt? That she loved him with all of her heart and that the gifts that he had given her made her happier than she had ever been in her life. "Oh, no," she explained breathlessly. "The music box is wonderful. I shall treasure it always. It's all so wonderful."

Dylon watched the tears stream down her cheeks as their eyes met. Why did he always react to her this way? He didn't want to make her cry; he just wanted to make her happy. She reached up and wiped the tears from her face, and smiled at him. "Dylon, you've made this a wonderful Christmas. Thank you, thank you so much."

Chapter 10

Holly awakened first; lying there, she savored the moment, loving the feel of Sam's lean, hard body pressed up against her backside. She had to keep reminding herself that this wasn't a dream. How could this have happened to her? Maybe it really was a dream. When she felt Sam's warm breath on her neck, she reached down and grasped his hand that was lying restfully on her thigh, and brought it up to her mouth. His hands were enormous and callused and his knuckles held a smattering of black hair, but his nails were clean and neatly trimmed. She took pleasure in the smell of his masculinity and shivered at the thought of the stench of the men that had used her so violently.

"If you're awake, why ain't you up fixing us some breakfast?" Sam whispered as he squeezed his hand over hers and nibbled on her neck.

She turned over in his arms, and their faces were inches apart. His breath was strong from the night's sleep, but not entirely unpleasant.

"Merry Christmas, Sam."

He gave her a lazy smile. "Merry Christmas, darlin'. Now get your tail up and fix me somethin' to eat, woman."

Holly jumped up, shivering from the cold. She quickly stoked the fire and put some water on to boil. Then she brushed her hair and tied it back with a faded ribbon she had in her sack. They had been sleeping in their clothes, so her dress was wrinkled, but she put on the new flannel shirt Sam had given her and buttoned it. She washed, dumped the pan of water outside, and poured in some clean water for Sam. Then she went out to the privy. When she came in, Sam was at the table fixing something in one of the fancy cups. He glanced at her, grinned sheepishly, then handed her the cup. "Happy Birthday, darlin'!"

"Oh, Sam!" She laughed gleefully. "It's hot chocolate." Throwing him a puzzled gaze, "but how did you get it?" She asked. "And how did you know it was my birthday?"

"I knew you didn't like coffee, so I had Chris fix me up a tin of chocolate." Chucking her under the chin, he winked. "And Duffy told me you were born on Christmas Day."

Holly closed her eyes and let the sweet hot liquid roll around her tongue before she swallowed it. Ned was right, she thought. There really are guardian angels and hers must be Sam Drew.

Ned had told Dylon that Sam and Holly were staying at the Drew's old cabin. So he decided to take a ride over and ask if they would like to have Christmas dinner with them. Chris really cared for the girl and seemed disappointed they didn't stay last night for dinner. His mind drifted to Chris. He hated the fact that he made her cry this morning. She looked so happy when she opened the music box. The delighted smile on her face was what he had hoped for. Then he remembered how she looked when he loomed over her, demanding to know if she liked it or not. He wondered, as he clicked the reins on the horse, why he always reacted to her the way he did. For reasons he didn't fully understand, he knew he wanted to make her happy. He could feel the guard he had wrapped around his heart slipping and he just hoped he could handle it if and when she rejected him.

Dylon realized Holly was afraid of him, but it really didn't bother him much, as he was used to the stares of people. She was a plain little thing; he thought and was surprised to see a guy like Sam take up with her. He liked Sam Drew; he seemed to be a hard worker. Dylon chuckled, remembering how uncomfortable Sam was when Rita and some of the other woman on the wagon train flirted with him. Rita, he thought, pulling his hat down further against the cold. That was a subject he was going to have to deal with, and it would have to be soon.

Sam and Holly were in the yard building a snowman when Dylon rode up. "There a problem, Clay?" Sam asked with some worry in his voice.

"Naw, just thought we would ask ya to come for Christmas dinner." Dylon glanced to where Holly was standing, half hiding behind the snowman. "Chris and the girls would sure like it. She's fixing a huge meal. We'll eat in a couple of hours."

Sam threw Holly a glance. "It's up to you," he stated.

Holly's eyes flicked to Dylon's face, then she glanced away.

"Holly, I know I look fierce," Dylon said as he glanced down at her from his horse. "But I won't bite you." He chuckled, "I promise." Sam walked over to where Holly was standing and grasped her hand in his. "Well, what do ya say? Ya want to go or not?"

Holly wanted to go. She enjoyed being with the girls and Ned, but she especially liked her new friend Chris. Sam smiled at her when she nodded her head and then he went over to where Dylon was sitting on his horse. "See you in a couple hours, then. And, thanks Dylon!"

Chris was in the kitchen, peeling the potatoes when Dylon rode up. She had been worried when he left; he had told no one where he was going. He had put on the new shirt and tie she had made and just rode off. A streak of jealousy ran through her as she realized how handsome he looked and hoped he wasn't riding to town to see Rita.

The emotional turmoil Chris was experiencing was unbearable. One minute he seemed like he was happy and cared about her, then the next he would get quiet and sullen or yell at her. Now he'd just up and left and he hadn't been gone long enough to ride to town. It doesn't matter; she thought. He's back, that's all that matters. He was here with her, and she would just live for now.

Dylon entered the cabin and saw Chris standing at the counter. He walked over and put his arms around her, placing his hands on both sides of the sink, trapping her in. Chills ran up her spine as he placed his mouth to her ear and whispered. "Better peel a few more of those potatoes. Sam and Holly are coming for dinner."

Chris swirled around in his arms weak-kneed with the nearness of him?" She smiled up at him as she laid her hand on his chest and gazed into his wonderful, clear blue eyes.

Bringing his face even closer, as he felt the branding of her hand on his chest, he smiled back. "Figured it would make you happy." Dylon drug his gaze down to her lips then back to her smiling eyes. Chris stood breathless, waiting.

"Papa! Papa! Come quick! There's a rabbit."

"Ah...Jeez!" He sighed as he stood straight and ran his hand through his hair. Pressing his finger to her lips, he spoke in a hoarse whisper. "We'll continue this later."

"Papa, come quick!" Karen squealed as she burst through the door. "There's a big white rabbit outside."

They were all outside trying to find the rabbit when Sam and Holly rode up. After seeing the radiant glow on Chris's face, Dylon was glad he had ridden over and asked them for dinner.

"Oh, Chris, everything tastes so good," Holly said as they all sat around the table; eating their fill of turkey, mashed potatoes, gravy, and cranberry sauce. There was pumpkin and mincemeat pie for dessert. Then, they all chipped in to help with the clean-up.

Gathering around the Christmas tree with Dylon sprawled

in his rocking chair and Ned half asleep on the bench, Holly and Sam sat on the floor playing with the girls and their new toys. Chris made a fresh pot of coffee and brought out a plate of gingerbread cookies and fudge that she had hidden from Ned and Dylon. "Well, boy," Ned teased as he glanced at Dylon. "That's the only place we didn't look."

Chris poured the coffee and set the cookies and fudge on the table. Then, with Karen and Sarah looking on in excitement, Dylon lit the tallow Christmas tree candles. Karen asked Ned if he would read the Christmas story from the Bible to them. Chris, Karen, and Sarah sat on the floor by the tree; Dylon sprawled out next to them. They cuddled together, Sam and Holly on the bench

Dylon loved the smell of the warm tallow from the candles. He also liked what the glow from them did to Chris's hair.

Ned sat down in the rocking chair and opened his tattered old Bible and began. "This is from Saint Luke, Chapter 2.

And it came to pass in those days, that there went out a decree from Caesar Augustus, that all the world should be taxed. And all went to be taxed, everyone into his own city. And Joseph also went up from Galilee out of the city of Nazareth, into. And so it was, that, while they were there, the days were accomplished that she should be delivered.

And she brought forth her firstborn son, and wrapped him in swaddling clothes, and laid him in a manger; because there was no room in the inn.

And there were in the same country shepherds abiding in the field, keeping watch over their flock by night.

And, lo, the angel of the Lord came upon them, and the glory of the Lord shone round about them; and they were sore afraid.

And the angel said unto them, Fear not: for, behold I bring you good tidings of great joy, which shall be to all people.

For unto you is born this day in the city of David a Savior, which is Christ the Lord.

And this shall be a sign unto you; Ye shall find the babe wrapped in swaddling clothes, lying in a manger.

And suddenly there was with the angel a multitude of the heavenly host praising God and saying, Glory to God in the highest and on earth peace, goodwill toward men.

And it came to pass, as the angels were gone away from them into heaven, the shepherds said one to another, Let us now go even unto Bethlehem, and see this thing which has come to pass, which the Lord hath made known unto us.

And they came with haste and found Mary and Joseph, and the babe lying in a manager.

And when they had seen it, they made known abroad the saying, which was told them concerning this child.

And all they that heard it wondered at those things which were told them by the shepherds."

Ned looked up from the words if the Bible and glanced around, taking in the warm peaceful scene in front of him. Feeling joy surging through his old heart he continued. "But Mary kept all these things and pondered them in her heart."

Dylon listened intently to Ned read from the Bible. He had never heard this story before and wondered how true it really was. Although, he did believe that Ned would probably give up his life, for what was in that old book of his.

He glanced over at Chris and the girls breathed in the heady scent of pine and tallow and realized he had never felt this much peace in his life.

Sam and Holly decided to walk back to the cabin, as it was only a couple of miles. Sam held the horse's reins in one hand

and Holly's small hand in the other. It was a clear, brisk night, and the sky held a multitude of stars. Holly pointed toward the heavens at one star that seemed to be bigger and brighter than most. "Look, Sam, do you suppose that's the star Ned read about in the Bible?"

"Could be." Sam agreed as he heard her give a deep sigh. "What is it, Holly?"

She squeezed his hand tighter and brought it to her face. "This has been the most perfect day of my life. I wish it would never end."

Sam thought he heard a little sadness in her voice. "There'll be other days, darlin', lots of them."

It was late when they got back to the cabin, and they were both exhausted. They fell into a relaxing sleep, wrapped in each other's arms. Sam awoke, startled when he heard the door bang open. He sat up and quickly reached for his gun, then he heard his name. "Sam!" He focused his eyes and saw that it was his brother, Ken. "Damn, boy, you scared me. Shut the door, it's cold."

"I was worried about you, Sam. You were supposed to meet me this morning." Ken glared in surprise as he watched the girl next to his brother sit up and rub her eyes sleepily. "I thought something might have happened to you, being all alone out here." Then he nodded toward Holly and sneered. "But I must have been mistaken. You'd rather spend your holiday with nothin' but a whore, instead of your family and friends!"

Holly quickly stood, grabbed her cape and shoes, and dashed out the door. Judaea, unto the city of David, which was in Bethlehem;(because he was of the house and lineage of David:) To be taxed with Mary, his espoused wife.

Sam shook his head in disgust and glared at Ken. "Real nice, little brother! Too bad there weren't a couple of crippled kids here you could kick on your way out!"

A glaze of chagrin covered Ken's face as he grabbed the back of his neck and began rubbing it. "Aw, Sam! I'm sorry, but I was worried about you. Remember, we got a meeting with the banker in Helena. If we don't leave today, we won't get there in time."

"Go on back to town," Sam told Ken as he got up from the makeshift bed on the floor and went over and threw some wood in the fireplace. "I'll meet you there in a couple of hours."

Sam felt a wave of disappointment in the way his brother acted toward Holly. He recognized that as long as she stayed in this town and lived in Duffy's saloon, she would have little if no chance at all for a normal life. And the realization hit him that he wanted to be a part of her life, but it wouldn't be in Pony, Montana.

When he went outside to look for Holly, he found her sitting despondently on a log by the snowman. As he walked over to her, she stood up defiantly and faced him. "You and your grand family and friends may think I'm nothing but a whore." She yelled as she slapped her hands to her heart and glared at him. "But in here I'm a virgin." Then Holly threw her hand out, with a look of disgust, pointed at his genitals, and gritted. "You men can force that thing in a woman, and all you get is a few inches. But you can never penetrate a heart, a mind, or a soul. Not unless you're allowed to!" She beat on her chest as the tears streamed down her face. "NEVER!" She wailed. "NEVER! NEVER! NEVER!"

Sam stood stock-still and watched her, stunned by the words she had just thrown at him. "Holly, I'm not the one that said it."

"Maybe not," she snarled. "But I'm sure you think it!"

Sam moved closer to her and grasped her gently by the arms. "Holly?" he asked sadly, his eyes searching hers. "Do you really believe that?"

She shrugged from his touch and spun around, her back to him, refusing to answer. He stood there for a moment, waiting. Then, shaking his head, he heaved a bitter sigh. "I don't deserve this."

Holly heard the crunch of his footprints in the snow and whirled around, afraid to let him walk out of her life.

"Sam," she whispered to his retreating back.

He kept walking.

"Sam!" she called out louder.

He stopped and turned around. They stood appraising each other for a moment. Holly is so young and carrying a world of rejection on her shoulders. Sam wanted with all of his heart to pull her out of that world but didn't know how.

Deciding to take a chance, he held his arms out to her. She moaned and ran into them. "I'm sorry Sam! I'm so sorry! So very sorry!" She sobbed into his chest with her frail arms wrapped tightly around his waist.

He held her close, wanting nothing more than to protect her from the viciousness that this life had heaped on her.

"It'll be all right darlin'." He whispered as he buried his face in her hair. "I promise it'll be all right."

"This meeting with the banker in Helena is real important to Ken," Sam explained to Holly as he helped her pack her things. "If we get the loan, then we can buy some cattle and start workin' the land."

Sam lifted a sullen Holly onto his horse and then swung on behind her. They rode back to town in silence. He stopped in front of Duffy's and as he helped her down from the horse; he held her small body close to his, then he gently set her to her feet. "Holly, I'll be back before you know it." Grasping her chin in his callused hand, he drew her face up to meet his and smiled. "Then we'll do some talking about our future." He let her go and stood watching as she walked through the saloon door.

The day after Christmas, the Watts family, TC, and Rachel Isdell rode over and spent the day with Dylon and Chris. TC seemed preoccupied and asked Ned if he could speak to him in private. Although Dylon was told that TC was engaged to be married, his stomach still felt sick with the thought that he was going to ask Ned for Chris's hand in marriage.

It was a little too chilly to go outside, so Ned invited TC into the bedroom. "What seems to be the problem, young man?" Ned asked as he motioned for TC to sit down on the opposite bed.

"Well, you see sir," TC said as he fidget with his hands. Then he finally stood up and started pacing the floor. "Chris tells me you're a Christian and...Well, I got a callin' of the Lord on me." He slumped back down on the bed, leaned over, and with elbows on his knees, he rested his head in his hands. "I run away from it and also from the girl I want to marry. And," he sobbed. "I don't know what to do."

Ned went over and sat next to him and placed his arm around his shoulder. "Seems to me, young man, that ya already took the first step." TC gave Ned a puzzled glance as he wiped his eyes with his forearm.

Ned just grinned. "You see son, your confessen' to the calling of the Lord on you, and you're miserable for running away from it. So now all you have to do is to decide when you're going to stand up and face the Lord and find out what he wants to do with you. And as far as that little lady of yours...Well." Ned said as he patted TC's shoulder. "You need to get on back to where ever she is and marry her, that is if she'll still have ya."

A couple of hours later, Dylon and Mr. Watts were at the table playing checkers. And Anna, Chris, Mrs. Watts, and Rachel were sitting on the floor cutting out patches of material for a quilt that Chris was learning how to make. Dylon's unease grew when Ned and TC came out of the bedroom. Chris glanced up at TC and when their eyes met, he smiled at her and she broke out into a huge grin. Dylon held his breath when Ned announced TC had something to say. "Well," TC spoke nervously. "I've decided to go back to Seattle and enter the seminary. And," he continued. "I'm going to find Ellie and beg her forgiveness and ask her to marry me."

Chris and the other ladies flew to him, hugging and congratulating him, while Dylon slumped back in the chair and let out a relieved sigh. They spent the rest of the day in pleasant conversation, and they all spent New Year's day at the Watts home.

The next few days were the happiest Dylon could ever remember. Just spending time with his family, something he thought would never happen in his life.

They were sitting at the table, just finishing with lunch, when they heard a rider come in the yard. Dylon got up and went and opened the door. "It's Sheriff Gallen. Wonder what he wants?"

Sheriff Gallen entered the cabin with hat in hand and greeted Chris and the girls. Then he asked Dylon and Ned to come out into the yard. He wanted to talk to them in private. When Dylon came back into the cabin, Chris could see the worried look on his face. "What is it? What's the matter?" She asked.

Dylon walked over to her and grasped her gently by the arms. "Chris, it's Holly. She's been badly hurt. She's asking for you and Ned."

Chris's face furrowed in shock. "What happened?"

"Seems she's been beat up pretty bad and stabbed several times."

Chris threw her hands to her face. "Oh, God! No!" she exclaimed in a horrified gasp. Then she glanced at Dylon questioningly. "Was it Sam?"

It surprised Dylon that she would think that Sam would be capable of such a despicable act. He realized then how little she could trust anyone.

"No," he answered. "Of course not, and besides, he's out of town."

Chris saw the baffled look on his face as he asked. "How could you think something like that, Chris?"

"Men do cruel things to women." She threw back at him in a trembling voice.

He gently grasped her chin in his hand and made her look at him. "Do you think I would be capable of doing something like that?"

"I don't know what to think!" She snapped back, bewildered.

Ned and Chris rode to town with the sheriff and Dylon took the girls to the Watts, then followed after.

"Sam! Sam Drew!" Sam heard Sheriff Gallen call his name as he and Ken rode into town. The trip to Helena hadn't taken as many days as they thought. But it had been a long and a hard trip and he was dusty and tired. All he wanted to do was get a hot bath, a good meal, and some sleep. Then he wanted to go see Holly and give her the blue gingham dress and frilly bonnet he had bought for her.

"What's up, Sheriff?"

"Need to talk to ya a minute, Sam."

"Meet you back at the room," Sam told Ken as he climbed down off his horse and threw the reins over the hitching post. As he walked over to where the sheriff was standing, he grabbed his battered Stetson off his head and beat it against his leg to rid it of some of the trail dust. Sheriff Gallen took off his own hat and twisted it in his hand. "Got some bad news, Sam. Someone got a hold of little Holly and beat her up." Sam went pale and grabbed the sheriff. "Where is she?" He yelled.

"She's at the saloon. Got Duffy locked up, he emptied his pistol on the guy." Sam turned and started running toward Duffy's as the sheriff called out after him. "She's cut pretty bad. It doesn't look too good for her."

Sam entered the saloon and took the stairs two at a time. Rose was coming out of one of the rooms crying. "Oh Sam," she ran to him, tears streaking her rouged cheeks. "I'm glad you're here. She's been calling for you."

As he entered the room, he saw Ned sitting at the foot of the bed and Chris standing on the other side of it, next to Dylon. He fell to his knees by the side of the bed and grasped Holly's hand in his, uttering a groan at the sight of her. Her face was a mass of bruises, her eyes were blackened, and she had a deep gash on the side of her cheek. "Holly... Holly... I'm here, darlin'."

When she heard his voice, she opened her eyes and through swollen lips whispered weakly. "Sam, oh Sam, I missed you so. I think you took my heart with you."

He held her small hand to his mouth and started kissing it. "It's right here in my pocket, honey."

She moved her hand to his face and gave him a weary smile. "I'm so very tired," she whispered. "But you know what?"

"What darlin'?"

"Ned was right. Jesus is a bright light. Can't you see it, Sam?"

Sam realized then that he was losing her. "Holly, you can't leave me, you hear?" His voice was quivering. "I love you. Do you hear me?" He laid his head gently on her chest. "Oh, God...Holly." He sobbed. "Don't leave me."

She began stroking his hair. "It's all right for me to go, Sam.

The voice in the light told me He had something special for you to do."

Sam lifted his head up and gazed at her, bewildered, tears streaming down his face. "Not without you, Holly. Not without you." Then he laid his hand on her forehead and gently pushed the stray locks from her battered face. He saw the worry in her eyes and instinctively knew it was for him.

"Sam, you've made me feel loved and I've been so happy with you. But...But the light and the angels. Can you hear them singing?" She squeezed his hand and winced in pain. "I...I wish I could be with them."

A peaceful gaze washed over her face, and Sam knew her mind had entered a different realm. It hit him then, what she had been through and all the terrible things that this world had done to her. With a gut-wrenching certainty, he knew he needed to let her go. Unchecked tears streamed down his face as he reached over and kissed her swollen lips. "Go ahead, darlin', I understand and I won't hold you here. You can go on home." She gave him a weak smile, exhaled a sigh, and fell into a deep sleep.

Sheriff Gallen let Duffy out of jail to be with her. When Holly heard his sobbing, she opened her eyes and reached her hand out to him. But her strength failed her, and she fell back into a coma. She died later on that night with Sam's hand in hers. Her face held a look of beauty and serenity. Ned placed his arm around Duffy's shoulder as they stood by her bedside, crying. Chris hadn't realized Dylon was there until she felt his powerful arms go around her, and she sagged against him, reveling in his support.

Holly was buried in her new blue gingham dress in a small plot behind the Community Hall. Duffy stood next to Sam and as they lowered her body on the ground. He spoke sadly. "She just made it to her twenty-first birthday." Then he glanced over at Sam. "The poor kid never traveled any further than that dirty little cabin of yours." Shrugging his shoulders, he threw out a harsh laugh. "Hell, she's better off where she is. Life has no place for women like her."

Dylon felt Chris stiffen at Duffy's statement. On the way out of the cemetery, she grabbed Duffy's arm. "If it weren't for men like you," she sobbed. "There wouldn't be a woman like her!" Dylon placed his arm around Chris and led her away, while Duffy hung his head and was led back to jail by the sheriff.

After Holly's funeral, Ned went to the Watts farm and picked up the girls and Dylon drove Chris home. She sat quietly next to him with her hands folded in her lap, and her eyes cast downward. He pulled into the yard, quickly jumped out, and threw the reins over the fence rail. After he lifted her down from the buggy, he gently wrapped his arm around her shoulder and led her into the house.

"I'll fix dinner," she spoke in a daze as she went to the stove and grabbed the coffee pot. "I had better hurry; Ned will be here with the girls in a minute."

Dylon heard the tremble in her voice as he went and gently retrieved the coffeepot from her hand, setting it back on the stove. "Let me help you out of your cloak." He said tenderly as he slid it from her shoulders and threw it across the chair. Then he placed his hands on her shoulders and steered her toward the bedroom. "You're tired, Chris, you're going to lay down. I'll take care of the dinner." He set her on the bed and slipped her shoes off. Then he reached behind her and undid a few of the buttons on her dress. Her hair was wrapped in a tight coil, so he pulled the comb and hairpins out and watched as it fell in thick waves down the back of her neck. "There," He said, laying her back and covering her with a blanket. "You try and get some sleep." Reaching down, he gently brushed a stray lock of hair from her forehead. "Are you going to be all right, Chris?". She gazed up at him, hearing the concern seeping through his voice. "Yes, I'm just so... tired." She whispered as she closed her eyes and drifted off into a fitful sleep.

Ned and Dylon fixed dinner for the girls and put them to bed. Then they cleaned up the dishes and filled the woodbox and called it an early night. Dylon had just crawled into bed when he heard Chris moaning. He rushed into the room in time to see her thrashing and kicking at the blankets. Not wanting to wake Karen and Sarah, in the bed opposite her, he sat down, placed his hand on her shoulder and cautiously shook her. Chris let out a gasp and woke up, her arms flailing. Dylon gently held her down and spoke very softly. "Shh...Chris, it's me, Dylon." As her sight focused, she relaxed, and he let her go.

Chris glanced over at the girls, then back at Dylon, and whispered. "I was having a horrible dream."

"What about?" He asked, propping the pillow behind her so she could sit up more comfortably.

"Jack Slade was chasing me, and...and you had the girls." She buried her face in her hands and muffled a sob. "I...I couldn't reach you."

Dylon pulled her hands from her face and enfolded them in his. "Slade's not a part of your life anymore, Chris. You're safe now, here with us."

She gazed at him and then down at his hands. They were excellent hands, big and calloused hands that had selflessly worked hard to take care of her and the girls. Now they were encompassing her small ones, making her feel safe.

"Dylon," she whispered affectionately. "I know that you're not anything like Jack Slade or that man that hurt Holly. You've been so good to us. I don't know if I can ever repay you."

Dylon gently began caressing the back of her small hand with his thumb. "You don't owe me anything. You brought Karen and Sarah into my life. That's payment enough."

You stupid fool, he thought, tell her, tell her now, tell her she owns your heart. Lay her back on that bed and bury yourself in her and tell her with your body how much you love her. But Dylon knew he had nothing but his love to offer her and that would never be enough for a girl like Chris.

"You better go back to sleep," he said as he stood and smiled down at her. "It's late and we don't want to wake the girls." Then he quietly left the room.

Chris lay in her bed, still feeling the presence of Dylon. She loved him with every fiber of her being. If only he could return that love. She thought about what he had said and it was true she was safe, but for how long? What was she going to do when Dylon married Rita? Time was growing short, and she was going to have to make some decisions. She had put it off long enough. Maybe if Ned was willing, and she got a job in town, they could stay here, in this cabin. She was certain that Ned wouldn't want to work for Rita. Chris had made many good friends in Pony, and she knew Dylon would let her see the girls. When she thought of Dylon, her heart ached with longing for him. He had been so much a part of her life, a life that would have been worth nothing had it not been for him. She thought of poor Holly, and knew, like Holly, she would rather die than live the life of a whore. Holly seemed so at peace with death. Maybe, Chris thought, she found it in the God Ned talked about so often.

The next morning, after breakfast, Dylon announced he had to ride back to the ranch site for a couple of days. He needed to check on things. He was really pleased to see how disappointed they all acted, especially Chris. "It'll only be for a couple of days." He told the teary girls as they hugged him goodbye.

***

It was a few days after the funeral, and Sam and Ken were standing in front of the dilapidated old cabin. Sam felt Ken's pleading voice pluck at his heart. "Sam, this is crazy. Your home is right here. We made plans and the loan for the cattle came through."

"Look, little brother, this is your dream," Sam said as he swept his arm across the vast rangeland. "And you got a nice little gal to share it with you."

Ken noticed the look of sadness cross Sam's face as he watched him sit on the log next to the melting snowman. "Is it because of the death of that girl?" He spoke with a touch of anger in his voice.

"That girl had a name and in all likelihood, Holly would have been your sister-in-law." Ken paled and the look of shock didn't go unnoticed by Sam. "Listen, Ken," Sam continued with a resigned sigh. "I would have moved on, anyway. It's time I find my own dream." He picked up some snow and started patching the snowman and spoke sadly. "Hope ya understand, boy. It's time for me to move on."

Chapter 11

Dylon saw everything was going along fine at the mine site. The men had all come back to work after the holidays and were cutting and stripping logs for the cabin. They had planned on working until the weather got too cold.

It was just as well, because Dylon had stepped in a chuckhole and wrenched his back, and was in great pain, so he decided to come home.

"Where's Chris?" He asked Ned as he was greeting the girls.

"She walked to town to see Rose."

Dylon winced from his back pain as he set Sarah to the ground. "Who?"

"One of the girls that works for Duffy. Wanted to see Chris about something."

"Ned!" Dylon ranted. "She's a whore!"

"Well now, son, I don't think something like that would rub off on another person. And I reckon even a whore needs a friend."

"How long has she been gone?" Dylon asked, worriedly.

"Not long, a couple of hours, maybe."

Dylon poured himself a mug of coffee and watched the girls play with their blocks. Then he gulped his coffee down and headed for the door. "I'm going after her Ned."

"Suit yourself, boy," Ned answered with a knowing grin.

Dylon painfully mounted his horse and started the two-mile ride to town. He hadn't ridden far when he saw them. Chris recognized him and started waving and running toward him, while Rose hung back. "Hi!" she said, smiling up at him. "I thought you would be gone longer."

"Yeah, I can see that." He answered curtly, reaching his hand down to her. "Come on, get up here. We're going home."

Realizing he was mad about something, she asked. "What's wrong?"

"Look, I got enough on my hands now. I don't need any more added burdens."

"What are you talking about?"

"You!" He snapped, the muscles in his jaw tightening. "Hanging around with whores!"

Her expression changed to anger as she spun around and stalked back to Rose.

"He looks like he's really mad," Rose stated with a look Chris could only detect as hard and uncaring. Chris understood the shell that this woman and women like her had to build around them. They had to make the world think that they didn't care. But Chris knew that like her mother, Rose wasn't asking for approval, just acceptance. She let out a bitter sigh as she realized that's all everyone was looking for in their own way: acceptance.

Chris shrugged her shoulders and shook her head. "He's always mad, about something or another." Then she glanced at Dylon worriedly. "But I guess I had better go. Thanks for walking me this far."

Dylon saw Chris wave to Rose, then he watched as she crossed to the other side of the road and march right past him.

He pulled the horse up in front of her. "Come on, I'll give you a ride."

Casting him an indignant scowl, she hurried her pace. "I'll walk, thank you."

He flinched in agony as he jumped from his horse and, in a few painful strides, grabbed her. "Look girl, I'm tired, hungry and hurtin' and I'm not going to argue with you. Either ya get on the horse or I throw you over it, butt up."

She yanked away from him, stalked to the horse, and grabbed the horn. Just as she put her foot in the stirrup, he placed his hand on her bottom and pushed her up. As he mounted the horse behind her, she heard him give a low moan. Glancing over her shoulder at him, just inches from his face, she could see that he was in pain. "What's wrong?" Chris asked. "Are you sick?"

"Naw, I tripped in a chuckhole and hurt my back."

Although she was holding herself ramrod stiff, Dylon could still feel the warmth of her body. The now so familiar scent of her wafted through his nostrils and dug a little deeper into his heart.

When they drove into the yard, Dylon painfully eased off of the horse. Then he reached his hand up to help Chris, but she ignored it and slid down by herself. It surprised him when she hesitated and then walked next to him. He figured she would be so mad at him she would stomp into the house and slam the door in his face.

Dylon was relieved when he heard Ned explain to the girls that their Pa hurt his back and he couldn't be lifting them for a few days. He didn't eat much that night and after dinner; he limped to his chair. Chris washed the dishes and got the girls ready for bed. Then she went out to the back porch and hauled in the old, round, wooden tub. Ned helped her carry in water from the well and they put it on the stove to heat. She went into Ned's bedroom and came out with a clean set of clothes and a large towel. Standing in front of Dylon, Chris reached her hand out to him. "Come on." She said as she helped him get up from the chair. "You're going to take a hot bath."

Just then, Ned came through the door with another bucket of water. "And, boy," he said firmly. "Don't you go trying to empty that tub after you're finished? Ya hear, Chris and I will take care of it."

Dylon sank back gratefully into the warm water, feeling it seep into his weary bones. He noticed Chris had her back to him as she spoke. "If there's something you need, just call. I'll be in the bedroom."

He chuckled to himself, thinking you'd be three shades of red if you knew what I needed from you.

Ned stayed by him and kept replenishing the tub with warm water. Finally, and reluctantly, he got out of the water. After pulling on his pants, he limped, bare-chested, to the cot in Ned's room. Lying on his back, he closed his eyes in agony, willing the pain away. When he heard someone enter the room, he thought it was Ned, but it was Chris's soothing voice above him. "Turn over on your stomach." Opening his eyes, he saw her standing with a bottle of liniment. "Chris, I'm sorry about the way I acted this afternoon. I know Holly was your friend, but I just don't want you to get hurt again."

She gazed at him with a sad smile. "Rose just wanted me to have some of Holly's things. Mostly the Bible and the books that Sam gave her. Then she offered to walk me a little ways home."

He reached out to take her hand, and she watched as he grimaced in pain. "Turn over, Dylon." She ordered kindly.

He rolled over with a groan and when she sat down; the bed sagged and their bodies touched his thigh to her thigh. She began rubbing his back, from the waist to his spine and finally up to his neck and shoulders. She only quit after she heard his deep snore and knew he was in restful sleep.

Chris sat there, allowing the touch of his thigh to radiate throughout her whole body. She watched him sleep, wanting nothing more than to lie down on the bed next to him and feel his powerful arms encircling her. In his own way, he was the kindest, strongest person she had ever met. She smoothed back the hair from his face and traced the angry red scars on his cheek with her finger. These scars aren't half as hideous as the ones you have hidden in your heart, she thought. Oh my love, I wish I could be the one to rid you of your hurts and take care of you as you have taken care of me, Ned, and the girls. "I will always love you, Dylon Clay. You are my life." She whispered, as she pulled the blanket over him and quietly walked out of the bedroom.

It was a few weeks later; Ned and Rachel had driven TC to Butte to the train depot. On the ride back home, Ned asked Rachel, "Do ya think TC's little Ellie will take him back?"

Rachel tucked the blanket around her legs a little tighter to help fight off the cool March wind. "He said he was going to try, but if she didn't want him anymore, he was still going to serve the Lord."

Ned flicked the reins impatiently to get some speed out of the horses and frowned. Rachel reached her hand over and patted his arm. "What's wrong, Ned? You seem preoccupied."

Ned and Rachel had become close friends because of their mutual love for the Lord. They also knew it would only remain a friendship. Through their many long talks, they realized that their true heart-mates were long dead.

"It's that boy, Dylon; he seems to be intent on marryin' that Rita Lewis. He won't listen to reasoning and he won't have nothin' to do with God or Christianity. He's so dang busy tryin' to get his fortune back." Ned ripped his hat off and smoothed his hand over his bald head, then slapped it back on. "I figure Chris's little heart is breakin' and I don't know what to do."

Ned had told Rachel the entire story about how Chris and the children had come into their lives. "What about Chris?" She asked. "Is she open to accepting the Lord?"

"You can tell she's listenin' when I talk to her about Jesus. But her eyes and heart are on Dylon."

"It's funny how people are," Rachel stated with a slight smile on her face. "They say they don't believe in depending on God or prayer. They think it's just for old women or weaklings." This time, her smile widened into a laugh. "Then they turn right around and find something or someone else to depend on. In Dylon's case, his God has become material things." She sighed and shook her head. "And poor Chris, her God has become Dylon and those little girls." They glanced at each other and shook their heads sadly. Then she patted his knee again and grinned. "Well, old friend, it looks like we got some real prayer work ahead of us."

***

As Dylon rode closer to the cabin, he could feel the overwhelming excitement of coming home. It was the end of March and it looked like winter was about ready to give up to the warmth of spring. He had been gone two months, and they had been busy months. The house was almost built, and it was going to be one of the finest and biggest around these parts. The mine was starting to show some gold, so all in all, his life was coming back together again. Now, if he could just figure out some way to get rid of the constant thoughts of Chris. No matter what he did or where he was, something would remind him of her. Especially when it came to the new house, he was building. He would always wonder if this is the way she would want this room built, or where she would want the windows put. He had to keep reminding himself that this was Rita's house. Although, she could have cared less what he did with it. She had only been to the property a few times and then only seemed interested in how much money the mine was bringing in.

His mind wandered back to the time he spent with Chris and the girls at Christmas. Except for Holly's death, it had been a wonderful time. He remembered the night Chris rubbed his back and how much better he felt the next day. The good time they'd all had at the Watts' on New Year's.

He chuckled, remembering the day he left when he had kissed Karen goodbye. She told him he needed to kiss Ned too, but Ned laughingly told him he could give his kiss to Chris. Karen agreed, and Dylon gladly fulfilled Ned's wish.

After they had kissed, he teased her about what a good kisser she was becoming. She must have been practicing. He saw the laughter in her eyes when she countered back that she had a couple fellers hid away in the barn and they had been teaching her. He was still chuckling when he came in sight of the cabin. There was a horse and buggy tied to the hitching post and Karen, Sarah, and Ned were sitting on the porch swing. When Karen saw him, she ran to greet him. "Papa, there's a fancy man visiting Sis." Dylon swung her up in his arms and grinned as she scrunched up her little face. "He's got funny clothes on and a funny hat, too." She stuck her sticky hand up and showed him the candy she had. "See, he brought us some candy."

Dylon climbed the stairs to the porch, put Karen down, and picked up Sarah, who was jumping up and down to be held.

"Howdy boy, good to see ya."

He glanced over at Ned, who was sitting on the porch swing. "What's up Ned, who's here?"

"Some fancy lawyer from Seattle, 'pears Chris has a rich aunt that has been searching for her and wants to see her."

Just then, the door opened. When Chris saw him, her face beamed into a welcome smile. "Dylon, how good it is to see you! Welcome home." She glanced over at the stranger that had followed her out the door. "I want you to meet Mr. Peevis. He's a lawyer from Seattle. He's tracked me down. It seems I have an aunt who wants to meet me."

Mr. Peevis stuck his hand out and grasped Dylon's in a warm, friendly handshake. "Well, Mr. Clay, I'm glad I finally got to meet you. I feel like I already know you from all the things your family was telling me. And of course, Herb Lavine extolled on your virtues as well."

Mr. Peevis was a short, rotund man who wore clothes of the best cut. He had a head full of curly black hair. His crystal blue eyes were framed in wire-rimmed glasses that sat on the edge of his rather enormous nose. He was an honest and well-liked man and known by his peers to be a lawyer of high scruples.

Dylon shook his hand and was impressed by his firm handshake and straightforward smile. "Herb Lavine?"

"Yes. I've been tracking Miss Spencer down for months now. Actually, it's her mother we were looking for. We didn't know about Christine." Glancing at Chris with a sincere smile, he continued. "But believe me, my dear; your great aunt will be thrilled to meet you." Pulling out his fancy gold watch, he gave a look of concern. "Dear me, I have a train to catch." Glancing at Chris, he said. "I'll be back this way in about a week. You can give me your answer, then." He smiled toward Dylon, Ned, and the girls. "Good meeting you. Hope to see you again."

As they watched him ride out of the yard, Ned commented. "Seems like a nice enough feller." Then he grabbed Karen and Sarah each by the hand. "Come on, little ones, let's go in and start dinner and let your Pa and Chris talk."

Chris explained to Dylon that her great aunt Christine Spencer had been looking for Megan for years. It appeared that her mother even named her after this aunt.

"Didn't your mother ever tell you about her family?"

"Not a lot that I can remember," Chris answered. "I was just ten when she died, and I really didn't get to see her that much. But I do remember her always saying I came from excellent stock. Mr. Peevis wants me to go to Seattle with him. It seems she is old and sick and wants to see me." She shot him a glance that made his stomach turn into knots. "Mr. Peevis said she's rich and my expenses will be paid."

Not wanting to deal with the fact that she might leave him, he grasped her by the hand and led her toward the house. "Come on." He smiled down at her kindly. "Let's eat. We'll talk about this later."

The next morning, he and Ned were doing repairs in the barn when Ned broached the subject. "When are you going to talk to Chris?"

"What about?"

"Come on, you know what I'm talkin' about. She needs to make some kind of decision about going to Seattle. You love her, don't cha' boy?"

Dylon paused from his work, chewed on what Ned had asked, then with a worried tone answered. "Yeah, Ned, I do. But I got a few things I have to take care of. How am I going to support them? Rita sure ain't gonna want me around when she hears how I feel about Chris."

Ned leaned heavily on his pitchfork and watched the young man with pride. He loved Dylon as if he were his own son, and knew within himself that Dylon felt the same way. Some might say it was pure luck or chance that they were together. But years ago, when Dylon pulled his old drunken carcass out of the horse trough that two young cowhands had tossed him in, Ned knew it wasn't fate but God's timely intervention.

"Let me ask you, somethin' son. Ya reckon those little girls are happy?"

Dylon jerked his hat off, pulled out his handkerchief, and wiped the back of his neck. "Yeah, I suppose so." He answered, slapping his hat back on.

"And Chris," Ned continued. "Well, now, it seems to me ever since Christmas she's been walkin' on air."

Dylon grinned. "What's your point, Ned?"

"My point is, son, the Lord dealt you a pretty good hand and you can't see it through your desires for things that will eventually rot away." Dylon listened intently to this old man that he had grown to love. Ned had become the father that he had never really known. Although Dylon wasn't sure about the God that Ned put so much faith in, he was sure of Ned and his wisdom.

"Dylon, material things have always meant too much to you and I'm a wonderin' if maybe that's why you didn't lose it all, so's ya could see what was really important." Ned lay the pitchfork down on a bale of hay and walked over to Dylon and patted him on the shoulder. "I got some money set aside so we won't starve. You think on it, I know you'll do what's right."

Dylon didn't have a chance to speak to Chris about the matter. There had been an accident at the mine site. One of his men had died from a rattlesnake bite, and he was needed in town to help with the funeral arrangements. It was late when the message came. Ned had just gone to bed, and the girls were already asleep.

Chris was standing on the top step of the porch, watching as Dylon saddled his horse. He grabbed the reins and led the horse to where she was standing. "I'll be home as soon as I can," he said as he turned and mounted up. Then he changed his mind and came and stood in front of her. They were almost at eye level. "Listen, girl, whatever you decide to do about Seattle is fine with us."

Before he could turn to go, Chris threw her arms around his

neck and kissed him. He stood, shocked for a moment, then began returning the kiss. "Wow! He chuckled as he put her at arms-length. "Maybe I should get those fellers you got hiding in the barn to give me a couple of tips." Kissing her gently on the nose, he mounted up and rode off. But then he hesitated, turned, and rode back to where she was standing. He dismounted and tied the horse to the post, then grasped Chris by the hand, and as he pulled her toward the barn, he whispered urgently, "Come with me."

She followed him willingly. When they entered the barn, he lit the oil lamp and turned it low. Dylon could see she was shivering, so he slipped his jacket off and laid it on a pile of clean hay. Then he sat down and pulled her with him, making sure she landed on the jacket. Gently grasping her by the shoulders, he turned her to him. "Seems like there's no little people around to disturb us." He shot her a sly grin. "Think maybe we can finish what we have been trying to get started?"

Her eyes met his. "We can try." She smiled, answering his grin.

He grasped her chin in his hand and pulled her mouth to meet his. The kisses were gentle at first, with little nips on the lips and face. But when he heard her sigh and felt her body relax as she wrapped her arms around his neck, a pounding desire for her seized him. He started at her mouth, devouring it, tasting her sweetness. Then his tongue began tracing the pattern of her long, silky neck as his hands began exploring her body. Her clothes became a hindrance, as his desire to touch her bare skin became an obsession. He reached for the top button of her blouse and his shaking hand fumbled at the tiny barriers. Chris realized the problem and brought her hand to meet his. Their fingers coiled and their eyes met. As she reached up and began opening the barrier, he noticed her shy smile. He slipped his hand inside her chemise and cupped her ample breast in his huge rough hand, and felt the fire of desire roar through his body at the touch of her naked skin. He raised his eyes to gaze at her lovely face and pure joy overwhelmed him when he saw the desire in her eyes. The love that he held for her soared to new heights as he kissed her deeply. When he heard her whimper, he tore his mouth away and rained kisses down her neck and finally to where his hand was caressing her breast; she gasped as his mouth took over the caressing. "Oh, Dylon." She moaned as she buried her face in his hair and molded her body closer to his. He yanked at her skirts until they finally released her bare legs, and he felt restricted by his own clothing as the surge of desire intensified.

An unfamiliar thrill had seized Chris, and she was lost in the feelings of intimacy that Dylon was plunging her through. She wanted to belong to him totally, but deep within her consciousness, there flamed a spark of purity that she could not or would not extinguish. When she felt Dylon's taut manhood pressed against her bare thigh, she stiffened as the childhood name, 'DAUGHTER OF A WHORE!' echoed in her mind. And though she loved Dylon with all of her heart and soul, she wanted a marriage bed and not a few passionate minutes in a bed of hay.

Dylon felt her hesitation and with a quickened breath, brought his eyes to meet hers. Seeing the doubt and fear in them, he knew he couldn't take her this way. She needed to know from him that she was loved and cherished and, most of all, that he wanted her for his wife. Pushing away from her, he sat up and ran his hand through his hair. "Aw...Jeez, Chris," his voice came in a low ragged whisper. "This is wrong." He stood, pulling her with him, gently brushed the hair from her face, and began buttoning her blouse. His chest constricted as he noticed her flushed face, the dazed set of her eyes, and the thick mass of chestnut hair falling around her shoulders. He clenched his fists at his sides, wanting so much to own her, body and soul, but with a reluctant sigh gritted. "Go in the house."

For the first time in her life, Chris felt valued. She had loved Dylon for longer than she could remember, but now, even though he hadn't said the words, she felt that love returned. She gazed up at him. "I love you, Dylon." She whispered as she placed a gentle kiss on his mouth. Then she turned and walked to the house.

It was a few days later, and Dylon still hadn't come home. But Mr. Peevis had returned to Pony and was very anxious to hear if Chris was going back to Seattle with him. They were sitting across from each other at the table drinking coffee and eating cookies Chris had made. Ned had taken the girls to town for a visit with Rachel.

"Are you sure, Christine?" Mr. Peevis' voice held a note of disappointment. "Your aunt so wants to meet you."

"Oh, Mr. Peevis, I want to meet her too, really I do. But right now is a bad time. Maybe in a few weeks." Chris couldn't bear the thought of leaving Dylon. Not now, not when they were so close to finding each other. "You see," Chris tried to explain. "Mr. Clay and I need to straighten some things out."

Rita snapped the reigns on the buggy in an impatient gesture, hurrying the horse to a faster gate. She knew Dylon was still in town, and she wanted to talk to Chris Spencer before he got there. It was obvious Dylon was falling in love with the girl. Bad timing, Rita thought. She couldn't afford to lose him now. At least not until she could find someone as dependable as Dylon. He was a valuable worker and could be trusted. Rita knew Dylon didn't love her, and she certainly didn't love him. But it wasn't good for a woman to be alone, especially a rich widow. She had made a wise choice in picking Dylon. He would never steal from her, and he was the type of man to remain faithful to the woman he married. He wasn't a terrible lover, although he hadn't touched her since the night of the dance on the wagon train, months ago. He used his daughters as an excuse and told her that it was best they wait until they got married. Karen and Sarah were cute little girls, as far as children go, but she sure didn't want children in her life. She had already sent for some information on boarding schools. That would get them out of her hair for at least most of the time. She was glad that Jim Gallen had told her about that lawyer, Peevis, coming from Seattle. Her face flushed as she remembered this afternoon with Jim in his bedroom. He was so handsome and more to her liking, in the looks department than Dylon. She liked dark, gentlemanly men and Dylon was big and gruff. Even without the scars, his blond hair, blue eyes, and harsh ways would have been a turnoff. But he had always been there when she needed him and she sure needed him now. And, she thought with a smile, she always had Jim to fall back on if Dylon couldn't supply her needs in the marriage bed.

Chris heard a buggy enter the yard and glanced out the window. Her brow furrowed when she saw it was Rita Lewis.

"What is it, Christine?" Mr. Peevis asked, noticing her worried look. "Is there a problem?"

"No...It's just a friend of Dylon's."

After introducing Rita to Mr. Peevis, Chris explained to her that Dylon hadn't come back from town yet.

"Yes, I know, dear." She gave Chris a coy smile. "I've been with him." Rita shrugged her jacket off and walked to the table as if she owned the place. "That coffee smells so good, mind pouring me some." Pulling the chair out, she sat down and reached for a cookie. "You do make the best cookies I have ever tasted. I wish you were going to be here. I would definitely have you make some for our wedding reception." Chris was reaching for a mug in the cupboard and swirled around, almost dropping it, when she heard Rita's statement.

As Chris poured her coffee, Rita patted her hand and spoke in a patronizing manner. "I'm really glad I was able to catch you before you left." Chris felt a prickle of apprehension run up her spine as she listened to Rita. "Dylon told me all about your aunt. I must say, he's certainly relieved." Rita glanced at Mr. Peevis and favored him with one of her breath-taking smiles. "You see, Mr. Clay and I are getting married soon, and he feels that Chris's leaving will be one less burden. Especially with all that talk about her friendship with the whore that was killed. Holly was her name, wasn't it?" Rita took a sip of her coffee and a bite of cookie and then continued. "He's really concerned for his children's reputation. Of course, dear," she said, as she turned to Chris with a sober expression. "Dylon really thinks a lot of you, knowing you're Ned's daughter, and he also knows how much the girls care for you." Rita's eyes narrowed into a look of concern. "With you gone, it will give me a chance to get to know Karen and Sarah. After all, I'll soon be their mother."

A queasy feeling erupted in Chris's stomach. She silently berated herself for being so brazen by kissing Dylon and then following him to the barn. When Dylon pulled away from her and told her what they were doing was wrong, she foolishly thought he loved her and wanted to wait until they were married. But she realized now that she was nothing more than a burden and an embarrassment to him. Her cheeks flamed, remembering how she had enticed him. She knew that Dylon Clay was an honest man and would never cheat on the woman he loved. And, she knew now, that woman was Rita Lewis.

Dylon had talked to Rita in town, but when he saw her wrapped seductively around Sheriff Gallen as they were going into his room, he decided to deal with her later. It had taken a couple of days longer than he expected, but at least he was able to get a job at the mill so they wouldn't starve. There was still his friend in Butte that would give him a job in the mines if it came to that. He wasn't going to worry about it. He loved. Chris, that's all that mattered. Dylon felt a rush of pure joy when he remembered Chris's words of love that night in the barn. Although he couldn't figure out why she would love him, with the way he had treated her, that was all going to change. He was determined to work hard for his family and become deserving of her love.

Dylon rode into the yard, dismounted quickly, threw the horse's reins over the hitching post, and took the porch steps two at a time. When he opened the door of the cabin, he saw Ned sitting in the rocking chair holding the girls; tears were streaming down his cheeks. "She's gone, boy." He sobbed. "Just took off and left with that lawyer feller, said in the note it was better this way."

Chapter 12

Chris gazed out of the smudged windows of the train and barely noticed her beloved mountains as they slipped past her view. She felt humiliated when she thought of what Dylon must think of her and her wanton actions in the barn. What if he hadn't of stopped, would she have stopped him? Her body went limp when she thought of how he had made her feel. The touch of his hand on her bare skin and the taste of his mouth on hers made her body tingle at the very thought. Tears streaming down her cheeks, she buried her hands in her face. "Oh, God, please!" She moaned silently. "Don't let me be like my mother." Chris tried to imagine doing the same things with another man and suddenly felt ill with the thought. She loved Dylon and always would; he had been so much a part of her life. She would never have to worry about Karen and Sarah. Dylon and Ned would give them the love and care they so richly deserved, and they would grow into fine happy women. A shiver ran through her as she thought of her love for Dylon. She truly wished for nothing more than happiness for her kind and the gentle giant.

Mr. Peevis's heartfelt sick as he watched the tears stream down Chris's face. He knew that Lewis's woman had really hurt her. Although, he still had a hard time understanding why the lady didn't know that Chris was not Ned's daughter, especially since she was going to marry Dylon. Old Ned had explained the situation to him the first day they had met. He had to agree with Ned that even though they didn't like the idea of a lie; it was probably the best thing to do at the time. It sure didn't make much sense that Clay's fiancée didn't know. Something fishy about that whole situation, he thought.

He had attempted to distract Chris by telling her about her Aunt Christine's mansion. He explained to Chris that when her husband died five years ago; the mansion was left to her Aunt Christine's stepson. It had been in his mother's family for years. He had graciously allowed his stepmother to remain living thereafter his father died. Mr. Peevis told her that the stepson, a fine young man named Marvin, lived in Europe with his wife and children.

After trying all that he could do to find out what was wrong with her, he finally conceded defeat. He fell asleep, his head bobbing with each bounce of the train.

The sights smells, and sounds of Seattle amazed Chris as the horse-driven hackney swerved through the cobblestone streets of the busy city. This would be her new home, and she was determined to find her place here and forget what lay behind.

Chris had been in Seattle a little over six weeks now and had grown very close to her great-aunt Christine. She had hoped that the terrible loneliness she felt for Dylon, Ned, and the girls would subside with time, but it had only seemed to grow worse.

Her aunt had arranged for her to be introduced to some of the young people in the area, and they had invited her to many afternoon teas, luncheons and parties.

The Spring Cotillion was one of the biggest events in Seattle, and Aunt Christine had insisted Chris attend. Not wanting to hurt her feelings, Chris reluctantly agreed. She felt out of place as she sat in the majestic ballroom of the Seattle hotel. The gaily-dressed couples danced around her as the orchestra music filtered through the room. Mr. Peevis and his wife Agnes were more than happy to escort Chris to the dance. They took special delight in introducing her to some of Seattle's most eligible bachelors from the finest of families.

Chris had been dancing with many young men and was glad

for these few moments of rest. Sitting next to Chris was a beautiful young lady named Mavis Peal. Chris had met her at one of the many luncheons she had attended in the last few weeks and they had become friends. "Chris, your dress is simply divine. Where on earth did you get it?" Mavis asked with a sincere smile.

Chris gazed down lovingly at the ball gown she wore. The low-cut, sapphire-blue, princess-style bodice was lavished with small white-simulated pearls. The short puffed sleeves of lighter-blue gossamer satin were also trimmed in tiny pearls. The overskirt of the ball gown flowed out into yards of expensive blue satin, while the bottom of the skirt and short train was lined in flounces of simulated pearls sewn onto handmade Swiss lace. "It is lovely, isn't it?" Chris answered as she smiled back at Mavis. "Aunt Christine is too sick to leave her bed, so she insisted the seamstress move the sewing machine in to her room and do the work where she could supervise." Chris stood, swirled around, and curtsied to Mavis. "And this, my dear friend, is the wonderful result."

Mavis covered her mouth with a white, satin gloved hand as she giggled. But then, suddenly, something or someone caught her attention from across the room. She reached for Chris's hand and pulled her back into the chair. "Oh, Chris! Look at that tall, dark-haired man speaking with my father. Isn't he handsome? I met him this morning when he visited our home. And Father said he's interested in courting me." Chris's eyes moved to where Mavis was looking and was shocked when she stared into the eyes of Jack Slade. She quickly turned her head, hoping that he hadn't recognized her. Bile rose in her throat as painful memories flooded her mind and she thought for a moment that she was going to be sick. "Chris, are you all right?" Mavis asked with concern as she reached for her hand. "You turned pure white. Can I get something for you?"

"No... No. I'm fine, thank you, Mavis." She said as an uncontrollable urge made her look to where Jack had been standing, but now was making his way across the room toward them.

Chris got up, knowing that she needed to leave before she had to confront this evil man. But Mavis grabbed her and pulled her back down in the chair. "Oh, Chris, he's coming over, please. You can't leave now."

"Miss Peal," Jack drawled as he grasped Mavis's hand in his. "I was in hopes I would get to see you tonight and have that dance you promised me this morning. Mavis giggled and arose from the chair at Jack's gentle tug. "I too was looking forward to our dance, Mr. Slade." Jack placed his arm around Mavis's tiny waist and steered her toward the dance floor, totally ignoring Chris, much to her relief.

It wasn't long before a young suitor swept Chris out on the dance floor. While dancing with the young man, Chris noticed Jack standing with Mavis and her father. A sickening chill went up her spine when she realized what a man like Slade could do to an innocent young girl like Mavis. She quickly turned her eyes when she noticed Jack staring at her.

"I hope you will give me permission to call on you some afternoon, Miss Spencer?" The young man asked as he led her from the dance floor. Chris hadn't had time to answer when she felt Slade's arm slide around her waist in a tightening grasp. "Excuse me, sir, but I think Miss Spencer has saved this next dance for an old friend." Then, as the music started, he swept her out on the dance floor. Chris held herself as far away from Jack as she could. But his powerful arms pulled her close as he whispered in her ear. "What happened? Did Scar's face get tired of ya and throw you out?" Chris stiffened and pulled out of his arms. But Jack's hold tightened. "Relax, Chris, I'm not going to hurt you, nor do I want to cause a big scene." He released his hold on her a little and Chris immediately backed away from him, still feeling his arm around her waist as they swirled around the dance floor. "Except for your height and weight, you look just like your mother did." Chris could feel his evil eyes piercing down at her. "I like my women meaty, like you. Megan was always too skinny for my taste." He leered as he pulled her roughly toward him. Chris forced her eyes to meet his as she remembered Mavis's slim figure and retaliated. "Then why would you want to have anything to do with a girl like Mavis Peal?"

"Well now, sweet-cakes, I just want to sell some property to her daddy, but he's so rich I'd stand to inherit a tasty little sum. That is if I was to marry her. But don't worry." He smirked. "I'd take you to warm my bed any time you say."

Chris jerked out of his arms, oblivious to the couples dancing around her. Glaring at him, she quietly gritted. "You really think I would allow you to do to my friend, Mavis, what you did to my mother?"

Jack glanced around him uncomfortably and then grabbed her arm as she started walking away. "I'd advise you to stay out of it or believe me, you will live to regret it."

"No!" she ground out, slapping his hand away. "I would regret it if I didn't do something about it." Then she turned away and walked over to where Mr. Peevis was standing, talking to some men.

Jack watched her rigid body as she stomped off. For a moment, he wondered if he should be worried by her threat. But then an evil grin crossed his face as he realized Chris Spencer had always feared him, and there was no reason to believe she still didn't.

Chris watched Jack hover over Mavis for the rest of the evening. But she was relieved that he had stayed clear of her.

On their way home that night, Chris told Mr. Peevis about Jack Slade. After he heard the entire story from Chris, he had told her not to worry about it anymore. He and John Peal were friends and the matter would be taken care of. They both agreed not to tell her aunt anything about seeing Jack Slade.

Before Chris went to bed that evening, she decided to check on her aunt. She knocked on the door before quietly entering. The bedroom, like the rest of the mansion, was grand. Charles Jessler, a rich lumber barren, built it in the early 1800. In fact, they even named the street after him. Henry Jacobs bought it for his first wife and family. His wife died, and he had been alone for a long time when he met and fell in love with Christine Spencer, a young schoolteacher. They married, with his son's blessing, and lived quite happily until Henry died five years ago.

Her aunt glanced up from the enormous four-poster bed she was lying in. When she saw Chris, she laid her tattered Bible on her lap and motioned for her to come in. "Chris, my sweet child, come and sit with me." Christine Jacobs watched as her great-niece approached her, and noticed not for the first time the unhappiness that always lingered in her lovely brown eyes. Chris had told her aunt about Dylon and the girls, and she wished she could do something to help her niece. But Mrs. Jacobs realized she had little time left on this earth. She could only hope that the inheritance she was planning on leaving Chris would in some way help in making her niece's life a little happier.

She certainly understood that money was of little satisfaction to the loss of someone you loved. When her beloved, Henry, had died, life seemed meaningless. It didn't matter how much money she had. The only thing that kept her going was her faith in the Lord. "I didn't expect you home so early." Christine noticed how lovely her young namesake looked in the blue satin evening gown, one of the few gowns that Chris would let her aunt have made for her. "Did you have a nice time?"

Chris sat on the edge of the bed and gently grasped her aunt's frail hand in her own. "Yes, it was a lovely evening, Aunt Christine." Her aunt noticed the tense lines on her niece's face. "Oh, Chris, I thought by introducing you to some young people it would help to ease your pain of loneliness." Seeing the tears creep down her cheeks, she pressed her lace hankie in Chris's hand. "But I see I was mistaken. Well, from now on, no more forced dinner dates. It will be just you and me." She reached her wrinkled, aged hand up and brushed the tear from her niece's face. "Although I can't imagine why you would want to be stuck with an old lady like me when you could be with people your own age."

Chris reached for her aunt's hand again and placed it in her lap. "There's so much I want to know about my family. Please, Aunt Christine, tell me more." Her aunt had told her quite a bit already about the Spencer family, carefully avoiding Megan Spencer.

The frail, genteel old lady leaned back on her pillows and sighed. "Yes, my child, you're right. I guess it's time we talked about your mother." Mrs. Jacobs smiled at Chris and weakly squeezed her hand. "You have her eyes, you know. Megan was an only child, and headstrong, but I loved her, and so did your grandmother. I'm afraid your grandfather was a different matter. He loved her but, she was much like him and they would continually butt heads. He had a drinking problem and although he wasn't mean, he was entirely too strict on Megan. When your mother was sixteen, she met a much older man and fell madly in love with him."

"My father?" Chris interjected with a questioning gaze.

"No, dear." Her aunt smiled back. "And probably just as well. When your grandfather refused to let them even see each other, Megan ran away with the man. I was just a young teacher at the time and lived with your grandfather, who was my brother. Your grandmother and I wanted to find Megan, but your grandfather was determined not to let us."

Christine pointed to the water glass sitting on the ornate bed table. "Hand me a sip of that water, my dear."

Chris noticed her aunt growing weaker. "Oh, Aunt Christine," she said, concerned. "You're tired. We can finish this some other time."

Christine sipped at her water and handed it to Chris. "No, now is the time." She reached over and took another hankie from the table and wiped her mouth, then sat back comfortably into her pillows. "Now let's see. Where were we? A year after Henry and I were married, your grandparents were killed in a carriage accident. It devastated me; it was the only family I had left. Henry recommended I look for Megan. But before we could get around to it, he became very sick. I nursed him for two years before he died." Her voice sounded shaky and her eyes filled with tears as she continued. "When I finished grieving, I decided to find Megan. I hired a detective and finally, after years of searching, we heard that she was working in Colorado for a man named Jack Slade." She glanced at Chris's eager face and sighed tiredly. "I'm afraid there's not much else to tell you. I sent Walter Peevis out to Colorado, and this Slade man wouldn't tell him a thing. But one of the girls that worked in his establishment told him to talk to the lawyer, Mr. Lavine, and my dear great-niece." Mrs. Jacobs smiled weakly at Chris. "That's how we found out about you."

Chris's shoulders slumped, and her face held a bleak look. She had so wanted to know more about who her father was and why her mother ended up with a man like Jack Slade.

"Chris dear, look at me." Chris brought her eyes to meet her aunts. "I know you're disappointed that there's not more to tell. But it's very important that you understand this. It's not where you come from, but who you become and how you get there, in this life, that really counts." She caught Chris's eyes with her own and gave her a loving smile. "Love, honesty, integrity, your service to others and especially to the Lord. These are the only things that really count in this world. You are a giving, gentle, loving, child and God has much in store for you. Oh, goodness," she chuckled. "I'm beginning to sound like your friend, Ned. Aren't I?" Then she reached her arms out and Chris came willingly into her embrace.

Jack Slade sat back in the seat of the train that was bound for Colorado and inhaled a long drag of the expensive cigar he had just lit. He ignored the irritable fanning and coughing of the lady sitting across the aisle from him. Chris Spencer had called his bluff. Jack leaned his head back and thought about the meeting he had this morning with John Peal. The man was furious, but being the businessman he was, he knew the property Slade had for sale was just what he had been looking for. After a heated discussion, he agreed to pay Slade a fair amount over the price. He was asking if Jack would agree never to see his daughter again.

Jack was satisfied; he got what he came after, money. Besides, Mavis really wasn't his type. He also realized that Chris now had friends in high places. So he decided to cut his losses and head back to Colorado.

He glanced at the woman across from him and saw that she was a fine figure of a woman. He quickly crushed out the offensive cigar and, with his most sincere grin, he leaned across the aisle, touched her hand, and spoke softly. "Mam, I do hope you will excuse my rudeness." He looked forward to the long trip ahead of him when he saw the return smile and the suggestive glint in her eyes.

About three weeks later, Christine Spencer Jacobs died peacefully in her sleep

It was just a few days after her aunt had died and Chris was sitting in the office of Mr. Peevis's Law Firm. Chris watched him as he paced back and forth in front of his elegant desk. "No! Christine, I can't." Exasperated, he continued. "Not all of it, that's unheard of."

She finally spoke up. "It's my money, isn't it?"

Walter Peevis walked around his desk and sank heavily into his expensive leather chair. "Well, of course, dear." He drew in a deep breath, realizing he had raised his voice to her. He and his wife had grown very fond of this girl.

He had been a friend to her great aunt for years, but what she was proposing was unheard of. "You are her only surviving relative. I could understand you giving Mr. Clay some of the money, but all of it?" Exasperated, he continued. "What about Ned and the little girls?"

"Dylon would never let Karen and Sarah go without," Chris spoke up with a firm voice. "Mr. Peevis, he lost everything he had for us, so this really isn't my money, it's his." Then she relaxed a little and smiled at him. "Besides, the time I spent with my Aunt Christine was enough for me."

"But what will you do, my dear?"

"I have a job as a kitchen maid here in Seattle. They supply board and room and a fair wage." She watched as Mr. Peevis shook his head in dismay. "I'll be fine...but I want you to get that money to Dylon as soon as possible."

Chapter 13

PONY MONTANA, *Two weeks later.*

"All of it! Why would she want me to have all of it?" Dylon exclaimed, baffled. He was sitting at the table, Sarah was nestled in his lap, Ned was pouring coffee, and Karen was helping him. "What about the girls and Ned?"

"Christine felt that you and your wife would see that they are taken care of." Mr. Peevis answered as he opened his expensive-leather briefcase.

Dylon threw the man a puzzled look. "My wife... I'm not married."

Mr. Peevis glanced at him, shocked. "But... Mrs. Lewis sat right here and told Christine and I that the two of you were getting married." He sat down rather quickly in the chair and continued. "She said that you had told her all about Christine's aunt and that you were hoping that Christine would leave with me." Confused by this new turn of events, his voice raised a notch. "She said you told her it would be one less burden on you."

"I didn't tell Rita nothin'." Dylon gritted. Then he realized Jim Gallen had told Rita about Mr. Peevis, and Rita, in her devious manner, took care of the rest.

"Where is Chris now?" Dylon asked, feeling his stomach turn into knots.

"Well, Mr. Clay, she has secured a position as a maid with a family in Seattle. You know, the day that I came back here, she had decided not to come to Seattle with me. She told me she wanted to get some things worked out with you first. But then, of course, when Mrs. Lewis came and told us you were getting married." Slumping back in the chair and pushing his glasses further on his nose, he continued thoughtfully. "I must say, now I know why Christine cried for most of the trip to Seattle. It had seemed strange to me that Mrs. Lewis kept referring to Christine as Ned's daughter when even I knew the truth." He sighed regretfully. "I should have put two and two together then."

Ned placed the hot mug of coffee before Mr. Peevis. "No sense in kicking a dead horse." He sat down across from him and continued. "Did Chris seem happy while she was with her aunt?"

"They were very fond of each other, and Chris was with her when she died. I don't think she regrets meeting her aunt and being there with her." Mr. Peevis pushed his glasses up on his nose, took a sip of his coffee, and shook his head sadly. "But, happy...no, I wouldn't say that. She had met some nice friends. And we introduced her to several eligible bachelors, but she showed no interest in any of them."

Dylon sat with his head in his hands, listening, silently berating himself. Why hadn't he gone after her? He should have told her he loved her that night in the barn. Then suddenly, an idea struck him. He jumped up; startling everyone as the chair fell over and hit the floor. Not bothering to stop and pick it up, he ran to the bedroom. He opened the drawer and found the metal box that held all of his important papers. Lifting the lid, Dylon took out the document that Herb Lavine had made Jack Slade sign. As he entered the kitchen, he grinned over at Mr. Peevis. "You say I got a lot of money?"

"Oh my, yes. Why?"

His grin widened as he took in the rest of the family. "Ya willing to help me get Chris back?"

"Yes, of course." Mr. Peevis answered. "If it would make Christine happy."

Ned threw Dylon a curious grin. "What's your plan, boy?"

Dylon shouted excitedly as he picked up Sarah and threw her in the air. Then he glanced at Ned. "Come on! Let's get packed! We're going on a trip."

Chris had been at her new job for almost three weeks now and was settling in quite well. Her room was comfortable, and she got along well with the rest of the staff. Her employers were kind and paid their employees a fair wage.

She was leaning over the big sink, washing pots, when the maid came into the kitchen. "Chris, there's someone at the door for you." She walked over and stood next to Chris and whispered apprehensively. "I think it's the law."

Chris quickly tucked her hair behind her ears, took off her apron, and smoothed her dress with her hands. She wondered as she walked to the door if it were more papers to sign from her aunt's estate.

There were two men standing just inside of the hallway. "Good afternoon, Miss." The man holding the document asked while tipping his hat. "Are you Christine Spencer?"

"Yes, I am," Chris answered, puzzled.

"And you were a bondservant to Jack Slade?" The other man asked briskly while stepping forward.

"Yes... But!"

"Well, Miss Spencer, I'm afraid you're under arrest."

"But I don't understand...I...my contract was bought by someone else."

"You'll have to talk that over with your new owner. Our orders are to take you to him. Would you please get your things?" Dylon warned the two men, whom Mr. Peevis had hired from a detective agency, that Chris was feisty and she might try to run.

"Miss!" The larger of the men spoke with a very serious note. "You will make it harder on yourself if you try to run. We will catch you, and then we would have to handcuff you. I'm sure you don't want to embarrass the people that you've worked for."

Chris sat in the buggy as it rumbled down the Cobblestone Street, stiff with fear. Why would Dylon want to sell her contract? Had she really been that much of a burden to him? She knew he didn't think much of her, after the way she threw herself at him that night in the barn. Of course, she couldn't blame him for hating her. He had lost so much because of her. She hadn't talked to Mr. Peevis since before she came to work. She could only hope that Dylon hadn't received the money yet. Although she knew how much he must hate her. Maybe when he received the money, it might help him to regain all that he had lost because of her.

She had asked the men who came for her if she could have time to get in touch with Mr. Peevis. She was sure he could straighten this matter out. But they had told her that their job was to deliver her. What she did after that was between her and her new owner. Fear ravaged her mind as she wondered if Jack Slade was involved in this. He would want revenge for what she did to him. Especially after having Mr. Peevis tell Mavis's father about him. She tried pulling herself together, determining in her mind that she would never be bound to a person like Jack Slade. If she had to, she would run away or die trying.

They drove a little way out of town and turned up a dirt road. She could see a small white church in the distance, with some people milling around. As she got closer, she saw a massive figure with a crop of unruly blond hair and knew instantly it was Dylon. Ned and Mr. Peevis were there too.

When she saw the girls, she jumped out of the buggy before it stopped. Karen and Sarah started running toward her and she fell to her knees as they ran into her arms. "Oh, Sissy, Sissy," Karen cried, tears streaming down her face and her arms wrapped tightly around Chris's neck. "Papa says you can be our mama if you'll marry up with us."

Chris felt Dylon's presence and let out a gasp of pleasure as she glanced up at him. She thought he was the most handsome man she had ever seen, especially in his silk shirt and black string tie. When he reached his hand out to her, she grasped it and he pulled her toward him, gazing searchingly into her eyes. Chris smiled up at him, and Dylon let out a relieved holler. Then he swung her up into his arms. "Girl...you have a choice. You can marry me or be my bondservant, but either way, I'm not lettin' you go. 'Cause, you're all that I ever want to own."

Chris grasped his face in her hands, turned his cheek to her, and began kissing each scar, starting at his eyes, down his cheek, and ending at his lips. With each touch of her mouth, Dylon could feel the years of hurt and pain ebb from his life. He moaned as he put his lips to hers. "Ah, Jeez, girl, I love ya."

Chris noticed the Wedding flowers when Dylon and the girls led her into the church. She was momentarily stunned when Mrs. Peevis, Mavis, and many other friends she had met while in Seattle ran up to greet her. "Come on Chris," Mavis said as she grasped her hand and steered her into a room off of the side of the church. Mrs. Peevis followed. She gasped with delight when Mrs. Peevis showed her a wedding dress, veil, and all the other necessities that went along with it.

Chris had Karen and Sarah come in to help her get dressed, and when she was ready, they opened the door. Dylon was standing there, with a beautiful bouquet of flowers in his hand. He gazed down at her.

"Are ya ready, girl?" He grinned as he grasped her small hand in his and they started walking down the aisle toward their future together.

Ned and Mr. Peevis were standing next to each other, watching the tender scene. Tears were rolling down their cheeks. Mr. Peevis reached up and took off his glasses, then he wiped his eyes with his neatly folded silk handkerchief. Ned used his sleeve.

"Well now, Lord... I wanna thank ya." Ned whispered as his eyes wandered upward. "It took us a bit a doin' but it looks like we finally got Your will accomplished."

They stayed for two more weeks in Seattle, enjoying Ned and the girls as they spent their day sightseeing. In the evening, Ned took care of the girls, while Chris and Dylon spent rapturous nights at the fanciest hotel in all of Seattle.

Chapter 14

5 years later in Kansas City, Kansas

Sam Drew leaned against the porch railing of the boarding house he had been staying at for the last few weeks. The sun was just pulling itself up from behind the rolling hills that bordered the city. He drew in a long drag of his cigarette and gazed upward toward the orange and yellow scene unfolding before him. He thought this was his favorite time of day, as he ground out his cigarette and breathed in the fresh morning air. He liked the quiet of the mornings. It gave him a chance to think, and he had been doing a lot of that lately.

He hadn't done much with his life in these last five years. Wandering aimlessly from job to job wasn't very rewarding. Three years ago he went back to Montana to help Ken build his house and then stayed long enough to help Dylon Clay build onto his house for their growing family.

Dylon had bought up all the surrounding property from Rachel Isdell and was building a nice size ranch. They had a baby boy two years ago, and he had just heard in a letter from Ken that they were expecting another soon.

He was proud of what his brother Ken had done with the farm and his marriage to Anna seemed secure. His little nephew was pretty great, too. He was just two years old and as smart as a whip. Sam grinned, thinking about how everyone had told him the boy looked just like his uncle.

A wave of sorrow pierced his gut, as his face of Holly appeared before him. He often wondered what life would have been like had Holly lived.

The tantalizing aroma of biscuits baking made him aware of the hungry rumble in his stomach. As he turned to go into the boardinghouse, he heard the clatter of a cart. He glanced up the street and realized that he had been hoping the strange little group would appear again.

For the last four mornings, two young boys, rather shabbily dressed, would push an old rickety cart filled with laundry down the middle of the road. A girl lagged behind. She had a severe limp and leaned on a thick wooden cane. He couldn't see her face because her head was covered with a ridiculous-looking big brimmed-straw hat. All, except the girl, would politely nod at Sam as they passed by. Sam assumed they were delivering clean wash to the back door of Floozy Flossy's Flop House, which was at the end of the street.

He watched them as they turned into the alley. Strange little group, he thought. Then he remembered his hunger pangs and headed up the porch stairs, only to be stopped by the sound of a crash, then shrill screaming and loud cursing. He realized the commotion was coming from the trio that had just passed him.

Jumping off of the porch, he dashed around the corner, almost tripping over the cart that was lying on its side. There were clothes scattered all around it.

Sam watched as the two young boys shouted and kicked at one of the men. When he heard a loud groan, he glanced over to see the girl bashing a stout young man over the head with her cane. The man shoved the girl and as she fell, her hat flew off and a mass of bright orange hair tumbled around her shoulders. When the man lifted his boot up to kick her, Sam quickly drew his gun and shouted. "The boot touches her, mister, and you loosen it along with your foot!"

As they heard Sam's voice, all stopped in mid-action and turned toward him. The man pulled his foot back and moved away from the girl. "This ain't your fight, mister. She's my woman!"

"The hell I am!" the girl retorted. "I wouldn't be caught dead with a cow turd like you!"

The man sneered and headed toward her, only to back off when he saw Sam raise his gun, pointing it straight at him.

"Listen here, Runt." He yelled. "Yer nothin' but a mud-ugly gimp and your Pap knew I was the only one who would look after ya!"

She pulled herself up with the cane but began to wobble. She yelled as she fell back down to the ground, "Pap thought more of nose snot than he thought of you!" When she waved her huge stick at him, her voice grew even louder. "Now you get on out of here, Eddie Riggens, and leave me and mine alone!"

Riggens eyed Sam, and the raised gun, then motioned to his sidekick, and they both started backing down the alley. He pointed to the girl and snarled. "This ain't over yet, Runt. I'll get you and those ragamuffin brats!"

The two boys ran over to the girl and started pulling her up. The tallest one yelled excitedly. "Hot! Dang! Twerp, we done got 'em on the run."

She steadied herself with her cane; then she reached up and cuffed him on the shoulder. "Dammit, Rocky, I told ya to quit yer gol-darn swearin'."

"Can't thank ya enough mister." Showing a mouth full of straight, pearly-white teeth, she grinned up at Sam. "Sure am sorry ya had to get involved in this here ruckus." Sticking her small hand out, she continued. "My name's Jenny Cramer and these here are my brother's. The small, feisty one is Corbin. The one over there with the nasty-soundin' mouth is Rocky."

Apple-green eyes stared out at Sam from a face drowned

in freckles, and a mass of burnt-orange curls tumbled around her shoulders. Sam realized his first impression of her being a young girl was wrong. This pint-sized lady was well into her womanhood. And, he thought, that the bum he had just run off wasn't far from being wrong. She really was a mud-ugly runt. Embarrassed by this thought, he said nothing, quickly spun around, and helped the boys turn the cart over.

His handsome features and expensive clothes didn't go unnoticed by Jenny. And neither did his rudeness, not having the decency to even shake hands. Old Pap would have called him 'one of those uppity-ups who thought their outhouses didn't stink'.

She watched as he ignored her and continued helping the boys pick up the scattered clothes. Her anger at his curt behavior rose as she yanked a petticoat from him. "That's all right mister, thanks, but we don't need your help no more."

She spun around and yelled. "Come on, boys. Let's get a move on. We need to go wash this stuff again." Then she grabbed Corbin's arm and started limping down the road.

Rocky helped Sam shoved the rest of the clothes into the cart. "Thanks, mister, sure do 'preciate the help." Glancing up the road, he yelled. "Wait up Twerp!" Then he started pushing the heavy load down the road.

They had only gone a few blocks when Rocky paused for a moment to wait for Jenny to catch up. "I'm scared, Twerp. Now that Pap's dead that Eddie Riggens is going to ruin it for us."

Jenny limped to the cart and released Corbin's arm, and leaned up against the solid structure. She smacked Rocky gently on the shoulder. "I said don't call me Twerp!" Then she wrapped her arm around his waist and motioned for Corbin to come stand next to her, wrapping her arm around his waist as well. "We've been through a lot, and with Pap's help, we made it out of that orphanage. And now, we're going to figure out a way to make it through this mess, too."

Jenny couldn't believe that it would be 21 years ago this month that Pap and Memaw Cramer picked her and her brother Jacob out of all the children in the orphan train that had stopped at the small railroad station in Kansas City, Kansas. She wasn't much older than eight and Jacob was around 13 or 14.

Jenny was too sick at the time to know much about what was going on. After their parents had died in the New York City influenza epidemic, Jacob scrounged for food and took care of his sick little sister the best he knew how.

When the people from the Children's Aid Society of New York found them, they were living in an abandoned storage shack that was unheated. The only belongings they had left were a few thin blankets. Jacob had sold everything else he could to buy food.

Jacob was relieved when the Aid Society offered them food and a warm place to stay.

When the Doctor checked Jenny, he told Jacob that she had rickets from being so malnourished. The prognosis was grim. They told him she would never walk and probably not live out the year.

When Jacob heard about the orphan train, he decided to take Jenny and see if he couldn't make a better life for both of them. He loved his little sister and would do anything he could to help her get well.

They had been on the train for days and although many families were willing to take Jacob, they certainly didn't want to be burdened with a sick child like Jenny.

Her legs were so weak that she couldn't stand on them for very long. So Jacob had her strapped to his back, standing at the railroad station in Kansas City. Mike and Julie Thompson had heard Jacob telling another family that if they wanted him, they would have to take his little sister too. When they watched the family walk away, and saw the dejected look on the young boy's face, their hearts immediately went out to the two children. They took both children home and showered them with love and attention.

Mike Thompson was a bit of a character. Foul language flowed naturally from him, but it never seemed offensive to anyone. He was uneducated but had a great insight into people and felt that honesty and hard work were the most important traits a person could have. He owned a small farm and also a small working gold mine. Between the farm and the mine, he was able to reek out enough earnings to support the four of them.

The first year was the happiest any of the four could ever remember having. Much to his wife's chagrin, Mike lovingly nicknamed Jenny Twerp. Although the child did not grow in stature, she was thriving in every other way.

Not long after their arrival, the children began calling Mike and Julie, Pap and Memaw Thompson.

Jacob had never been so happy. He enjoyed working the mine and farm with Pap. And, best of all, he and Jenny were finally able to feel the peace and security that they had so longed for.

Julie Thompson saw through the rough exterior of her man, Mike, and loved him unconditionally. After years of trying, with no success, to have a family of their own, it wasn't hard to let Jenny and Jacob into her heart and love them dearly.

One day as Memaw and Jacob were coming back from shopping in town, they were caught in a rainstorm, when a bolt of lightning flashed across the sky it spooked the horse and the carriage tipped over and fell down a steep ravine killing Memaw and Jacob instantly.

Mike had lost his wife, his partner, his better half, and also the adopted son he had grown to love as his very own. He realized he could do one of two things: go out into the woods and lay down and die, or raise the crippled little girl that he had grown to love. With little thought, he chose the latter.

He had decided that he would do everything in his power to allow his 'little Twerp' to have a happy, productive life. He would exercise her legs three times a day. See that she had the full cream from the cow's milk. He only gave her the best vegetables from his garden and plenty of good red meat.

The doctors had told him it was too late to stop the leg curvatures that the vitamin-D deficiency had caused. Severe malnutrition at such an early age caused improper development and hardening of her bones. That is what made her legs misshapen. Because of this, she would always be in pain and short of stature. But despite everything, she thrived on the unconditional love of her Pap.

Because of her disability and the fact that they lived so far from school, Jenny missed a proper education.

Although Pap was unlearned, he had taught Jenny how to love life and survive in any circumstance she would be put into. He had a deep love for children, animals, and nature. Jenny easily and happily followed in his footsteps.

After taking Jacob and Jenny off of the Orphan Train, Mike and Julie stayed involved in helping find other children good homes. As years went by, Pap stayed very involved in the work, even taking some of the older children into his home until they were old enough to be on their own.

Three years ago, he and Twerp took in two young brothers, Corbin and Rocky. They were seven and nine years old. There was also a younger sister named Malinda. At Pap's request, the mission society started a search for her. Two months ago, the Society had finally located her. While they were preparing for her arrival, Pap died of a heart attack, leaving Jenny the soul support of the two boys.

After Jenny and the boys got back to the farm that day, they washed the clothes that were ruined. While they were hanging them on a line that was strung across two trees, she told Rocky they could deliver them tomorrow and pick up the money Flossy owed them; before going to the train station.

Jenny fixed dinner for the boys and sent them up to bed. Then she poured herself a strong mug of coffee, sat down at the table, and did some serious thinking. The train was due in tomorrow and Corbin and Rocky's little sister would be on it. She needed to keep Pap's death from Mr. Post, the society's agent that traveled with the children. The rules were very strict. There had to be two adults, and they had to have the financial means to support the children. Jenny realized she had neither, at least for now. But Mr. Post didn't need to know that. They would be at the train station tomorrow and pick up Corbin and Rocky's little sister. She would get that gold mine working again and support her family, no matter what. After all, didn't Pap always teach her that she could do anything she set her mind to?

The next morning, Sam decided to go to the train station to find out the cost of a ticket and also to find out if they would ship his horse. He hadn't really decided where he wanted to go, but he had decided it would be a welcome change to ride on a train. Bow, his horse, had become a faithful partner in the last few years and it would be worth the cost to ship him to where ever he decided to go.

Sam had prospered in the last five years and he had made some excellent investments, so making money was of no real concern to him.

He noticed the train station was unusually busy today, so he had asked the ticket agent what was going on. He was told it was the Orphan Train that came into town every few months. Sam had read stories about the New York orphans, so he decided to hang around for a while and see what was going on.

"Look, Twerp, there's that nice man that helped us yesterday," Rocky said, motioning toward Sam.

Jenny wasn't paying attention. She was too busy watching a blond-haired, handsome, young man waving and coming toward her.

Jenny steeled herself as she returned his friendly greeting. "Howdy, Mr. Post. Where is she? Me and the boys are anxious to get her home."

Her heart sank as she watched Mr. Post's face. "We heard about Mr. Thompson dying, so I didn't bring her. With him dying and you being alone the society didn't feel like it would be a good idea."

Jenny leaned heavily on her cane as Rocky whispered something into his brother's ear. Corbin took off running and went and stood right next to Sam. Sam smiled down at him and then looked stunned as the little boy stuck his thumb in his mouth and then reached up and grabbed his hand.

"Gee, Mr. Post, you must not have heard about Twer... er I mean Jenny getting married. See, there he is over there" Rocky pointed toward Sam and Corbin. When he noticed the thumb stuck in Corbin's mouth, he thought, nice touch, as a renewed respect for his little brother's acting ability grew.

Allen Post nodded and waved at them, and then looked down at Jenny. "Congratulations! That really changes things." Just then, someone called his name. He looked toward them, then glanced quickly at Jenny. "I want to meet him as soon as I talk to this couple about another child. I'll meet you back here in a few minutes." Then he quickly rushed off.

Jenny glared at Rocky. "What in the gol-darn, dag-nabbit, blue-blazes do you think you're trying to do?" She hissed at him.

"Come on, Twerp, what have we got to lose? Let's go ask him if he's willing to play the part. We can offer him a few dollars. Mr. Post will meet him; we'll get Malinda and no one need know the difference."

Sam watched the little lady limp toward him, leaning heavily on her cane. He wondered by the way she swayed and her short legs if she hadn't had rickets as a child. From what he had read, the lack of proper nourishment, especially vitamin A could really do growth damage to a young child's bones.

"Good work, Corbin!" Rocky exclaimed enthusiastically as he slapped the boy on the back. "The thumb was a nice touch."

"Get that blasted thing out of your mouth!" Jenny growled, glaring at Corbin. "Look, mister," she continued as she shot Sam a worried look. "I'm sorry we got you mixed up in this. But there are a few dollars in it if you'll act like we just got married."

Sam glared down at her.

"It's really important; it'll only be until the train leaves." Rocky pleaded, seeing Mr. Post heading their way. "We can't get our little sister unless he thinks Twerp's married."

"I'm sorry I took so long." Allen Post smiled as he joined the little group. He stuck his hand out to Sam. "I'm Allen Post, sir, and I understand congratulations are in store."

Sam's interest was peaked by this odd little group, so he decided to play along. He grabbed the young man's hand. "Sam Drew, Yeah, thanks."

"Well, Miss Thompson, or I should say Mrs. Drew; it looks like things have changed. I'll be able to bring little Malinda along on the next trip." When he heard someone calling him, he glanced over in their direction and motioned to them. "I'm sorry. It looks like I'm going to have to take care of some more business. Nice meeting you and again, my congratulations to you."

Jenny breathed a sigh of relief. She was glad to see the back of him. But then he stopped, turned, looked at them, and said. "I should be out to your farm for a visit in a few hours."

"Our farm?" All three of them shouted in unison.

"Yes." He glanced at Jenny. "Surely you remember the policy. There must be a home visit before we place a child." He glanced again impatiently toward the group that was calling for him. "I've got to go. See you in a few hours."

Jenny glared at Rocky. "Now what? How you plannin' on getting us out of this dag-blasted mess?"

Rocky scratched his head and shuffled from one foot to another, then pleadingly gazed up at Sam.

But Sam quickly recognized that look and threw a pointed finger at him. "Don't even ask, boy, you said just a few minutes. And I played my part."

Jenny watched as Rocky's face fell and she knew that his heart was breaking. He had always felt that it was his fault Malinda was taken away. She and Pap had told him over and over again that it was not true. He was just a child himself and there was nothing he could have done about it.

For months, after he came to live with them, he'd have horrible nightmares about losing his baby sister. Now here they were so close, but because of her and her appearance, no one would marry her. Not that she really cared, other than Pap. She hadn't met a man worth the shucks from a rotten ear of corn. She figured it was one of two ways; take a chance on this stranger that had at least been kind to them or that no-account jackass Eddie Riggens. The only thing of value that she owned was the gold mine Pap had left her, and that was useless unless they could get someone to work on it. "Mister, I don't have much money and I realize this is a lot to ask." She watched Sam as he emphatically shook his head no. Well, she thought, she would just have to sweeten the pot. "Look here, mister, I own a gold mine, and if you'll just come to the farm and act like you're going to take care of us, just for a few hours, mind ya, until he leaves. Then I'll give you a half share in it."

She had definitely caught his attention he had always liked mining. "Is it a working mine?" He asked.

"No sir, at least not now. But when Pap was alive, we dug enough gold to keep us all going."

Sam ran his gaze up and down her small, deformed body, then raised his eyebrow in a doubtful glare. "You?"

Jenny could feel the blood rush to her cheeks and she was just about ready to give him the what-for when she felt a nudge from Rocky. She checked her temper and pasted a friendly grin on her face, and repeated what her Pap had often said about her. "Maybe the outside package don't look like much but you ain't seen the inside package yet. And I don't reckon yer ever gonna." She sneered up at him as she turned and limped away.

It was Sam's turn to blush now. Actually, he found he liked this little lady. She had more grit than he'd seen in a long time, man or woman. "O.K., Mrs. Drew." He grinned as he drawled. "You got a deal."

Sam pulled his horse, Bow, to a stop and turned around in his saddle, and waited for them to catch up. They were in a rickety old wagon with a mule pulling it. Rocky kept yelling. "Get a move on, Pompous, move your ass." Each time he would yell the phrase; Jenny would reach over with her cane and smack his arm, yelling. "Quit your damn swearin'." Which Rocky's reply was. "Hell, Twerp ass ain't swearing. That's what these crazy animals are called."

Sam had finally tired of waiting for them and jumped down off of his horse and tied him to the back of the wagon. Then he strode to the front of the mule and yelled for Rocky to throw him the reins. Using his full strength, he tugged on the mule and soon the animal realized that he had lost control and began to amble along behind Sam.

As they entered the yard of the small farm, Sam noticed that the cabin and barn were in much need of repair. Although, the yard was neat and had a nice size garden growing along the side of the house. He noticed a big hog wallowing in a mud puddle by the leaky pump. There was no doubt in his mind that she needed a handyman's touch.

"Ain't much, but we call it home," Jenny said, grabbing Rocky's hand as she clumsily climbed down from the cart.

At the sound of her voice, the huge hog's head pulled up out of the mud and he began waddling toward her. Sam realized he was headed straight for him and jumped out of the way as the hog passed him, leaving a trail of stink behind. The hog skidded to a stop right in front of Jenny. Jenny leaned on her cane, bent over,, and began patting his muddy head. "Hi Petunia, did ya miss us? "The hog snorted and rubbed up against her. Sam was amazed when he noticed how very gentle the hog acted toward her as if it knew she was not very strong.

Rocky came and stood next to Sam and pointed at the hog. "She calls that old smelly pig Petunia. He's been blind since birth and Pap wanted to do away with it. But Twerp wouldn't have nothin' to do with that. He's been around here for years. Blind as a bat, but he can sure smell ya and if he doesn't like what he smells, ya had better watch out. He can hear a pin drop from a mile away. He makes a hell of a watchdog; he'd protect Twerp with his life."

Sam tied Bow up to an old fence rail and, as he was walking across the yard to the house, he noticed Jenny had a rooster in her arms. She was just setting it on the ground when he walked up to her. He blinked twice and did a double-take, and still could not believe his eyes. The rooster had a wooden leg. A piece of thin wood shaped much like his other leg was harnessed to his body. Jenny grinned up at him. "That's my rooster. Pap's named him Major Pain-in-the-butt and kept threatening to throw him in the stew pot. But I reckon he liked him all right cause he was the one who fixed up the peg leg for him." He's been around here for a couple of years. Seems to be doing all right." She walked up the steps of the cabin and motioned for him to come in. As he entered the room, he was in for another shock. The biggest, meanest-looking black dog was coming toward her. The dog had one full ear the other looked like it had been ripped off. Half of his top lip had been torn away; showing part of his teeth and making him look like he had a permanent sneer. There were patches of black fur spread over his body. The bare spots were covered with ragged cuts that had been neatly stitched.

Jenny fell into the nearest chair and the dog gently laid his ugly head in her lap and whined loudly. She patted his head and soothed him. "Hello, my Black Beauty, did you miss us?" Glancing up at Sam, she explained. "We found him out in the woods a few months back. A pack of wolves must have got a hold of him."

Just then, Rocky and Corbin came through the door and the dog waddled over to them. "How ya doin' Beauty?" Rocky said. "Did ya take good care of the place while we was gone?" Corbin fell on the floor and hugged the big dog's neck. Rocky glanced at Sam and explained. "Twerp thought if she gave him a pretty name, he'd think he was pretty."

Sam felt he had better not say it, but he was thinking the only thing about this dog's name that related to him was Black. He was also realizing for the first time that he had never heard the young boy, Corbin, speak.

Sam liked what he saw of the sturdy built cabin. It was a large room, and in the corner, a partial wall and door were built. The partition separated the small bedroom. The front part of the room served as the kitchen. In the corner was a big cast-iron cookstove. A sturdy sawbuck table with benches on either side sat in front of the window. At the other end of the room was a small pot-bellied wood stove. A rocking chair sat in front of it and along the wall was a deacon's bench with brightly colored pillows on it. There was one window in the front part of the house and one in the back above the bench. They were both covered with crisp, white muslin curtains. The place was clean and homey. Sam could smell the ham hock and beans simmering on the back of the stove, and a happy, familiar feeling surged through him.

Jenny went to the cast-iron stove and started piling wood in it. "Rocky," she said, pointing to the near-empty wood box. "You had best get the wood and water in right away. It looks like the sky's gonna give us a good dumpin' here in a minute." She glanced at Sam. "Recon' you can go help if ya want. We can eat when I get the cornbread baked."

"That sounds great," Sam grinned back at her as he followed Rocky out the door. "I can't tell if it's my stomach or the sky that's rumbling."

Jenny watched as he walked out the door, taking in his hard, lean body. Her cheeks reddened, and she looked away, busying herself at the stove. It baffled her with the way this stranger made her feel. Actually, he didn't seem like a stranger at all. It felt like she had known him all of her life. A part of her wanted to be afraid of this new feeling. Then another part made her feel that everything would be all right. She shook her head, trying to make some sense out of this whole thing.

She knew as she got older that there would never be a husband and family for her. She had come to terms with that fact long ago. The love and security she had received from Pap and Memaw had always seemed sufficient enough. And, her work with the Children's Aid Society, taking children from the Orphan Train, was very important and gave her a feeling of fulfillment. Now with Rocky and Corbin and soon, with any luck, their little sister she had a family. But when she looked at this man, she realized how empty her life would be without a husband and children of her own. The sense of peace and security this stranger gave her was the most puzzling feeling she had ever experienced. Frustrated by these unfamiliar thoughts, she shoved the cornbread in the oven and set the table.

Chapter 15

Allen Post tried to nudge the old horse he had rented at the livery stable to a faster pace. He wondered if this old nag would get him to the Thompson place before the gray, clouded sky opened up and drenched them both.

There was something bothering him about Jenny Thompson's marriage. Why he wondered, would a man like this Drew fellow be attracted to someone like her? She was a good person and had proven repeatedly that she could do anything that she had set her mind to do. He really liked and respected her and did not want to see her hurt.

He remembered the first time he had ever met her. It was about five years ago. He had to admit that at first; he was a little upset by her appearance. Her frail, little crippled body, face full of freckles, and her crop of bright red hair would shock anybody. But once a person got to know her, they would notice her big, bright green eyes and her pretty little mouth that formed around a set of straight-pearl white teeth. She was never selfish with her radiant smiles.

Mike Thompson's death saddened him. He was a good man, and they had become friends. Jenny and her Pap had been such a value in their work with the Children's Society and had done wonders with Rocky and Corbin. He knew that she would take good care of their little sister, too.

Although he believed in the work of the Orphan Train that the Children's Aid Society had formed almost twenty-five years ago. Some of their rules were too stringent, especially the one where two adults were required to take a child. He cringed, remembering some of the people that he had to release the children to, knowing that the only reason they were taking the child was to become a workhorse for them. He had heard horror stories from some of the other society workers where the children were even asked to show their teeth as if they were some kind of animal. He had been working with the Society since he graduated from Seminary four years ago. He had often thanked God in his prayers that something like that had never happened to him on one of his trips with the children. Because he would have a real hard time retaining a Christian attitude.

The regulation stated that a society worker needed to spend at least one night in the home of a new family. That had already been done at the Thompson's years ago and really need not be done again. But something about this whole thing bothered him and he wanted to get to the bottom of it.

Allen grinned, remembering the shocked look on their faces, even the new husband's face when he told them he would be coming out to visit with them.

Glancing up at the sky again, he ground his heel into the horse's side a little harder this time. Then he patted the bedroll on the back of the horse and chuckled, thinking of what their reaction would be when he told them he would be spending the night there.

After Sam's third helping of beans, ham, and cornbread, he pushed himself away from the table, declining the peach cobbler that was offered to him. "I could probably find room for that cobbler in a while." He told her as he stood and began gathering the dishes.

"You go ahead and rest. I reckon you did enough by helping the boys with their chores." Jenny told him as she grabbed the dirty plates from his hand. "Rocky, you get on your bookwork now and Corbin, you get ready for bed."

Sam went and stretched out in the wood rocker by the potbelly stove. It had been a long time since he felt this full and this content. It was strange, but for some reason, he felt that this is where he belonged, in this house and with these people.

He watched as Corbin scurried up the loft and came back down with a book. Then he came over and stood in front of Sam and laid it on his lap.

He grinned at the boy as he picked up the book. "The Adventures of Tom Sawyer by Mark Twain. This is one of my favorites. You like to read, boy?"

Corbin nudged the book toward Sam. "You want me to read it to you? Is that what you want?"

Corbin grinned and shook his head excitedly.

Sam glanced at where Jenny was standing in front of the table. "If your sister doesn't mind, I'd be glad too."

"That would be a real treat to all of us," Jenny answered as she nodded to Rocky, who was sitting at the table studying. "Ya can do that later. Listen to the story tellin'."

Jenny was washing the dishes, trying to pay attention to Sam as he read to the boys. But her mind kept wandering back to Mr. Post and what would happen when he arrived? She had to find some way to hide the truth from him. It was getting late, and she needed to get Sam out of her house. She hesitated in her thoughts for a moment. This man was a total stranger to them. Yet, she felt as if she had known him all of her life. A peculiar feeling flowed through her. She would have sworn she heard a small-still voice saying that Sam Drew was where he belonged.

Maybe, with luck, she thought, Mr. Post had gotten too busy to make the ride all the way out here.

Her heart sank when she went out into the yard to empty the dishwater and noticed a rider coming up the road.

Allen Post got off of his horse and tied it to the hitching pole in front of the house and walked toward Jenny. "I'm sorry I'm so late, but I got tangled up in some business that had to be taken care of." When he heard a loud rumble, he glanced up and saw a lightning bolt flash across the darkening sky.

He rushed over to his horse and began leading him to the barn. Jenny quickly went into the house and slammed the metal dishpan on the table, startling Sam and the boys.

She glared at Rocky. "Gol...darn it! Rocky, I hope you're happy we're stuck with him for the night.

The two boys and Jenny stared at the door wide-eyed as they heard the knock, then they gave a startled jump when they heard the deep rumble of thunder. Sam stood up and laid the book on the chair when he heard the knock again. "We sure can't leave the poor guy standin' in the rain." He said as he strode toward the door.

Rocky stood up from his place on the floor and glanced meekly at Jenny. "I...I'm sorry Twerp, I'll tell him the truth."

Jenny chewed on her bottom lip and screwed her face into a worried frown. "Naw! You and Corbin head on up to bed. This is my problem. I'll handle it."

Allen rushed into the cabin, and Sam quickly slammed the door against the wind and the rain. He noticed the boys climbing the ladder to the loft. Then he grinned at Sam. "Looks like I made it just in time." Slipping out of his jacket and throwing his bedroll by the potbelly stove, he ran his hand through his wet hair. "I can sleep right here tonight. I'll try not to get in your way."

Sam watched as Jenny's face paled. It would be interesting to see how she was going to get herself out of this mess.

"Would ya be wantin' somethin' ta eat a'fore ya bed down, Mr.

Post?" Jenny asked.

"A cup of coffee would be great. And if you don't mind, your Pap called me Allen. I'd be pleased if you would too."

Jenny brought both men a mug of coffee to the table where they were sitting. "Honey, I'm going to bed. You and Allen can go on ahead and chaw a while. She said as she placed Sam's coffee in front of him.

Sam was dumbfounded and threw her a puzzled glance. She avoided his gaze, mumbled a quick goodnight, and shuffled into the bedroom, quietly closing the door.

Sam stiffened in irritation. That little sneak, he thought to himself. He shoved away from the table, thinking if she expects me to get her out of this mess, she's in for a big surprise.

"You will have to excuse me, Allen. It's been a long day and I'm beat." He glanced out the window at the downpour and went and threw some more wood into the fire, banking it for the night. "Looks like the rain's not going to let up for a while. You should be warm enough, but if not, just throw some more wood in."

"Goodnight!" Sam called over his shoulder as he headed for the bedroom door, a plan forming in his mind.

Jenny was sitting on the side of the bed. Her feet resting on a box that she always used so it would be easier for her to climb up on the bed. She didn't look up when he came through the door. He walked to the other side of the bed and sat down, feeling the bed sag and the old springs squeak from his weight.

"Did ya tell him?" Jenny asked, keeping her eyes on her hands that were folded in her lap.

"Nope!" Sam answered, kicking off his boots.

Jenny's head jerked up, and she glared at him as he stood and unbuttoned his shirt.

"What in the gol-darn, blue-blazes do ya think you're doin'?"

He slipped out of his shirt and undid his belt buckle. "I'm getting ready for bed."

"Wha... what are ya talkin' about? Yo...You can't do that!"

"Why? It's late and I'm tired."

She watched as he slipped out of his jeans, stripping to his unmentionables. When his bare, hard-lean thighs appeared, she quickly turned her eyes, feeling her cheeks blazing.

"We ain't married." She sputtered. "Ya gotta go tell him so!"

Sam sat on the edge of the bed and pulled off his jeans. Then he swung his naked legs onto the bed, throwing the patchwork quilt over them. He propped up the pillow and lay up against it, resting his arms behind his head. His piercing eyes glared at her. "This is your ball of wax, lady! You're the one that got yourself into this mess. I'm just along for the ride.

Jenny lifted her eyes and felt the heat rise to her face as she skimmed over his naked chest and met his stare. "Ya didn't tell him then?"

"Nope! That's up to you."

"Yeah, I reckon you're right." She sighed as she slipped off of the bed and grabbed her cane. Then a thought struck her, and she hesitated. Sam watched, puzzled, as she laid her cane up against the wall and crawled back up on the bed. "I got a plan and I'm a-thinkin' it's gonna work." She propped the pillow up against the headboard and arranged herself comfortably on the bed. "This is the last Orphan Train trip Allen's gonna make." She glanced over at him but hurried on not waiting for a response. "'Member he told us he wouldn't be back this way cause he was quittin' to go to a preaching school. There'd be a new feller a-comin'."

Sam was feeling like a fool. His plan seemed to backfire. Here he was lying half-naked in a strange woman's bed and she wasn't the least bit embarrassed or afraid. "Lady!" He snapped. "You got about as much sense as a flea."

"What did ya say?" Surprise covered her face as she glanced over at him.

He growled out quietly, not wanting to disturb the visitor sleeping on the floor in the other room. "A naked man you don't know anything about climbs in your bed and you're not even afraid!"

"Naw!" She grinned back at him. "A good lookin' feller' like you wouldn't want to mess with the likes of me. But forget about that." She waved her hand in the air at him. "Here's my plan." She rambled on. "He'll be leaving in the morning and the new feller won't know what ya look like. So's I'll just get that fool, Eddie Riggens, to wed up with me." She shook her head in disgust. "That crooked-necked horse turd will do anything for a price. Course I'll have ta renege on my promise about ya gettin' half the mine. Taint worth much anyhow. Could a been, but like Pap always said, If ya ain't got ya, don't get. And we never had no money ta do anything with the mine anyhow."

Sam watched in awe as she chattered on. This weird little lady, so engrossed in her plan, totally amazed him.

He liked her; he didn't even mind the way she looked. When she smiled, her entire face would shine with radiance. Her green eyes sparkled with a joy for life, and she had more spunk than anyone he had ever met. Her handicaps didn't seem to hinder her. He realized he hadn't felt this interested about anything or anybody since Holly was killed.

Sam couldn't throw off this strange feeling that he had. From the moment he first laid eyes on this peculiar little group, he felt a kinship to them, almost like a prearranged plan for his life. He couldn't shake the thought of the night Holly died. She had told him that God had a special plan for his life. And, now, laying here in this stranger's bed, listening to her half-baked plan, he felt a deep peace and knew that this is where he belonged.

He had to chuckle to himself at her tenacity, a naked stranger climbs into her bed and she wasn't the least bit afraid of him. She just keeps rambling on about some stupid plan. Suddenly Sam realized he didn't want another man to be the head of this family, least of all a piece of scum like Eddie Riggens. "Hey! Hey!" He loudly interrupted, ignoring her whispered shh as she pointed to the door. "Don't even think about backing out on our deal!"

His abrupt manner startled Jenny. "Well, I...I."

Sam swung out of bed and slipped on his pants, then he glared down at her. "I'm going out there and tell that fellow the truth. Then, if that's what it takes to give those kids a safe home, I'll marry you myself." He shoved his hands through his hair and gritted. "It's a darn sight better than that, Riggens, getting his hands on those kids."

As Sam marched out the bedroom door, Jenny felt a surge of relief flow through her. He was right she would much rather deal with a man like Sam Drew than scum like Eddie Riggens. She felt that his kind would stand by his bargain. She had absolutely no fear of him. It was strange, but she felt like she had always known this man and that he was a part of her existence.

Sam had a long talk with Allen and after telling him the whole story. They discussed the plan Sam had for the family. They both chuckled over Jenny and her stubborn streak.

Allen told Sam all that he knew about Jenny, Pap, and Memaw Thompson and their work with the Orphan Train. Sam gained a renewed respect for his future wife.

Allen agreed to stay for a few more days while Sam and Jenny went to another town to get married. He felt that it would stem any gossip that might hurt the arrival of the boy's sister.

Sam went into the bedroom and told a relieved Jenny the plan. Then he went out to the barn and got his bedroll. As he stretched out on the floor next to Allen, he glanced over at him. "Tomorrow morning, let's take a ride out to the mine and check it out." Allen agreed, and then they both turned over and fell asleep.

The next morning, Sam and Allen stood in front of the old mine shaft, silently shocked by what they saw. Allen watched as Sam lifted his foot and pushed on an old sluice box. It immediately fell apart. "It looks like there is going to be a little more work than we thought," Allen said as Sam shook his head in disgust.

Allen had agreed to stay for a while and help in any way he could. He now realized that this was a lot bigger job than two men could handle.

"Something's not right here, Allen."

"What do you mean?"

Sam reached down and grabbed a piece of wood from the sluice box. "This hasn't fallen apart from age. It looks like it's been destroyed with an ax. Look around. Someone has purposely torn up this place."

Allen raked his fingers through his hair and looked around at the wreckage, shaking his head, puzzled. "Sam, I'm sorry, but I don't know anything about mining and this looks like more than just the two of us can handle."

Sam was in deep thought and half-ignored Allen's statement. "What? Huh? No! No! That's all right. I got a friend that I'm going to wire to come and help us. He worked in the mines for a while. Dylon Clay will know what to do."

After they left the mine, Sam and Allen rode into town. Sam wanted to rent a horse and buggy so Jenny could make the long trip with some comfort. He wasn't in any mood to deal with their old mule, Pompous.

Allen sent a wire to his family, telling him he would be delayed for a while, and Sam sent one to Dylon Clay.

Sam dropped by the Sheriff's office and see what he could find out about the Thompson mine. Something didn't seem right to him.

Sheriff Lindale greeted Sam with a firm handshake. He was a big, friendly man in his late fifties with a protruding belly and a gray handlebar mustache. "Sam Drew, yeah, I heard about you and Jenny Thompson. You're married, right?"

"News sure gets around fast," Sam answered as he sat down in the chair that the sheriff offered him.

The sheriff chuckled. "Someone heard you talking to that Post fellow from the Orphan Train. Then it went through the gossip line till it finally reached me."

The Sheriff listened as Sam told him what he saw at the mine, then started fingering the curl on his mustache. "Old man Thompson told me that someone was trying to sabotage the mine. He thought it was Eddie Riggins. Seems Riggens wanted to marry up with Twerp, so's he could get his hands on that mine. Mike wouldn't have nothing to do with that." The sheriff went to the counter, grabbed a couple of mugs, then poured coffee in them from the wood stove burning in the corner of the office. He set a cup before Sam and continued. "I went out to his place to talk to him but couldn't prove anything." Riggens is a real piece of trash. His old man wasn't a half-bad sort. When Eddie was around 7 or 8, his father brought a squaw home. They had a baby girl. Then, about three or four years back, he and his wife died from influenza or some sickness like that. So the breed-girl lives there with her brother. From what I saw, I get the impression he treats her like a punching bag."

As Sam stood to leave, the sheriff said. "The folks around here like Jenny Thompson and the boys, so I hope you're planning on treating them well."

"Well, it looks like we got something in common, sheriff because I like them too."

As Sam and Allen rode into the yard, Rocky and Corbin came dashing out the door. "Where in the hell-fire ya been?" Rocky yelled." Riggen's sister is here all beat up and Twerp took off through the woods with the shotgun to shoot his balls off." Sam leaped off of his horse and grabbed Rocky. "Settle down, boy! Now tell me, which way did she go?" Rocky took a deep breath and pulled away from Sam. "I was going to go with her, but the girl is bleeding real bad and Twerp told me to stay."

Sam yelled over at Allen, who was tying up the horses. "You and Corbin go see about the girl. Rocky and I will go find Jenny."

Rocky told Sam that it was only about a half of a mile through the woods and she had been gone less than an hour.

As Sam followed Rocky, he figured with this rough trail and her carrying the gun and trying to maneuver with her cane, they couldn't be too far behind. They came out into a clearing and saw a dilapidated old cabin. As they came closer, they heard someone screaming. Rocky glanced over at Sam. "That sure ain't Twerp." Then he grinned. "Lay ya odds, she's got him strung up by the balls."

They rushed into the cabin and saw Eddie cowering in the corner with his hands covering his privates. Jenny had the gun aimed in that same direction. And the dog, Beauty, was standing next to her, growling and looking like he was ready to tear Riggens to pieces. "Hot-Damn! Twerp! Ya got a skunk cornered!"

"Help me, mister!" Riggens pleaded. "She's crazy as a loon and so's that dog!"

"Ha! I'm crazy, am I? Maybe you're right Eddie Riggens. I'm crazy enough to shoot a cow turd like you who catawamptiously chawed up your sister. Lilly is the kindest, sweetest person I know, and I can guarantee that it won't never happen again." Just as she shouldered the gun, Sam reached over and grabbed it from her hand. Then he glared at Riggens. "Don't move!"

Jenny scowled up at Sam. "What in the tarnation do ya think you're doin'? You ain't seen what he did ta that girl!"

"Rocky, take your sister and head on back to the house. I'll finish up here and be right with you."

Rocky grabbed Twerp's arm and then grinned. "You're gonna shoot him, ain't ya, Sam?"

"Rocky, do what you're told." Then he pointed to the door and yelled. "Now!"

Rocky jumped and grabbed Jenny's arm. She argued, but when Sam's glare turned on her; she allowed Rocky to lead her out the door.

"Thanks, man. I thought that crazy witch was going to shoot me." Riggens squeaked with a relieved sigh.

Sam strode over to him, reached down, grabbed him by the nap of the neck, and shoved him roughly up against the wall. "Listen here, you dirtbag." He gritted his face inches from Riggens. "You ever come near my family again and I'll kill you myself." Then he dropped him and grabbed the gun and started walking out the door.

Eddie yelled after him. "Your family, what cha' mean, your family?"

Sam turned around and growled. "Jenny is my wife. That now makes her Mrs. Sam Drew to the likes of a scumbag like you."

Jenny and Rocky were sitting on the steps when Sam came out of the cabin. Jenny pulled herself up, but when Sam heard her quiet groan, he went over and handed Rocky the gun. When he swung her up into his arms, Beauty started barking, and Jenny started yelling. "What in the blazes do ya think you're doin'. I can walk! I ain't crippled!"

Sam's eye's narrowed and with his face inches from hers, he gritted.

"Twerp, just shut up!" Then he glared down at the barking dog and yelled. "You too, Beauty!"

Both woman and dog instantly became quiet.

When they entered their yard, Sam set Jenny down. She yelled at Rocky to hand her the cane and at the sound of her voice Petunia came waddling to her. The hog brushed against Sam, almost knocking him over, leaving a trail of stench and a patch of mud on his pants. Old Major Pain, the one-legged Rooster wasn't far behind.

As they entered the small cabin, Allen came out of the bedroom and greeted them with a worried frown. "Whoever did this to that girl in there did a good job. She's pretty beat up."

Visions of Holly's death from a beating flashed through his mind as he followed Jenny and Allen into the bedroom.

The girl was sitting on the edge of the bed with her hands held over her face, sobbing. When Jenny went to her, she wailed. "Oh! Twerp, ya didn't do it, did ya?" Rocky approached her and gently grasped her hand. "Naw! Lilly," he said disappointedly. "She didn't cut him. Sam got there too soon." Lilly smiled up at them through her swollen lip. "I'm glad I didn't want you to go to jail because of him and his doings."

Lilly was a beautiful young girl of twenty. She carried more of her mother's Indian looks than that of her white father. She was tall and slender with long black hair, and a smooth olive complexion, and her almond-shaped eyes were more black than brown. Like her mother before her, she had a kind and gentle spirit. Eddie had always treated her badly, but now, since their father died, it seemed to get worse.

"You crawl into bed and rest now," Jenny said, as she turned and motioned everyone to leave. "You won't be going back to that hellhole anymore. You're going to live here with us."

Lilly grabbed her hand and brought it to her face. "I'll help good, Twerp. I'm a good worker."

"Yes you are, Lilly, and there's nary a better or kinder person alive. Now go on ta sleep." " said as she pulled the blankets up around her.

Jenny figured one more mouth to feed wasn't going to make much difference. But Eddie Riggens wasn't going to like the idea one bit. Dang!" she muttered. Wish Sam hadn't gotten there when he did. Might a been able to take care of that situation once and for all."

Sam and Allen went out into the yard to get some chores done. They would be leaving first thing in the morning to get married, and then be back late the same night. That way, it wouldn't put Allen in a compromising position with Lilly staying there. "Do you own a gun?" Sam asked Jacob as he began collecting the wood he had chopped.

"Yeah."

"You better have it handy. Because I don't think we have seen the last of Riggens."

Allen slumped up against the fence railing. "How could someone be so mean to that beautiful young girl?"

Sam's heart lurched in sadness, thinking of Holly. "It happens, Allen. It happens more than it should."

They were just finishing up with the chores. Rocky had come to fetch them for dinner when they saw two riders coming up the road. "Holy-she-et! It's Riggens and the sheriff." Rocky cursed fearfully as he ran and stood behind Sam.

When they rode closer to Sam, Riggens pointed wildly and yelled out. "That's him, Sheriff, and the brat behind him was there too! They kidnapped my sister!"

Sam walked over to the sheriff as he dismounted.

"Afternoon Sheriff. What's the problem here?"

"Riggens here say you came over and beat him up, then kidnapped his sister, Lilly."

"Well now, sheriff, there is some truth to what he says. But I didn't beat him up. That was Jenny. Me and the boy came in after and stopped her from doing more damage." Sam yanked his hat off, raked his hand through his hair, then slapped it back on. "And as far as Lilly is concerned; it seems like he got the story backwards. She came here all beat up saying that he did it."

Sheriff Lindale shot Eddie a disgusted glance. "Is what he say's true, Riggens?"

"That runt threatened to lop my privates off, Sheriff!"

The sheriff chuckled. "It looks like this here fellow did you a favor and saved you from that vicious woman."

At that statement, Sam, Allen, and Rocky joined the sheriff with a loud laugh. Riggens spat out a curse and yelled. "This ain't over yet!" Then he yanked his horse around and galloped off.

Sam asked the sheriff to stay for supper and told him about their future plans. The sheriff agreed not to tell anybody that they weren't already married.

Thanks for the good cookin', Jenny." The sheriff said as he grabbed his hat and followed the other men out the door. He warned Allen to keep a watch out for Riggens. He agreed with Sam that he was a back shooter and would try to get Lilly back. "Eddie Riggens is too lazy to do his own cooking and cleaning. So he'll get drunk and get some of his no-account buddies to help him." As he climbed on his horse, he continued. "I'll ride out tomorrow and check up on you."

The next morning, as they were riding down the road in the rented buggy, Sam glanced over at Jenny. "You all right? You haven't said a word since we left the house."

Jenny threw him a worried glance. "I'm fine, I was just a-thinkin'."

"Would you care to share it with me?"

"I sure do appreciate all that you're doin' and as soon as we get little Malinda, I'll give you an annulment."

Sam pulled on the reins and brought the buggy to a stop, then he turned and faced her. "Look, I've already had one bad marriage and I'm not planning on having another. This one is going to be for good. And if that doesn't suit you, then we'll just turn around and go back the way we came."

Jenny glared at him, stunned. "Why would a good lookin', a smart man like you want to be stuck with the likes of me for the rest of your life?"

"There's nothing wrong with you." Then he chuckled. "Course you could probably clean up your mouth a little. And maybe think before you go off half-cocked ready to de-man a person."

"Umph! That blasted Eddie Riggens ain't no man no-how. So's it probably wouldn't of done no good." She shook her head and gazed up at him. "It's just a puzzlement why you would want to be stuck with me."

Sam detected fear and confusion in her voice. "I like you,

Jenny. I feel at peace with you. Your house is more of a home than I have had in a long time." He glanced over at her and grinned. "And I think you're cute."

Her face turned beet-red. "Sam Drew, don't ya be throwin' no bull at me."

Sam chuckled. "You're not getting no great prize in me, Jenny. But, I think we could do all right together. And,

The boys could sure use a man around the house. As far as the marriage bed. Well, I'm willing to wait until we know each other better. Except, I won't sleep on the floor, we can share the bed. I'm willing to wait until you are ready to consummate the marriage.

Jenny's cheeks reddened. She wasn't sure what the word consummate meant, but she figured she had a good idea. And, wondering if she would ever be ready to share her deformed body with anybody. It was something at least for now she would throw to the back of her mind and just be satisfied that someone was willing to share the responsibilities and burdens of her life. And, if all it took was just sharing her bed, that was fine with her.

Chapter 16

Dylon entered the master bedroom of the new home he had just built for his family. He stopped and stood still, taking in the sight of Chris sitting in the big old wood rocking chair. Their newborn son was suckling at her breast. He watched her as she gazed down at the child. Her face was radiant with love and tenderness.

Dylon felt he would never tire of watching his wife. Their love grew stronger as the years went by.

She noticed him standing there and smiled. "Hi, what did the telegram say? Is everything all right?" She whispered as he moved toward her and knelt down, taking the baby's small hand in his. His hand grazed her bare breast and their eyes met with a mutual desire.

"Sam needs me to come and help him. It seems he is married and inherited a gold mine."

Come to your Papa, little Ned, he whispered as he took the baby and placed him over his shoulder, and began patting his back, while Chris buttoned her dress. They both laughed as the baby let out a loud belch.

"When will you leave?" Chris asked as she took back the baby and laid him on the bed to change his wet diaper.

"I don't know if I'll go or not. I hate to leave you, especially now; so soon after the baby's birth."

"We'll be fine. Ned's here and Rachel will come over any time I need her. Besides, Sam's our friend and he was here when we needed him." She placed the baby in his cradle and went and wrapped her arms around his waist, laying her head on his chest. "Just hurry home and don't go picking up any strange women."

Sam and Jenny had been married about three weeks when Dylon arrived. Allen was still there, claiming that he needed to help build a new room onto the house since it was getting so full. But they all felt it was more because of Lilly than anything else.

The three men, with Rocky's and Corbin's help, built the new room. Also, with their help, the mine was just about ready to become a working mine again.

Little Malinda would be on the train tomorrow morning, so Dylon decided to stay and meet the new member of Sam's family. He was getting homesick for his own family since he had been away close to a month. But he felt good about helping Sam.

He liked Jenny and the boys. They were a strange bunch, but good people. He could hardly wait to get home to tell the family about Twerp, her brothers, and the motley crew of animals that she owned. He grinned when he thought of the first time that he had entered the yard. When Jenny and the boys came out of the cabin to meet him, the ugliest dog he had ever seen followed them. Sam ran over to help her off of the porch. Dylon had to admit that he was a little shocked by her appearance. But then he had to chuckle to himself again by her reaction to his appearance. She had glared up at Dylon and with a slight gasp whispered. "Holy Shii!" But, before she could get the rest of it out of her mouth, Sam quickly grabbed her around the waist and drew her up to his side, and loudly interrupted. "Twerp! I want you to meet Dylon Clay." She threw Sam a surprised glance, then stuck her small hand out, craning her neck up at the giant before her. "Howdy, there." Then she ran her eyes up and down his gigantic frame. "Whew-eee!" You're a big one, ain't-cha? Recon, no one would want a throw a catch like you back!" Before Dylon could reply, Sam yelled. "Step back Dylon, quick!" Dylon followed Sam's eyes and saw a big old hog rambling toward him. He quickly jumped back, but not before the hog brushed against him, rubbing his dirty carcass on his pant legs. He didn't think he would ever get the stench out of them. Then, to top it all off, an old rooster with a wooden leg hobbled up to her and rubbed against her like it was a cat. Sam had only grinned at his surprised look and told him he knew exactly how he felt.

At first, he had thought Jenny and Sam had made an unlikely couple. But as he got to know her, it was obvious they were good for each other. There was no doubt that Sam loved the boys, and the feeling was mutual.

They had discussed the fact that Corbin didn't talk. Sam had reassured Dylon that he was going to pursue some answers into the reason why.

In all the years they had known each other, he could never remember Sam being so happy. Except maybe with young Holly, but that didn't last but a few days before she was killed.

The morning they were to pick up Malinda, Dylon rode to the train station with Jenny and the boys in the wagon. He thought it was strange that Sam rode on his horse instead of riding in the wagon. That is until the mule stopped, and Rocky yelled. "Get a move on Pompous, you ass!" Then Jenny smacked Rocky with her cane and yelled back. "Quit yer gol-durn swearin, Rocky!" Sam got off of his horse and grinned at Dylon as he tied it to the back of the wagon. As if by ritual, he grabbed the reins that Rocky handed him. The mule began moving when Sam gave him a good smack on the nose and a hard tug. Then he began leading the mule the rest of the way into town.

The train station was hectic. So, Dylon leaned up against the wall of the depot, away from all the commotion, and took in the sights. When he felt a pair of eyes staring up at him, he glanced down to see a little girl not much older than five. She was giving him the once over. He noticed she had heavy metal and leather braces on both of her legs and was leaning on a pair of crutches. He grinned down at her, and she just kept staring at him. Finally, he scooted down on his haunches in front of her. She didn't take her eyes from him as she reached her small hand up to his face and gently touched the scars. "Do it hurt?" She asked a concerned grimace, covering her face.

Dylon smiled at her. "Not anymore." Then he glanced down at her legs and asked. "Do they hurt?"

She scrunched her face up and sighed. "Sometimes, but then my brother Danny, let me ride on his back." She placed her little hand on his shoulder, and it amazed Dylon she wasn't the least bit afraid of him. "Do ya have anybody to love ya?" she asked him with a concerned look.

"Yes, I do. I have a wife named Chris and two daughters and one almost brand new son."

She dropped her face to the ground in disappointment. "Then you're not lookin' for a couple of kids to take home with ya, are ya?"

"Well now, I don't know. Are you lookin' for someone to take you home?"

She again sighed and dropped her hand from his shoulder. "Naw, you wouldn't want me. I'm damaged goods."

Dylon felt a wave of hurt and compassion flow through him. This beautiful little girl must have been told at every train stop she wasn't wanted. He wondered at the cruelty of people. "Now that's funny, I see nothing but a beautiful little girl that cared enough to find out if this ugly old man was hurtin'." Then he chucked her under the chin. "I sure don't see no damaged goods." She threw him a toothless grin. "You wantin' to take us home, then?" Dylon stood, as a young boy of about thirteen ran up to her and eyed him suspiciously. "Ya all right, Kathy?"

"Yeah, did ya find someone that wants us?"

"No, Kathy, not here. But that's all right; we'll find someone at the next stop. I'm sure there will be something to eat there, too."

Dylon caught Lilly's eye and motioned her over to where they were standing. "Lilly, there are a couple of hungry children here. Do you think we can fix them up with some food?" Lilly smiled down at Kathy and reached for her small hand, then glanced at Danny. "Come on, there's food in the wagon." They watched as Danny scooted down and Kathy climbed on his back.

Dylon's heart caught in his throat, and he knew he would be adding two more people into his life. He also knew without a doubt that Chris, Ned, and his family would be thrilled. They would accept these two children with open arms.

Allen agreed to start the process in motion, and he assured Dylon that there would be no problem with him taking them back to Montana.

Dylon walked over to where the two children were devouring the sandwiches that Lilly had given them.

"Kathy, how would you like to go home with me?" She glanced at Danny. "No sir, I couldn't do that. Not without my brother."

"Well, Kathy, I wouldn't have it any other way." Kathy and Danny grinned at each other, then at Dylon. "I'll work hard for you, sir," Danny said eagerly. "I'll earn our keep."

Dylon placed his arm around Danny's shoulder. "Son, you will be a part of our family. There will be work to do, but no more or no less than any of the rest of the family."

Dylon sent a telegram that afternoon.

PICKED UP A STRANGE WOMAN. WILL BRING HER AND HER BROTHER HOME SOON. LOVE, YOUR HUSBAND.

Chapter 17

Sam leaned up against the porch railing and let the early morning sun warm his bones. It was times like these that he missed his cigarettes the most. But when Allen had led them to the Lord, Jenny agreed to clean up her foul mouth if he would give up smoking. That had been almost a year ago, and both of them had stuck to the bargain.

Although Sam had to chuckle to himself, it had been a lot tougher on Jenny, especially when she got her dander up.

Allen and Lilly were married yesterday afternoon, and by now should be in Seattle. They all breathed a sigh of relief when the train pulled out. Everyone was expecting trouble from her brother. But Riggens must have realized it was a lost cause.

Sam would miss them; Allen had become a close friend and a spiritual brother. And Lilly, with her sweet Christian spirit, was like one of the family. He knew she would be a real asset to Allen in his ministry.

He and Jenny had been married for over two years now. They had built a new house, with the help of Allen, Dylon, and his brother, Ken.

Dylon and Chris's adopted children, Danny and Kathy, were happy and thriving in Montana. Kathy had had an operation on her legs, and although she still wore braces, the prognosis looked good. Even his brother Ken and wife Anna had adopted a little girl from the Orphan train.

The gold mine was showing a profit, and he was able to hire

Abe Edwards to work for him. Abe and his wife, Millie, were good people. They had a big family and owned a small farm not far from the mine. He was a hard worker and a good friend.

All and all, life had been good for them. Because they had been worried about Corbin not being able to talk, he took him to Seattle, to see what the doctors there had to say. Sam figured they needed a vacation, so he took Jenny, Rocky, and Malinda with him. After a barrage of tests, the doctors could find nothing wrong with the child. They had told Sam that when Corbin was ready, he would talk. So, they gave him all the love and security that he needed and let the Lord take care of the rest.

The thing that Sam was most thankful for in his life was that Jenny was six months pregnant. He had been afraid at first that maybe it would be too hard on her to carry a child. But the doctor said that she was doing just fine. The heaviness of the child made it a little harder for her to walk. But her stubbornness pulled her through.

Breathing in the fresh morning air, Sam thought to himself that he had never been happier. Allen and Dylon were right when they had told him that, when you commit your life to Jesus, there is a real peace that passes all understanding, placed in your heart.

That afternoon while Sam, Abe, and Rocky went to the mine to work; Corbin and Malinda stayed home to help Jenny weed the garden. "Corbin, you be careful with that hoe. Sam just sharpened it and it'd likely slice a toe-off of ya." Jenny scolded as she scooted Petunia, Beauty, and Old Major Pain-in-the-butt out of the garden. "Skedaddle; on out of my garden before I throw ya in the stew pot!"

When she heard Beauty barking, he glanced up and saw Eddie Riggens stagger into the yard. She quickly snatched the hoe from Corbin and told him to take Malinda and put her down for a nap. Corbin grabbed his sister and hurried into the house.

Spewing foul curses, Riggens lurched toward Jenny.

Fear and anger coursed through Jenny as she frantically swung the hoe at him and shouted. Get on out of here, ya good for nothin' drunk!"

Riggens reached out and savagely knocked the hoe from her hand. It landed with a thud on the ground. The sharp edge of the hoe was facing upward. Hatred, filling him full of rage, he raised his fist and viciously smacked her on the side of the head, knocking her to the ground. "Ya stole my sister from me." He ranted. "So now you're gonna pay. Ya gimpy, ugly, bitch!" The dog, Beauty, was barking ferociously at him. But, when she loudly moaned as Riggens with a vengeance brutally kicked her in the stomach, both the dog and pig went wild and attacked him. Beauty jumped on him, his front paws pushing on his chest, snarling and biting while the huge hog wildly rammed into him, snorting and gnawing at his legs. Riggens let out a horrified scream and tried to fight them off. But when he tripped over Old Major Pain, pecking at his ankles, he lost his balance and fell to the ground. The back of his neck struck the sharp edge of the hoe. The enraged animals continued mauling him, shoving his neck further into the sharp blade. A sickening gurgle erupted, as blood flowed from his mouth.

The animals, sensing the death of Eddie Riggens, backed off and went immediately to where Jenny was lying. Beauty laid his head in her lap, and the hog gently shoved at her hand with his snout, while the rooster strutted back and forth, clucking frantically.

Corbin, hearing the commotion, placed Malinda in her bed, and whispered. "Please, don't move from this bed, Malinda. Try to go to sleep. Do you understand?" Malinda, sensing a problem, nodded her head yes, grabbed her doll, and pulled the blankets over her head.

Corbin dashed back outside, and what he saw horrified him.

Riggens was dead, lying in a pool of his own blood. When he saw Jenny lying on the ground, he ran to her and knelt down before her. She grabbed his hand and moaned. "Get Sam." Then she plunged into a world of darkness.

Corbin pushed his legs as fast as they would go, ignoring the stitch that was piercing his side. "Dear God," he shouted loudly. "Let her be all right. Please, God! Please, God!" He kept muttering as he ran as fast as he could down the path to the mine. Not realizing that he was speaking for the first time in years.

Sam glanced up from his work as Corbin came dashing into the camp. "Sam! Sam!" He yelled. "Twerp, she's hurt! Help!"

Fear paralyzed Sam for an instant, then he dropped what he was doing and took off running, leaving the others to follow in his trail of dust.

As Sam dashed into the yard, he saw Jenny lying on the ground, ignoring Riggens as he rushed to her, almost tripping over Old-Major-Pain. He shouted a loud curse as he kicked at the hog and yelled for Beauty to move. Then he swung Jenny up in his arms, feeling the sticky heat of blood coming from her skirt. As he was rushing toward the house, Abe, Rocky, and Corbin ran into the yard. "Ride for the doctor, Abe!" He yelled as he carried Jenny into the house.

Abe grabbed a tarp out of the shed and threw it over the body, then he jumped on his horse and rode for the doctor.

After Abe told the doctor what had happened, he went and got the sheriff. Then he rode to his house and asked his wife, Millie, to come over and help in any way she could.

When the doctor arrived, he went directly to the bedroom; and saw a frantic Sam kneeling at the bed, holding Jenny's hand. Just then, Millie quietly entered the room. "There is nothing you can do in here. Millie will help me. You go see about the children." He said as he shoved Sam out the bedroom door.

Corbin was talking to the sheriff out in the yard, and Sam went over and placed his arm around the boy's shoulder. Corbin, haltingly, tried to piece together what had happened. He sobbed and as the tears rushed from his eyes. Sam pulled him closer and gave him a tight hug. "Ya, did good, son. I'm proud of you."

Sam sent the boy into the house, then he helped the sheriff throw Riggen's body in the wagon. He watched as the wagon rattled down the road. Then he glanced around the yard, looking for Rocky. When he couldn't find him, he went to see if he was in the house. Rocky was crouched in front of the bedroom door, his knees pulled up to his chest and his head buried in his arms. Silent sobs were erupting from him. When he heard Sam approach, he glanced up. Sam cringed when he saw the hatred that the young boy's face held. "I shoulda killed that good-for-nothing bastard." Sam grabbed him by the arms and pulled him up. Rocky thrashed out at him, trying to push away. But Sam held him tighter until the boy gave up and fell into his arms, sobbing. "Rocky, don't let anger and hatred wrap around your heart like a vice, or it will cut off your whole existence. This family made a commitment to the Lord, and we have got to trust that God will honor that commitment." The sobs subsided into a quiet weeping and Rocky relaxed in Sam's arms. "Come on, boy, let's get Corbin and Malinda and do some serious praying."

The somber family was sitting in the front room together, Malinda on Sam's lap and the boys on either side of him. Abe was at the table. They all glanced up worriedly as Millie and the doctor came out of the bedroom. Millie went and whispered something to Abe, and he followed her back into the bedroom.

The doctor went to the stove and poured himself a mug of coffee, and sank tiredly down in the chair. Then he gazed at the family sitting on the couch, waiting for the news. "She'll pull through." He said as he took a big swig of the hot coffee. He set his mug on the table and shook his head tiredly. "I'm sure sorry. I couldn't save the baby."

Relief for his wife and deep sorrow for his child encompassed him. "Can I see her now, Doc?" He asked as he choked back the tears.

"Not now, Sam. She's sleeping, and she needs the rest. When she wakes up, you can all go in for a few minutes."

They all glanced up as Abe came out of the bedroom. He was carrying a small bundle wrapped in a blanket. Sam asked Millie to take care of Malinda while he and the boys went out to the barn. Abe had started to build a wooden box. Sam went to where the small-still bundle was lying and pulled the blanket open. He trembled with sadness as he viewed his frail, tiny infant son. As he gently placed his hand on the baby's head, he began to pray. "Lord, be with this family and give us the grace and the strength that we need to get through this terrible time." Abe and Corbin bowed their head in agreement while; Rocky angrily glared off into the distance. Sam wiped the tears streaming from his eyes with his shirtsleeve and wrapped the blanket back over the still form. Then he turned and went to help Abe and the boys.

Later, when the doctor said it would be all right for him to go see her, Sam leaned over the side of the bed and grasped Jenny's hand in his. When she opened her eyes, he smiled down at her. "Hi." He whispered. "How are you feeling?"

The pain in her heart was inconsolable, and tears welled in her eyes. "Oh, Sam, our baby, I'm so sorry."

"What have you got to be sorry for?"

"I lost our son, and the doctor said there won't be any more young'uns."

Sam brushed a kiss across her forehead. "I know, honey, he told me. But you're alive and that's all that matters right now. I don't think we could survive without you, Jenny."

"But, I... I wanted this baby." Wracking sobs spilled from her as she turned her head from Sam.

"I know Jenny, I did too. But we have to remember that our plate is already full. We have three wonderful kids that need us. They are outside that door, right now, waiting to see you." Then he gazed down at her. "Honey, God has been good to us and I believe that He'll help us get through this."

Sam had never told Jenny about the night Holly had died, or the vision she had seen; now, he thought, would be a good time. "Someone told me a long time ago that God had a special plan for me. And now, I believe, with all of my heart, that you are a part of that plan." He reached over and gently wiped the tears from her eyes. Remembering all the times that she had made him laugh, and the safe, peaceful feeling he had when he lay next to her at night. The total fulfillment he had after a night of their lovemaking still amazed him. "You have made me so happy. And I'll never be able to tell you enough how much I love you." He placed his hand under her chin and gently pulled her face to meet his. "You know what? It was the smartest move I have ever made when I decided to go along with Rocky's plan to pretend that we were married." Then he thought of what Beauty, Petunia, and Old Major Pain-in-the-butt did for Jenny. "Although I did have some second thoughts when I met your motley crew of animals. I sure am thankful for them now." He said as he breathed a sigh of relief.

Feathering light kisses on her lips, he smiled down at her. He was so thankful that she was alive, and he knew that the future held many great and wonderful blessings for them. "I want you to know something, my little Twerp; I look forward to spending the rest of our days together."

Every word that Sam had said to her was filtering through the pain and sadness of their loss. Because of his love for her, she realized she would be able to live through this time of darkness.

With God's help and the help of Sam and the children, Jenny

Drew was determined to carry on the work with the Children's Aid Society. And, like Pap and Memaw Thompson, their first concern would be the children on the Orphan Train.

An overwhelming peace flowed through her as she gazed at Sam and through trembling lips recited her favorite bible verse. "Peace I leave with you, my peace I give to you. Not as the world gives, give I unto you. Be not troubled or afraid.'" Their eyes met, and they smiled knowing that God would honor His promise.

Chapter 18

Allen Post sat at his office desk, at the Children's Aid Society, and drummed his fingers, worriedly. The letter he and Lilly had received yesterday from Sam had them both deeply distressed. It had been almost three months now since Jenny had lost the baby. They rushed to Kansas as soon as they had heard the news and did what they could to help. Jenny had been putting up a good front, and Allen felt she would eventually pull out of it. Lilly didn't agree. She had worried and prayed constantly for Twerp since they had come back to New York.

Sam had written that Twerp had never seemed to regain her enthusiasm for life. He had asked them to continue in prayer for her and also to remember Rocky. He had hardened his heart after the terrible ordeal with Eddie Riggens and losing the baby. He refused to go to church and would go off on his own, for hours at a time. He wrote that Rocky and Jenny had been arguing a lot lately, and Rocky was even talking about leaving. Sam told them in the letter, please pray. Although I trust in the Lord; I am at a standstill and do not know what to do.

Now, Allen realized that Lilly had been right all along. But what should they do about the situation? Lilly was going into her eighth month of pregnancy. So a trip to see them was definitely out of the question.

His thoughts were interrupted when he heard a knock on the door. Glancing up, he saw Lilly enter, carrying a small bundle in her arms. "I'm sorry to disturb you, Allen. But I have somebody I want you to meet." She smiled at him endearingly as she walked over and laid the bundle gently on his desk.

"Well, who do we have here?" Allen grinned as he opened the top of the blanket. Big blue eyes peeked out at him. They were sunk into a tiny pale face, with tuffs of reddish-orange fuzz covering its head. Allen glanced up at Lilly and asked. "Boy or Girl?"

"A little girl." She answered.

"Girls are harder to place, but with her being a baby, it should be a little easier."

Lilly glanced at him and smiled. "Uncover her."

Allen reached down and finished unwrapping the small bundle. He released a shocked gasp when he saw the little pink stub that should have been a leg sticking out from under her gown. "What else is wrong with her?" He groaned.

"The doctor said she seems to be perfectly healthy, except for the absence of the leg."

Allen suddenly realized that Lilly didn't appear upset over this baby. This, he knew, was totally the opposite of her usual reaction. She would cry and worry for days when a sick or deformed child came into the Society. He glanced up at her quizzically. When he saw her grinning from ear to ear, the same thought struck him. He returned her grin as they both yelled. "Twerp!" Startled, the small bundle before them began kicking and screaming indignantly.

Not being able to go themselves, Allen wired Dylon and Chris.

*****

Chris gazed out of the train window as it rumbled down the tracks. Then she glanced over at her sleeping husband, a little envious that he could sleep through so much jarring and noise. When the wire from Allen Post arrived, they had only two days to get ready before they caught the train to New York. Now, only being able to spend a couple of days in New York, they were on their way to Kansas. They would arrive in Kansas City in the morning, and she was relieved. A wave of exhaustion hit her as she realized they had been traveling for almost two weeks. Thank God for Rachel Isdell. She had enthusiastically agreed to stay and take care of the children. With Ned there also, Chris knew she had nothing to worry about.

She felt the small warm bundle she was holding wiggle and looked down to see the baby impatiently sucking on her fist. "Here, little one, you'll get more out of this," Chris whispered as she grabbed the bottle from her satchel and placed it in her mouth, and smiled as she watched this precious baby sucking intently. While feeding the baby, Chris's thoughts roamed to Jenny Drew. She had not met her yet, but Dylon had given her high praises. The family had enjoyed the stories Dylon had told them about her and the children and her animals. She felt like she knew her already and was looking forward to their meeting. "Lord," she silently prayed. "Help me be a witness to Jenny and help her love and accept this baby."

They had wired Sam that they were coming and he, Corbin, and Malinda met them at the train station. Sam gave Chris a big hug and introduced her to the children. When he glanced over at Dylon, holding the baby, he grinned. "A new addition to your family, I see." Dylon pulled the blanket from the baby and handed her to a stunned Sam. "No, Sam, she's your daughter if you'll have her."

Sam gazed down at the tiny infant in his arms. When he noticed her stub, he gently ran his hand over it. Then he noticed the orange-red fuzz covering her head and grinned as he kissed her forehead. "Howdy, little girl, welcome home."

An excited Corbin and Malinda sat in the back of the wagon holding the baby, thinking of names for their new little sister. It was amazing, Chris thought, that not one of them seemed to take notice of the baby's missing leg. This certainly was a remarkable family.

She was sitting in the middle of the two men as the wagon jounced down the road. A wave of apprehension flowed through her as she listened to Sam tell them about Jenny. "Sam," she said. "We need to stop and pray right now before we get there. We need to ask God to go before us and speak to Jenny's heart."

Sam felt the peace of Jesus enter in as he bowed his head and listened. When Dylon finished praying, Sam added. "Lord, thank you for my family and this new addition to it. Help me be all that you would want me to be. Thank you for going before us, Lord. Amen." All, including the children, chimed in with an Amen.

Jenny glanced out the window when she heard the wagon roll-up. Sam had told her he was taking the children and going into town. She had wondered why he hadn't asked her to go with them. But then quickly realized that she hadn't made for very good company, as of late. She was a little surprised to see Dylon jump down from the wagon. Then, irritation hit her as she saw him lift a woman with a baby in her arms down from the wagon. "He has a lot a grit, bringin' his Mrs. and new youngin' here at a time like this," she mumbled as she limped to the door, threw it open, and yelled. "I reckon I ain't in no mood for no company." Then she slammed the door and went and sank down on the bench by the table.

Dylon, Sam, and the children stopped. But Chris, with the baby in her arms, continued on, yelling over her shoulder at them. "You stay here. I'll be right back." Then she walked up the porch stairs and barged through the door.

Jenny glanced up, surprised, as Chris marched over to where she was sitting and laid the squirming bundle on the table, in front of her. "Jenny Drew!" She said in a firm, loud voice. "God has used Allen and Lilly Post and Dylon and me as His instruments to deliver this little girl to you. We have done our jobs. Now it's up to you!" Then she turned and walked out of the door, shutting it behind her.

Jenny glanced down at the wiggling bundle before her. When the baby started whining, he opened the blanket. She gazed up and down at the baby, taking in her little pink stub and the red fuzz covering her hair, and instantly bonded with her. Hurt, anger, and an unforgiving spirit flowed from the top of her head out of the bottom of her feet, sinking into the depths of hell. Jenny placed her hands on the baby and bowed her head as she felt the presence of the Lord. "Lord, I reckon I've been a big disappointment to ya lately. Haven't paid much attention to ya or all that ya have given me. I'm a-thinkin' that it's time to set things right with ya." She continued as she felt the long, held-back tears flow down her cheeks. "Please forgive me, Lord, for the hatred that I held onto for that cow-turd, Eddie Riggens. I reckon you made him, sos he's yer problem now." The baby started to wriggle and Jenny picked her up and cuddled her to her shoulder, rocking back and forth. "Lord, I know our little son is in yer hands and I'm askin' ya to maybe let Pap keep an eye on him for ya." She grasped the baby's tiny fingers and brought them to her lips, kissing them gently. Her face brightened and she smiled as she felt the peace and forgiveness of Jesus fill her heart. Then she grabbed her cane, pulled herself up, and brought her new infant daughter outside, to greet her family and friends.

It had been almost two weeks since Chris and Dylon had brought the baby to them. Twerp and the children had accepted her with unconditional love. When Sam had told the family about Holly, everyone, that is, except Rocky, had agreed that it was a perfect name for the new member of the Drew family. Rocky had said nothing, and when asked, mumbled he didn't care one way or the other what her name was.

That same night, after the children were in bed, he approached Sam and Jenny. "I reckon I'll be leavin' at first light. I'm lookin' ta see some of the country." Then he glanced over at his sister. "It's O.K. here now for ya, Twerp. And, there's things I wanna do."

Sam had tried to talk him out of the idea and they got into an argument. When Rocky slammed out of the cabin and Sam followed, Jenny laid her hand on his arm. "Ya sit on back down; I'll be a takin' care of this." That night in bed, Jenny told Sam that Rocky felt he needed to go back to New York and see if he could find some of his family. Sam was lying on his back with his arms behind his head, sadness covering his face.

Jenny understood how Sam felt; he loved Rocky as if he were his own son. "Ya know Sam, he's got a lot a hurts that he needs to tend ta." She remembered how she had felt when she was a young girl, and one of her foster brothers had left. "Pap told me once that a mama bird will push their young'uns out of the nest when it's time, sos they'd fly." Jenny turned to him and laid her head on his shoulder. "I'm afeared it's his time to leave the nest. Don't matter how much it hurts us who stay back. I reckon it's just nature's way for some."

Sam threw the ax to the ground and leaned up heavily against the tree, ignoring the pile of wood that needed to be chopped. It was at times like this that he felt he needed a cigarette. He couldn't quit worrying about Rocky. It had been three weeks now since he had left, and he missed him.

He felt in some way that he had failed the boy. But Jenny had told him he was going to have to quit gnawing on it and spit it out. He sighed as he picked up the axe. "Lord, I'm sorry. I know I don't need a cigarette. I know all I need is you."

*****

Twenty years later, in springtime, 1913

Dylon headed toward the old cabin Ned had moved back into not long after he and Chris were married. Ned, in his ultimate wisdom, had felt that the newlyweds needed their privacy.

A wave of nostalgia flowed through him as the old cabin came into view. He couldn't believe that it had been twenty-five years ago in the springtime that Chris and the two little girls had blasted their way into his heart.

There had been so many changes in his life since then. He had a beautiful wife, nine healthy children and so far 11 grandchildren.

Prosperity had finally come to him, but not in the way that he had always thought it should. It was true that he had many wonderful material things and more than enough money. Right after he and Chris married, he had worked hard to regain all that he had lost. He had always held a fear in his heart that without material things, he could not hold his family together.

Twenty years ago, Ned and Rachel Isdell helped to form the First Community Church of Pony, Montana. Rachel's nephew, TC, with his wife Ellie, moved from Washington State and became the pastors. Rachel had died two years ago, leaving a void in all of their lives.

Not long after, Dylon finally agreed to attend church, and he listened with interest to the sermon. All the things about serving the Lord that Ned and Chris had been preaching to him for years began to make sense. He accepted Jesus in his life and found the internal joy and peace that he had always sought for.

Now, the Bible verse, 'Set your affection on things above, not on things on the earth,' had finally made sense to him. Ned had been preaching it to him for years, telling him. "Someday, boy, it'll get through that thick skull of yours." Ned was right. Dylon realized that if he lost everything of earthly value, it wouldn't matter because he had a family that loved him, good friends, and most important of all eternal salvation, through Jesus Christ.

Their work with Sam and Jenny Drew in placing children from the orphan train had also been very rewarding. He and Chris had adopted three children from the Children's Aid Society and helped to place many more.

Kathy, although she still wore braces and would always walk with a limp, did not let it hinder her from entering nursing school. Danny had grown into a fine young man and had made the army his career. Actually, he felt blessed; all the children had grown into fine young men and women

Dylon wasn't sure how many children Sam and Jenny ended up with. He had lost count some years back. Just last month, the Children's Aid Society decided to honor them for all of their years of work. So they brought Sam and Jenny to New York and threw them a big banquet and presented them with a special plaque. Dylon and Chris were going to try to be there, but with Ned being so sick, they decided it was best to stay home.

Thinking of Ned, and all the years they had been together, he realized how much he loved the old man. Their relationship couldn't have been any closer if they were blood father and son. And now, Dylon knew the end was near for his beloved friend.

Dylon inhaled a deep breath, preparing himself before he entered the cabin. He felt the peace of the Lord surround him as he took in the sight before him. All of their children and some of the grandchildren were standing around Ned's bed. He noticed Karen and Sarah, tears were streaming down their face and he felt especially sad for them. Ned had been so much a part of their young lives. He was there for them during the good and the bad times in those earlier years. He also had played a significant part in how the beautiful young women that were standing before him today had turned out. Karen had married a college professor and had two little girls. Sarah married a young man interested in politics and had a boy and a girl. All of them were serving the Lord.

Chris was sitting in the chair holding the newest grandbaby. She glanced up at him as sorrow was devouring her face.

Ned's old eyes gazed up at Dylon and motioned for him to sit down on the bed. Then he grasped Dylon's large, work-worn hand. "I love you, boy." He gasped in a frail voice.

"You have been more to me than a son. You and Chris and the young'uns have given me much joy. But it's time for me to go be with my Martha and the babies now." Then he turned his eyes toward heaven and, through smiling lips, he uttered his last words. "Thank Ya, Jesus."

THE END

<h1 style="text-align:center">About The Author</h1>

Jeam M. Teasdale

Jean M. Teasdale and her husband Tom have been married for over 60 years and have nine children. They were missionaries in an Athabascan Indian Village of Alaska. Jean is currently living in Montana and doing volunteer ministry in a local nursing home.

Her readers comment on the fact that her characters are not always thin and gorgeous. They have physical deformities that must be overcome to be accepted by society.

Although her stories are Christ-centered, some of her characters appear crude. She felt that the language they use is a part of their personality and did not want to hide that part of their character.